A
Garland Series

VICTORIAN
FICTION

NOVELS OF FAITH AND DOUBT

*A collection of 121 novels
in 92 volumes, selected by
Professor Robert Lee Wolff,
Harvard University,
with a separate introductory volume
written by him
especially for this series.*

MARK WILTON

Charles B. Tayler, *Benjamin* *III* *1797- 1875*

ERIC

Frederick William Farrar

Garland Publishing, Inc., New York & London

1976

Library of Congress Cataloging in Publication Data

Tayler, Charles Benjamin, 1797-1875.
  Mark Wilton.

  (Victorian fiction : Novels of faith and doubt ; 42)
  Reprint of 2 works, the 1st originally published in
1848 by Chapman and Hall, London; the 2d originally
published in 1858 by A. and C. Black, Edinburgh.
  1. English fiction--19th century. I. Farrar,
Frederic William, 1831-1903. Eric. 1976. II. Title.
III. Series.
PZ1.T1596Mar7 [PR1304]   823'.7   75-490
ISBN 0-8240-1566-5

MARK WILTON.

Bibliographical note:

this facsimile has been made from a copy in the
British Library
(1261.b.39)

MARK WILTON,

THE MERCHANT'S CLERK.

MR. ARNOLD'S MANSION IN MARK LANE.

MARK WILTON,

THE MERCHANT'S CLERK.

" Unstable as water, thou shalt not excel."

GENESIS, xlix. 4.

[See p. 242.

The Condemned Cell in Newgate.

BY CHARLES B. TAYLER, M.A.

AUTHOR OF " RECORDS OF A GOOD MAN'S LIFE," " LADY MARY," &c

LONDON:

CHAPMAN AND HALL, 186 STRAND

MDCCCXLVIII.

LONDON:

VIZETELLY BROTHERS AND CO. PRINTERS AND ENGRAVERS,

PETERBOROUGH COURT, FLEET STREET.

JOSEPH M. EDLMANN, ESQ.

MY VERY DEAR FRIEND AND BROTHER,

AFTER long years of intimate friendship and affectionate intercourse with you, my high respect for your principles can only be equalled by my esteem and love for yourself. I know, not only from your words, but from your character and conduct, that you will approve the principles which I have sought to illustrate in the following pages, and agree with me that there are no principles, worthy of the name, but godly principles. I have thrown my views on this subject into the form of a narrative, for two reasons—first, because, if I have any talent to benefit others by my pen I believe it is rather in this style of writing than in any other; and secondly, because I am well aware that those whom I am most anxious to serve by this Volume, would perhaps turn away from the same lessons in a didactic shape. I have a high aim under what may seem to some a mere tale of amusement. Your name is an honour to my pages, and I beg you to accept the Dedication of the Volume, as a slight token of the deep attachment of your Friend,

CHARLES B. TAYLER.

OTLEY RECTORY,

December 16, 1847.

Guildford Grammar School.

MARK WILTON,

THE MERCHANT'S CLERK.

CHAPTER I.

I AM about to return to the well-spring of my young
and warm affections. Alas, the stream has long
ceased to freshen its deep and fretted channel. I must
stand by and tremble, (for I am not what I was), while
memory unseals the prisoned spring. Tremble, do I
say? Surely the full gush of those young and gladsome
feelings will make me lose awhile the consciousness of
what I am, and bathe my spirit in delights which but
very lately seemed lost for ever.

I well remember a morning in the month of July, 17—, that I passed in this chamber, this very chamber where I am now sitting; I was then about ten years of age and at home for the holidays. Let me look around me? Yes, all about this room looked then as it now does. The weather was, as it now is, very cheerless. The rain beat against the window panes in large drops, and then streamed down the glass; there was the same little pool of water oozing over the sill of discoloured oak. The foliage of the vine then grew, as it does at present, partly over the window; and in the upper corner there seems to be the same martin's nest, with the dark shining head of the little bird peeping partly forth. There hangs the well-known picture of my Great Uncle, painted in crayons, by Cotes, when he was at Westminster School. They used to reckon me like him. I had when a boy the same mild ingenuous countenance, the same clear healthy skin, the same untroubled brow, and thick brown hair.

I am sitting at the same old round-table, which I loved to spread over with my books and drawing materials, when a boy; I remember that I found it among some rejected lumber in one of the garrets, and I brought it down to my own favourite room, and with it the two worm-eaten, high-backed chairs which have remained here ever since. Oh, merciful God, what am I, that Thou hast been so gracious to me—that I should be thus snatched as a brand from the burning? What a world of wretchedness have I known since that summer day. It will be, I fear, but a loathsome task for me to write down the feelings of my vain and sinful heart, the events of my useless life. I would not do it; I would content myself with mourning over the past in secret, with repentance and anguish of spirit before my God, did I not hope that from my story others might receive a timely warning. I feel that I may unveil the naked deformity of vice, but I must be faithful. I will make no needless display of what my soul now sickens at, and if I must describe iniquity, I will disgust my reader with the view, shewing its hideous form. Useless indeed are those warnings where the senses are provoked into sin while a pretence is kept up which the cold tame judgment is asked to disapprove. I wish to exhibit the process by which the young and inexperienced may gradually and almost insensibly be initiated into the common everyday vices of a guilty world; and virtuous and genuine feelings may be changed into worthless habits! And how a man may still display those qualities which are current among the loose moralities of the unprincipled world, and become more maudlinized, (I can't find a better word,) more pitifully, more wretchedly lost to his God and to himself. I could weep when I think of the many, fine, ingenuous youths who leave the house of their childhood full of noble and honest simplicity, confiding in themselves and in others, with a real enthusiasm for truth and honour: but who soon learn the

cold calculating lessons of worldly, carnal—nay, in-
fernal selfishness; and, with ruined health, aching
hearts, and enfeebled intellects, become at last unfit for
anything that is good or great.　And this is still going
on; it was but yesterday that a frank, simple-minded
lad left this village, as I did many years ago, to become
a clerk in London.

My father was an officer in the Navy, and having
been severely wounded under the famous Lord Rodney,
he retired on a pension, broken down in constitution,
to the little town of Petersfield, in Hampshire.　He
was an upright and kind-hearted man, but I was
only five years old when he died, and can remember very little about him.　He was rather severe at
times, and I always feared him, till the day before
he died, when I was taken at his desire to his bedside.
He spoke very kindly then, and smiled upon me and
stroked down my curling hair with his thin hand.
When my mother was called out of the room my
father begged her to place me upon the bed near him,
and I sat there very quietly, and half afraid, for many
minutes.　I did not like to look at him, so I bent
down and played with the little tufts of cotton upon
the counterpane.　I remember that I pulled out one or
two of those little tufts which stuck up above the
others, and when I had done so, I looked round slyly
and fearfully to see whether my father had observed
me, and half expected a scolding.　He was looking
full at me, but had not a thought to notice the coun-

terpane. Large tears were streaming over his pale thin
face, yet he smiled very tenderly again, and I felt that
all at once I loved him without any fear. I crept up
close to him, and kissed him gently, and then drew
his arm close round my neck, with my head leaning on
his arm. The Holy Bible was lying on the bed, and
he said to me with a very faint voice, " Mark, I have
little to leave you, but if I had heaps of golden money,
I could not leave you any thing of such real value as
this one book; I pray that God may give you grace
to know its value. I fell asleep, and when I awoke I
found myself in my own little bed; it was then
morning, and I was an orphan. I remember another
circumstance at that time, within two days after my
father's death. I was very disobedient to my poor
mother, and after trying for some time to make me
mind her, she took me by the hand and led me up
stairs. She unlocked the door of a chamber, and we
entered. She gently lifted up a sheet which covered
something that stood in a corner of the room; but ere
she could speak, she burst into tears and sat down,
covering her face with both her hands. I knew not
why, but my passion had now passed away; I stood
beside my mother without moving or speaking. Slowly
she recovered her composure, and then, taking me in
her arms, she again approached my father's coffin.
" Listen to me," she said, with a very low, but firm
voice. " You must learn to conquer your own passions,
you have no earthly father now; your dear father has

left this world. This is all we can see of him. He has prayed for you, and I hope that you and I may be with him again when our bodies are as cold and as changed as this. You will, I hope, grow up to be a man, and when I am old and feeble you will be my friend and protector, will you not? My heart was quite softened by her gentle appeal, and I could only answer by my loud sobbing. I never can forget the last look which I took of my father's countenance. It was awful but not unpleasing. The smile, though rigid, was still a smile about the bloodless lips, and I could have believed that I saw my father sleeping calmly before me, had not the shroud and the coffin declared too plainly that his sleep was that of death.

My grandfather and aunt—my mother's only sister —came to us till the funeral was over, and then it was settled that we should return with them to Tancred's Ford, and make that our future residence. I never saw my dear mother look so happy after my father's death as on the day when we drew near to the home of her childhood. We met my aunt and my sister Alice walking upon the heath. My aunt had taken Alice home with her after the funeral, and my sister clapped her hands, and danced with joy when she saw the chaise approach which brought my mother and myself to our new home.

I shall pass over the history of my boyhood, though it was not altogether without events which might possess some interest to others. I do not wish to detain my reader on that part of my story. I went to school when I was about seven years old at Farnham, and came home every Saturday afternoon till Monday morning. Those Saturday afternoons were happy times. Our old servant, Thomas Frost, used to bring a grey pony—my pony, for me about two o'clock, and to walk by my side on our way back. With what a glow of delight did I always gaze around me, when I had quitted the long narrow lane, and passed the Fox hill, and the bridge over the Bourne stream, and climbed the long hill of deep yellow sand, and reached the spot where the grand open landscape burst upon me; the swelling hills of rich purple heath; the dark woods of Waverley, with the fir clothed summit of Crooksbury rising above them: Tancred's Ford, half hidden by the tall trees beneath, and Hindhead forming the distant horizon. Ah, with what a light heart have I cantered over the turf, or stopped to ask a thousand questions of my grave careful attendant. Then as I grew old enough to take care of myself, in what delicious day dreams have I sauntered along over the heath. If the day was hot, every breath of wind blew freshly there. I cannot remember on what subjects I was then wont to meditate; indeed I can scarcely call such unconscious musing, meditation. I only know that I was held in sweet communion with all that was beautiful in nature, and received into my heart her pure and silent influences; which, though undefined to me, have been ever since held as treasures by memory. Time itself has left them undisturbed, or touched them, as it does some fine old paintings, saddening their hues with a shade of rich and tender mellowing. The feelings of which I speak grew with my growth and strengthened with my strength, but I scarcely knew how dear the haunts of my childhood were to me till I was called away from them. My mother had much tenderness of heart, but no enthusiasm of any kind about her character. My aunt, who was many years the elder of the two sisters, openly professed her dislike to every feeling of the sort; but in spite of her assertions, and though she decried all works of imagination, and read the dullest and gravest books, her repressed feelings constantly escaped, and spread over her every day words and actions.

When I was about eleven years old, I left my Farnham school and was sent to the fine old grammar school at Guildford, which was founded and built in the reign of King Edward the Sixth, and where Archbishop Abbot, the determined opposer of Laud, and his arbitrary proceedings, had been educated. My father and a nephew of my grandfather's, a man of high character, and a rich London merchant, had been sent there when about my age, and it was by the advice of that same cousin Mr. Arnold that I went. I felt very desolate as the old yellow chariot (or as my grandfather always called it—the chaise) drove away, and I stood upon the steps looking after it till the tears blinded my eyes. But my kind schoolmaster, who had stood by me till the carriage was out of sight, patted me on the head, and then taking my hand in his, led me across the old court-yard and through the school-room into the play-ground, and calling one of the elder boys, who was standing in the midst of a group assembled under the grove of old walnut trees, which then stood there, commended me to his care, and left me. The first look of Halsted drew my heart towards him, and his kind voice confirmed the feeling that I had found a friend. He was a noble fellow, the best and the bravest boy in the school. Even now I can recal his fine ingenuous countenance, and many of his acts of kindness to me. No one in after life, with the exception of the friend whose likeness to him was so remarkable, ever gained such an influence over me as he did, but his advice and his example were always on the side of what was right. "Come, Wilton," were his first words, "I see by your red eyes that you love home, but you can't love your home better than I love mine, and you will soon be as happy here as I am. We were just holding a council which way we should go this afternoon, for we have to thank your grandfather for a half-holiday. Come and see the other boys, and give your voice in the decision; and mind," he said, in a lower voice, as we drew near the walnut trees, "if any boy claims you as his fag, you may tell him you are mine. It will be your own fault if you find me a hard master." I did not quite like the thought of being a fag, but I soon found that it was better to be Halsted's fag than another boy's friend, and it was out of real kindness to me that Halsted had claimed me as his fag. He knew that the bully of the school was intending to do so. He was, I fear, the only boy that had any real sense of religion in the school. He made no parade of his religion, but he was never ashamed to own it, though he was often laughed at for doing so. He knelt down morning and evening to pray by his bedside in the long chamber in which we slept, and he never allowed himself to be laughed out of what was right. He was with me at Guildford school, however, only during my first year; and my heart sunk, when, on my return after the holidays, I was told that Halsted would never come back, that he had died during the holidays, and left his mother, who was a widow, childless. He had written to me only a day or two (as I afterwards learned) before he was taken ill, and his letter was sent to me after the funeral by his poor mother. She added a few lines to it, in which she told me that her son Charles had loved me as much as if I had been his younger brother, and she sent me some of his books, and begged me to keep them for his sake. His letter was written to invite me to come and pass a week with him, before returning to school, at his mother's cottage, by the seaside, near Selsey, in Sussex. I had never seen the sea, and he told me he wished to witness the effect of so glorious a sight upon me, when I should see it for the first time. He sent me in his letter a sketch of the little sandy cove on the eastern side of Selsey Bill, where the narrow promontory joins the mainland, a wild looking, desolate spot, very picturesque, and finely sketched. There were a few words of excellent advice in that letter, which showed how well he had read my character. They might have been of great service to me, had I heeded them but half as much as I loved their writer—" Almost all your troubles at school, dear Mark, arise from your not having the manly courage to say—no. when you know a thing to be wrong. I would give you, as my own friend, the same advice which my dear mother has often given me,—learn to ask yourself this question, 'Is the thing right or is it wrong before God?' If it is right, do it, though you stand alone, and every one is against you. If it is wrong, suffer any thing, be willing to die, rather than to do it." Such were the last words to me of a boy of godly principle—a rare character! Surely he had this testimony, that he pleased God. God took him, and I wake up at the end of a long course of sin and folly, to own the worth and the wisdom of his admirable words, and to lament that I did not profit by them.

There were many dull old novels and romances at Tancred's Ford; but my sister and I were not allowed to open them. We used to read their titles through the glass doors of the book-case in the breakfast-room, but that book-case was always locked. The book-case, however, was locked in vain, for I managed to read others; and I look back with no little sorrow of heart to the time I wasted in novel-reading.

It was after Halsted's death that I first read a novel. One of my school-fellows allowed me to look over him as he read; he was a very different character to Charles Halsted, but he was now my favourite companion. He had nearly finished the book when I began to read with him; but he told me the beginning of the story. He was taken unwell shortly afterwards, and I remember stealing up into his room one half holiday with some books he had sent me for, and reading aloud to him through two volumes at one sitting. The book (I have since looked at it from mere curiosity,) was a tissue of inflated sentiments written in the vilest style. Its interest was then so absorbing that I do not think my companion and I exchanged a word till we had finished reading. That night I could think of nothing but the novel; nay, even in my prayers my thoughts wandered away to the senseless tale, and I forgot that I had knelt down to worship God. The thirst of my mind for this sickly excitement increased; I soon began to spend all my pocket money in paying for books from the circulating library. I read them whenever I could find an opportunity; sometimes I carried a volume home with me and stole up into my own room, or into the garden, to read them. One night my mother and aunt came into my chamber when I was in bed; they had been passing the evening at Waverley, and had not returned home till after my bed-time. They bent down to kiss me, and as my dear mother smoothed the pillow on which my sleeping head was laid, she discovered the greasy cover of a romance beneath it. I woke up just in time to see the sharp eyes of my aunt fixed upon the open book, and to hear her say, "nonsense! trash! enough to ruin the boy!" The book was taken away, and sent back to the library, and I was called upon to promise that I would get no more books from the circulating library. I did promise, but that promise has often been broken.

My school-fellow, who had allowed me to look over him when he was reading the entertaining novel I mentioned, was a high-spirited fellow, not at all romantic in his ideas. His chief passion was for horses and field sports. His conversation generally turned on such subjects, and I gradually began to acquire the same tastes.

I often smile to myself when I recollect the importance which Jack Burton and I (taking my tone from him), gave to his favourite topics. He seldom smiled except at the height of his enthusiasm when speaking of horses. If he saw anything in the shape of a horse in our walks, he would stand still instantly, and call my attention to it, beginning at the same time a grave dissertation on its merits. He had at home, he assured me, a horse for which he would take no money that could be named, though his father had bought it of a neighbouring farmer for thirteen guineas. I have always found that horse-fanciers possess some such invaluable steed, the former owner of which had not discovered its surpassing merits. Burton had much delight in going, and I, of course with him, to see the stage-coaches enter the town. I know not how he managed, but he seemed to be well acquainted with all the coachmen; and we both looked upon them as belonging to a race of superior beings. Our pleasure was at its height when we could hold a few moments' conversation with a stage-coachman. They certainly kept up their dignity; for sometimes when we both spoke at once with great eagerness and animation, our companion would answer like one whose mind was occupied by other subjects, looking perhaps another way, and addressing some other person with a short, dry monosyllable. We felt honoured if our heroes deigned to unbend and give an opinion, or a hint of any news in the sporting world. I am half inclined to pass over these accounts of my boyish days, for I feel that they must seem mere idle and unprofitable descriptions; but they may be useful in shewing to those who have patience to read to the end of my narrative, that a boyhood like mine, though disgraced by no glaring sins, but passed in what was little else than forgetfulness of God, was anything but a fit preparation for the trials and the temptations of after life; and yet I was called a Christian, and the unfailing resources and privileges of a Christian might have been mine!

After I went to Guildford school, I came home

once a month, and I often sighed on my way to school on those Monday mornings, when returning I sometimes heard the hunter's shouts blended with the barking of the dogs, or the horsemen and their hounds in the distance.   One morning, as I was returning on my pony alone to school, and picturing to myself the hot crowded school room with my dog's-eared Livy, and sundry other books for which I had no particular affection, in contrast with the breezy heath, and the laughing sunshine which I then enjoyed, it suddenly occurred to me that I had twenty lines of Homer to say by heart that afternoon, and that I had not even looked at them.   The book was in my pocket, and I took it out, with the manful determination of learning the lesson at once, and as fast as I could.   I had scarcely repeated to myself the first two lines when I heard the cry of the hounds at a short distance behind me.   I looked round, but they were not to be seen.   I had often read a novel with ease on my pony, but I now found it very difficult to keep my little Homer open at the right place.   Still I determined to learn, and tried not to notice the hunt; but suddenly the fox fled past me, and in a few minutes up came the hounds and hunters in full chase.   My pony seemed to possess even less resolution than myself, for he set off at full speed with the other horses.   I was taken by surprise, and in my care to keep my seat my book fell.   For a few minutes I went forward at full speed, and gave myself up to the ardour of the chase;

I was just thinking that I would stop, when I heard a voice crying out close to me, " Well done, my little fellow! famously sate!" and now I was so well pleased with myself that I did not care to stop. Soon after the fox was lost, and when our speed slackened, whom did I see, to my surprise, but my friend Jack Burton. "Ah, Mark," he said, holding out his whip-handle for me to shake instead of his hand, " I 've seen you all the while, but I could'nt stop to speak to you before. I say, you 're a capital rider, and that little grey of your's is a good goer, I like her paces prodigiously, I did'nt think to meet you here. Nay, my fine fellow, you 're not going?" he said at length, perceiving that I was about to leave them. " You must stay and see the end of the sport with us." " You must indeed," added Burton's uncle, the gentleman whose applauding voice I had heard behind me. " We shall be happy to have you with us. But come along, my boys," he shouted, riding off. " The fox is found, and we must be off." " Aye, come along," cried Burton, giving my pony a smart stroke with his whip. Of course the pony could not resist galloping off with them, and I did not choose to think till we were riding quietly towards the house of the squire, Burton's uncle. My mother had positively forbidden my visiting at the house of this man, whose company she judged very unfit for me. His house was well known as the resort of the lowest society; and there was scarcely a night in which the party went to bed sober. All this I remembered, but while I hesitated, every step took me farther from what was to me the path of duty. At last I said something to Burton about leaving them, but he called out at once to his uncle to forbid my doing so. The squire declared, with an oath, that he would not hear of it, and bade me hold my tongue. "You keep by his side, Jack," said he, "and tell me if he talks of playing the truant again." Jack did keep by my side, and said in a friendly expostulating tone, "My dear fellow, what is the use of your going to school now? if you had meant to do so you should have gone at first, but now it is near sunset. Why, you have lost the whole day! You can but get a rowing to-morrow morning, and you know you would be quite as sure of one to-night. Come along, and we'll have a rare time of it at the squire's; you shall see the hounds fed to-night; and go over the stables with me, and you shall have a capital dinner, and a bowl of punch, and there'll be plenty of singing, and I'll get Tom Fowler the huntsman to tell us all about Eclipse. Think of the dull school-room, and the old can of the very small beer, and the stale bread, and the slice of single glou-cester, and the going to bed at eight o'clock. Come along, and we'll sit up till twelve, and, if you like it, you shall smoke a pipe. Did you ever try one? I often do. If it makes you sick, you can lay it down, but I know, I mean to smoke." He went on talking, and so did I, till we stopped at the squire's gate.

"That's a fine fellow," said the squire, as we ran up

the broad steps before the door of the house, "Welcome to Liberty Hall. We have no tom-birch or horn-books here!"

We passed the rest of the day merrily, though I must own I often opened my eyes widely with astonishment at the ways of that same Liberty Hall, and I heard strange conversations between the squire and his riotous companions. But all seemed to me afterwards as a confused dream; for what with the hard riding of that day, and the noisy laughter, and the roaring fire, and the ale and wine and smoke, and the novelty of all the sights and sounds about me, my head was in a whirl when I went to bed, and I was quite astounded when I woke the next morning in a strange bed, and felt that all the pleasure was over, and the pain to come. I was growing very melancholy when Jack Burton burst into the room, laughing loudly, and crying out that it was time to be off to school.

As we rode leisurely towards Guildford, we consulted together how to conceal my offence, for Burton knew as well as I, that my mother had forbidden my visiting at his uncle's house. It was determined that I should ride at once to the little public house where I was accustomed to leave my pony, and where it was taken care of till one of our servants or neighbours came to Guildfrod to ride it back. The good humoured landlord came to the door as I rode up. "Well, master Mark," he said, "just come from home I suppose?" "Yes," I replied, and I felt with shame that one lie could not be told without adding others to cover it. The landlord continued speaking, but, hardly stopping to answer, I jumped off the pony and ran away. I entered the school-room just as morning prayers were over. The master was quitting the room, but he stopped when he saw me, and asked what had prevented my coming the day before, I felt myself colouring and about to make a confused answer, when Burton who was already there, passed close to me and said nodding, "Ah, Mark! how d'ye do?" as if he had not seen me for days. I recalled my confidence, and said boldly that "I had been ill, and that my mother thought it better for me to remain at home, and—and—" I was going to say more when my master cried out, "Very well, Mark, I believe your word. You need not stand there—I do n't doubt you—*You always speak the truth.* He passed on, but I remained standing where he left me, and the thought came quickly into my mind that I would go and confess the whole, when some one seized me roughly behind by both my arms, and, shaking me, exclaimed "Why, man, what's the matter? I'm afraid you are not recovered now from your illness, master Mark! Would not your mother think it better for you to return home for another day? Why, I never saw such a milksop," continued Burton, for it was he who spoke; "you have a poor face indeed to get out of a scrape. Where's the harm of an innocent, little white lie. Your mother's a very good sort of woman, I dare say, but she can't expect you always to be tied to her apron string. Besides she does not really know my uncle, if she did, she would never have refused his invitation. Some persons have been telling stories about him. If she knew what a good fellow he is, she would have wished you to visit him, therefore, in fact, you have not committed so great a crime, since her forbidding you only proceeded from her not rightly knowing him." I could not see the force of this argument, nor, I believe, could Burton, for in the midst of his serious and impressive reasoning he caught my vacant eye, after staring at me in silence for a little while, he almost shouted with laughter, and cried, "Ah, I'm a poor reasoner, I'm sadly puzzled, but you know what I mean of course, don't you? You know I mean that you—that I—that your mother."—"Yes, yes," I replied, as he paused. "But,—well, well," he cried, "I see you understand me." I could have said, indeed I do not, I am as much puzzled as yourself. I turned away with a heavy heart; I do not remember that I had ever told a deliberate lie before that day. I had often been deceitful and false, but I had now deliberately sinned. I felt myself a liar.

I joined in the wild merriment of Jack Burton, but the very excess of my mirth left me afterwards the more dispirited and thoughtful. I felt as if I had become an altered creature—I had lost my self-respect. I did not for some weeks dare to look another full in the face as I had been used to do. This may seem a strange fancy to some, but, bad as I have since been—to this day, the feelings I then experienced are present to my heart in all their freshness and reality. My mother, my aunt, my poor father had constantly spoken to me on the vital importance of speaking the truth at all times. I had fallen, and I knew with what a contemptuous pity I should be regarded if my conduct had been made public. My falsehood was never discovered, but it lay for a long time like a dead weight at the bottom of my heart. I could not bear to keep it unconfessed, yet I had too much care for my character, in a worldly sense, to own myself a deliberate liar. My sin was never confessed, or even mentioned till a few days ago, when I related all the circumstances to my aged mother. She smiled at the earnestness with which I described my behaviour, till she saw how deeply I grieved over it, and then laying her knitting upon the little table before her, she said very gravely, " You are right and I am wrong in the view which you have been led to take of that first deliberate lie. No one can trifle with his conscience without one day or other finding that he has been putting out the light which is given to him by God himself to warn him from the downward path. You may date much of your past wretchedness and your past errors, my dear repentant son, from that early day. ' See how great a matter a little fire kindleth !'"

CHAPTER II.

Tancred's Ford

I REMAINED at school till I was about seventeen years of age. I believe I should have stopped a year longer, had not a circumstance occurred which changed the plan that my relations had agreed upon.— No, not agreed upon, for they had determined only to tell me their wishes, and to let me decide as to what profession I should follow. They rather wished that I should be educated for the Church, for although I had no prospect of a living, they thought that with a curacy, and the comfortable fortune which my grandfather intended to leave me I should be a happier man, than in any more lucrative business or profession. I would rather have been a soldier or a farmer, but I did not like to disappoint them by saying so; indeed I did not think much on the subject, I knew there was time enough before me, and as they shewed not the least inclination to oppose me, I cared little about the matter.

One Saturday afternoon, when I returned home from school, I found a very handsome carriage in the stable-yard. It was drawn out from the coach-house, and the coachman was washing the wheels. "Whose carriage is this?" I asked. "My master's sir," replied the man, respectfully, "Thomas Arnold's, Esq." "Who can Thomas Arnold, Esq. be?" I said to myself, for just then I had forgotten that Arnold was the name of our rich cousin. I was much occupied by the elegantly built carriage, and after I had surveyed it on all sides, I walked to the stable, the door of which was open. "Why, coachman," I cried as I entered, "you seem to have some fine cattle here!" The coachman hastened towards me, well pleased at my admiration, but saying as he passed me, "By your leave, young gentleman, I'd warn you not to go too near the tallest of them,—that horse in the right-hand stall,—for he has a bad trick of kicking out at a stranger, though in harness he is as quiet as a lamb." He had scarcely spoken, when the horse verified his words, and lashed out so violently, that he almost broke his halter. I heard a scream behind me, and beheld our house-maid standing on the threshold, dressed out in her best gown and cap. "Dear me, master Mark," she cried, "how can you go so near those vicious beasts? I'm sure

my mistress would be finely frightened if she could see
you. Oh, coachman, I wonder at you!" "You
need'nt to be no matter alarmed, Mary, not in the
least," he replied, "for I'll take care your young
gentleman don't meet with no harm, and I'm sorry you
are so timbersome, Mary, though I'm glad to see you
at the stables. If you will walk to the left hand, sir,
you may see Boxer there, without any danger what-
somever, or stop, sir, I'll lead him out, and you'll see
him better."

"Oh, that I'm sure you must not, coachman," said
Mary, simpering. "You are very civil spoken, I'm sure,
but dear me, master Mark, why, you mustn't stand
dawdling here, Missis and Mr. Arnold are waiting for
you in doors, and I did not think you would go first
to the stables. I just came to call you; for I thought
it was you that slammed the yard door as you came in.
Dear me, master Mark, you can't go into the parlour
that figure, you had better just creep up stairs, and
slip on your best clothes in a moment."

I was in the act of just creeping up stairs very
quietly, not to let my steps be heard, when the drawing-
room door opened suddenly, and a loud hearty voice
called on me to come down directly. I turned round
and saw a tall portly stranger at the foot of the stairs
—"Come down, Mark, what are you going up stairs
for, we are all here. I wish to see you, boy—Well,
how do you do, Mark," said he kindly, shaking me
by the hand. "Why, cousin," he added, turning to

my mother, as we entered the room, "he is as like his father as he can stare. God bless you child!" and he stroked down my head, as if I had been a child; I coloured, for I felt I was seventeen. "His father, my old school fellow, was just such another at his age, a little shorter perhaps, eh, Katharine!" turning to my aunt, "you remember poor Harry, just such a youth, don't you? My aunt did not answer, but walked to the window and coughed; my mother bent her head down over her work, but her eyes filled with tears.

Mr. Arnold looked at them both in silence, and then sitting down, he began to talk to me, and to ask many questions, turning his attention entirely to me. "What do you mean to make of Mark, madam?" he said at length to my mother, "you must be thinking of something, for he will soon be a man." "We have determined on nothing yet," replied my mother, "but my sister and I rather thought of the church." "Nonsense, nonsense, cousin," he cried, interrupting her rather roughly, "the church! what, to be a church mouse all his life! That will never do. You must make your fortune, boy, and be a rich man. Come, tell me yourself what you wish to be?" I replied, that I did not care—that I did not know. "Now that's but a fool's answer, boy," he replied, "I like a direct answer, for I'm sure you care both and know what you wish to be. You have settled it, I daresay, in your own mind; so speak out.

I had not liked his manner of putting down my

mother's opinion, and, therefore, I had not told him my mind. I still hesitated, but my mother said to me, " If you have any particular wish, Mark, tell it to Mr. Arnold. So I said that if I were to have my choice, I should prefer being a soldier.

" God forbid," I. heard my aunt say to herself. My mother went on working, but made no remark. Mr. Arnold repeated my words, and added to them the dry little monosyllable, " Hem!" " Why, as to that," he continued, after a pause, in which he pinched his chin with his finger and thumb several times, and looked very thoughtful, " why, as to that, perhaps I might manage to get him a cadetship to India—but that is all a chance."

I looked round at my mother, and my aunt, so did Mr. Arnold; we saw but a blank expression on each countenance, which shewed very plainly that they felt no very great admiration of any plan for sending me out of the country. My aunt's words soon explained this. " Cousin Arnold," she said, with a decided voice and manner, " to tell you the truth, neither my sister nor I would willingly part with that rough-headed boy of ours, nor do I see any great necessity for sending him to India. I hope he won't think of going, and that you will not wish him to go, though I am sure you are very kind to take an interest in him.

" Not at all kind, cousin" replied he, rather sharply, " I shall not interfere with your wishes, or those of your sister."

My mother made some little remark, I forget her words, to soften my aunt's blunt speech, and the conversation turned to other subjects. The next morning Mr. Arnold received a large packet of letters from London, a few of which required immediate replies. After breakfast, he called for me, and bade me sit down, and take a copy of a letter he had been writing. "I am sorry to trouble you, Mark," he said, "but as my answers to these letters must be sent off by return of post, you might as well sit down and help me. First, however, mend my pen, Mark," he added, as I was beginning to write for him. "Your son writes a fine clear hand, madam," he said, when he next saw my mother, "and he makes a very good pen, I'll tell you what I have been thinking of, madam. What would you and Katherine say to my making a merchant of Mark? I mean, of course, a merchant's clerk? We must all begin as clerks; for, trust me, to be a good merchant a man must serve his apprenticeship. I am what they call a rich man, but I began life as a clerk in old Tresham's counting-house. How would you like it, cousin Mark?" he said, pulling me towards him. "Suppose you were to take your seat in my counting-house. I have no objection to have you for a few weeks on trial, and if we suit one another, you can stay."

My mother did not like to refuse this offer. My aunt thought it too advantageous to be refused. Nothing, however, was determined on that evening; but

before breakfast the next day, Mr. Arnold had examined me in arithmetic, and looked at my cyphering
books, and puzzled me with I know not how many
questions. He was pleased to find that I could speak
and write French very tolerably.

I arrived in London about five o'clock one afternoon, in November, 17—. The carriage took me to
Guildford, and the Guildford coach set me down at
the Horse-shoe, in the Borough, and after some little
delay, I called a hackney-coach, directing the coachman to drive to Mr. Arnold's house. He had kindly
offered to receive me into his own house for a few
days.

I had never been in London before, and the gloom
of a November afternoon in the Borough gave me no
very favourable idea of the vast city. The only thing
that pleased me was the view of the Thames, which I
caught in passing over London Bridge. Much confused with the noise and bustle of the crowded street,
through which I had with difficulty passed along, (the
coach meeting with long and frequent stoppages), I
arrived at last at Mr. Arnold's house, in Mark Lane.
Mr. Arnold's house and offices formed of themselves
a small court, and the entrance to this court was by
wide gates, and a wicket door. The porter, whose
lodge was just within the gates, had orders to shew me
to the house, and I looked around with amazement at
the windows of the counting-house, on the right hand
side of the court, they were then blazing with lights,

it being post night.   A footman, in a plain livery, opened the door into a large well lighted hall, paved with black and white marble, and then led me up a magnificent staircase of very dark mahogany, into a spacious drawing-room.   " My mistress or some of the young ladies will soon be down, sir," he said, as he stirred up the fire, and left me alone.   I turned round to survey the apartment, and, for the moment, thought that another person was in the room.   The dim light had deceived me, I had only seen my own figure, reflected at full length in an immense pier-glass.   I walked on tip-toe about the room.   Every now and then, when I thought I heard some one approaching, sitting down on a chair near the door.   I once peeped into a book that lay open on the table, but it was too dark for me to read the title.   I just touched one of the strings of a glittering harp, which stood in a dark corner of the room, but that one string sounded so loudly, that I again stole back quickly to my seat.   I was walking to one of the windows, but in doing so I tumbled over a low footstool, and fell at my full length on the floor.   I now determined to sit still, but no one came, and insensibly I fell fast asleep.

I was awakened by a scream, which, as I opened my eyes, and rubbed them with both my hands, turned into a laugh.   At first I could scarcely see the young lady that stood before me, for my eyes were dazzled by the light she held in her hand.   " I suppose I know who you are now," she said, " though you quite startled me when I came into the room. I'm sure mamma does not know you are here, at least they never told me." I now could distinguish her. I saw a young and smiling girl, about fifteen, with eyes and complexion and hair as bright as the dazzling light she carried. "How could you fall asleep behind the door?" she said, "you are quite tired after your journey, are you not? but I'll go and tell mamma that you are here," and she left me. In a few minutes Mrs. Arnold appeared, and with her my new acquaintance, peeping over her shoulder, and laughing. "Why, you are still sitting behind the door," she cried, "you must be very cold there." "Pray come to the fire," said Mrs. Arnold, holding out her hand to me, and as soon as I heard the sound of her voice, I felt that it was the voice of a friend. She enquired in the kindest manner after every one at Tancred's ford, and asked so many questions, to which I could easily reply, that I soon found myself conversing as freely as when at home. Another daughter entered before dinner was announced. She seemed rather quiet and reserved, and her manner was perfectly different from that of her sister, but she was, I soon found, quite as good tempered. On going down to dinner, we found Mr. Arnold in the dining-room. "Ha, cousin Mark, you are come!" he exclaimed, and he shook me heartily by the hand.

The first evening of my arrival in London I caught but a glimpse of the counting-house. Mr Arnold rose up as the cloth was removed, and saying it was post-

night, passed by a small door at the farther end of the
dining-room into the counting-house. He came back
before he had closed the door and called me to follow
him. I entered the brilliantly lighted office, and was
surprised at the number of clerks, and much abashed
as some of them turned round and stared at me. Mr.
Arnold, however, soon sent me back to the ladies. He
did not come up stairs till after tea, but when he joined
the party, his presence seemed to bring with it new life
and spirits to his wife and daughters. Mrs. Arnold laid
down her book, the harp was brought out of its dark
corner, and the piano-forte opened. The rest of the
evening past very pleasantly, and as they bade me good
night, with smiles and kind voices, and warm shakes
of the hand, I felt that I was very happy.

The next day I rose early, and I must own, I dressed
with more than usual care, and stood at the glass some
minutes arranging my hair and my dress. I hurried over
my prayers, for my thoughts were occupied with worldly subjects. I was too well satisfied with myself, as I
cast a glance on the dress of my outward man, to think
whether my spirit was clothed with christian graces for
the day. Full of myself I walked down stairs. The
housemaid was sweeping the drawing-room as I entered,
and (not seeing me) her whisk broom sent up a cloud
of dust into my face. I retreated suddenly, and was
standing in the passage, brushing off some of the dust
with the cuff of my coat, when Mr. Arnold came down
stairs in his dressing gown. "Well," he said, "I'm

glad to see you are an early riser, cousin Mark. Come, you may as well go with me into the counting-house, and I will give you something to do." I sat down near my new friend for the first time in the now silent counting-house, he gave me an immensely long letter to copy, and he left me there when he went to finish dressing. As soon as I was left alone and heard only the loud clicking of the clock, I could not resist looking round me and surveying the place where so much of my future life would probably be spent. Then I fell into a mood of thoughtfulness, and, alas! Mr. Arnold came back, with an unfolded newspaper in his hand, to call me up to breakfast, and found me with the pen in my hand, but the ink dry in it, and not another word written. "Why you have forgotten yourself," he said, as he looked over me, "you do n't hear me now, and you look as if you were thinking of anything but that letter before you; but come up to breakfast; you will do better when used to these walls and desks. He led the way to a large and cheerful breakfast room, hung round with pictures, chiefly landscapes, of rare beauty and value. The windows opened upon a garden court, in the centre of which a little fountain sent up its playful waters. The morning was clear and the sun shining brightly, and that room seemed to me one of the pleas-antest I ever entered, though in so dull a quarter of the immense smoky city. I sat for a few moments alone in the breakfast room, for Mr. Arnold, finding none of the ladies there, rang the bell rather violently, and called with somewhat of a stentorian voice at the foot of the stairs to say that he was waiting breakfast. "Oh I have been down, father," I heard Susan his eldest daughter saying in a playful yet expostulating voice, "you will find the piano-forte open, and my music book upon it. I have indeed played a long concerto of Haydn's, and half of the overture to Sampson." "Nonsense, child," replied her father, "what is the use of having been down, if you are not here when I come to breakfast? You know, Susan, how often I have said that I must have you ready to make breakfast the instant I enter the room." "Yes, dear papa, I know I'm wrong, but I only went up stairs just to ask Janet if she had seen the key of"—"No excuses, Susan, you know I hate excuses, but come in child. Well come and kiss me first, for you have forgotten to kiss me this morning." Susan entered the room with a smiling countenance, "How do you do." she said, holding out one hand to me, as with the other she moved the tea-pot nearer to the urn. With her quick and delicate fingers she soon prepared breakfast, but I observed that on rising up to take her gloves and handkerchief from the piano-forte where she had left them, she stood a moment before the instrument and turned over a page of the music book. I thought she did so to attract her father's attention to the instrument, and to remind him indirectly of what she had said, of the way in which she had employed her time. Mrs. Arnold now entered the room, her husband did not say a word to her, but he

took out his watch, announced that it was eight minutes
after nine, and asked, in rather a solemn tone, why Janet
was not down? and when she was coming down? "Susan,
my love," said Mrs. Arnold, turning to her daughter,
"you had better go up to your sister, and tell her to come
down immediately." "No, no," interrupted her father,
"pray don't hurry her—let her take her time—we shall
see how long the indolent young lady will be."

Ten minutes had elapsed before Janet appeared.
We heard her running down stairs, and she threw the
door wide open as she entered and cried out, "Now
pray, father, don't scold me. I know I'm very wrong,
and very disobedient, and that I dress very slowly, and
that I am an old offender," and kissed her father and
her mother, and nodded to me, and said to her sister,
"You know I've seen you before, Susan!" Mr. Arnold
looked very grave, but he received her kiss with an
affectionate smile, and then again he looked grave, and
said, as she sat down beside him, "What on earth have
you been about, Janet?" She looked at him, but did
not speak. "What have you been about, Janet?—why
don't you answer?" "Because," she replied, "I know
you do not like excuses, nor do I wish to make them,
though, perhaps, I could find a few very good excuses
for being so late to-day, but an excuse is so like a lie
that I would rather be silent, and bear a scolding, than
offer what I feel to be a very fair, correct sort of excuse.
But really, father, I could not always give a satisfactory
account of my mornings before breakfast. I am called

early enough, but I generally lie thinking about getting up, and hesitating and delaying till I fall asleep again, and on waking with a start, I hear that Susan is half dressed. Then, when I do get up, I always find that part of my dress needs a string, or is torn, or that Hannah has forgotten some order that I gave her; indeed, there is always some hindrance to being dressed in time, and at the time I always blame every one but the right person."

"Yourself you mean," said Mr. Arnold. "Indeed I do, I must own that afterwards I feel that almost every delay proceeds from my own inconsiderate self. I do not know when I shall get free from this terrible habit."

"Nor do I," said he, "till you determine to do so in good earnest. You'll make me angry with you every morning, Janet, I know you will, because you never take the right way to break this vile habit. But do make haste. Why, child, you have not even began to breakfast yet! You do nothing but talk. Good bye— I can't wait to talk longer with you. Come cousin Mark, we will go to business."

"I hope you have been brought up in regular habits," he continued, as he walked towards the counting-house; "for I tell you plainly that you will never do here, nor nor will you get on in life anywhere else without habits of regularity and order." "Wait a moment," he said, as he pulled open a drawer in his large writing table, "here is the little printed paper that you will do well to study. Learn it by heart, look at it often to see that you do n't forget it, and above all put it in practice. It was given me by John Maxwell, one of my religious friends, who got it printed; and I think it came from the lips or the pen of a good man, a clergyman, whose preaching he attends. I knew nothing of the son, but my father knew his father, old Cecil of Chiswell-street, and his grandfather before him. However, that is no-thing to the question—if you want to rise in the world, be punctual and regular—take time by the forelock, as the old saying is. You 'll know the value of this advice when you have learnt to practise it. This is a copy of the paper which Mr. Arnold gave me—I have kept it carefully.

THE IMPORTANCE OF PUNCTUALITY.

Method is the very Hinge of Business; and there is no Method without Punctuality. Punctuality is important, be-cause it subserves the Peace and good Temper of a Family: The want of it not only infringes on necessary duty, but some-times excludes this duty. The Calmness of Mind which it pro-duces, is another Advantage of Punctuality: A disorderly man is always in a hurry; he has no time to speak to you, because he is going elsewhere; and when he gets there he is too late for his business; or he must hurry away to another before he can finish it. Punctuality gives weight to Character. "Such a man has made an appointment:—then I know he will keep it." And this generates Punctuality in you; for like other Virtues it pro-pagates itself. Servants and Children must be punctual, where their Leader is so. Appointments, indeed, become Debts. I owe you Punctuality, if I have made an Appointment with you: and have no right to throw away your time, if I do my own.

Mr. Arnold was in the act of putting the paper into my hand, when the door of the room opened, and a gentleman appeared, whom he received with much cordiality. "You are the very man I was talking of," he said, " for I was giving one of your printed papers to my young cousin. I think, Maxwell, that you have met his father at this house. Poor fellow, he was a gallant officer, and an honest man, and a loss to his country." " I knew him well," said the kind man, and held out his hand to me, " and I wi·n to know his son, for the sake of the father. I shall be glad to see you at my house," he said, " and to introduce you to the excellent clergyman whose remarks about punctuality, my friend Mr. Arnold has given you. Your father has met Mr. Cecil more than once at my house; and he has been with me often to St. John's Chapel, where he preaches.

When Mr. Maxwell took his departure, we went on to the counting-house, and there Mr. Arnold introduced me to his clerks and particularly commended me to a little sharp-featured man, who I soon found was a person of some importance. Mr. Dawson had been an inmate of that counting-house between twenty and thirty years, and he had gradually become a most serviceable friend to his employers. His knowledge of mercantile concerns always appeared to me quite wonderful, though he possessed none of the talent necessary for a director.

Mr. Dawson was then perhaps about five and forty

years of age; the other clerks were generally much younger. I sat very stiff and quiet on my high stool, referring every now and then to Mr. Dawson for instructions, and the first day passed without any incident worth mentioning. I felt very strange, and stared and gaped with astonishment when I accompanied my new acquaintance, Mr. Dawson, to the Bank, and the India House, and many other houses and offices; and I took off my hat, and made a low bow, which nobody noticed, when I entered or quitted any office with him.

The next day Mr. Arnold begged Mr. Dawson to look out for a lodging for me in the neighbourhood where he resided. And I soon after heard that a Mrs. Thompson, a widow lady, whose house commanded a view of Kennington Common, then a green and airy spot, had consented to receive me as a sort of boarder into her family. Mr. Arnold, however, declared that I should remain as his guest till after Christmas.

I have little to relate of the few weeks which passed during my stay in Mark Lane. I became better acquainted with the clerks. I saw more of London. My hand-writing improved. Mrs. Arnold and her daughters called me by my christian name. I received a long letter from my dear mother, and a very few lines from my aunt. I wrote also to them the longest letter I had ever written.

It was about the beginning of December that the partner of Mr. Arnold, who had been, on some affairs of consequence to Holland, returned home.

Mr. Ernst Von Brekelman, or as he was called in England Mr. Brekelman, was by birth a German, and had passed the first years of his life at Frankfort on the Maine, his native place. At the age of fifteen, he came to England, and was received into the house of Mr. Arnold's father. He wrote in the counting-house as a clerk for three years, and then returned to Frankfort. His father had been long a friend and correspondent with the firm of Arnold and Co., and both parties were well pleased, when, after an absence of ten years, Mr. Ernst again visited England, and declared himself the suitor of Miss Henrietta Arnold. The marriage was celebrated within two months afterwards, and the firm of Arnold and Co. was soon changed to that of Arnold, Brekelman & Co. Mrs. Brekelman died about a year after her marriage, but her husband still remained in England, and devoted himself most unremittingly to business. He was the sternest and the strictest man I ever met with. I saw that from the day of his return, the counting-house became an altered place. The clerks had before freely indulged in conversation, and paid little attention to the mild shrill voice of little Mr. Dawson. They had sometimes gathered in social groups before the fire. But when Mr. Brekelman came back, and resumed his place in a small inner room, the door of which, unlike that of Mr. Arnold's, was never allowed to be closed, the clicking of the clock might be heard for hours during the awful silence,—a silence interrupted only by the visits of persons on business, whom he always dismissed with as few words as possible. No intimate acquaintance from a neighbouring office sauntered in, and lounged about the desk of any one of the clerks, recounting in an under-voice, the adventures of the past evening, while many a pen was suspended, and many a head stretched eagerly forward to hear what had occurred. No newspaper was carelessly taken up, and conned over with a feeling of increasing interest, till the day-book or the ledger were forgotten. All was carried on in exact and quiet re-gularity, and if a person quitted his desk, and whispered to another, the whisper was generally audible enough to convey some such sense as "When did we last re-ceive advices from Foster's house?" "What sum was paid into Price, Lloyd, and Co.'s." If a person chanced to raise his head, he was sure to find the stern countenance of old Brekelman raised at the same moment, with his large owl-eyes scowling beneath his frowning brows, or to hear his loud harsh voice sud-denly calling out, "Any thing you wish to know, Saar? You had better look to your books, Saar." Mr. Bre-kelman was remarkably tall and thin; but being large boned, and large featured, there was a strange sort of gauntness about his whole appearance: he dressed in the old style, with knee and shoe buckles, and ruffles at his wrists. I have often heard him abused for his formal and unrelaxing strictness; but he was so con-sistent in his conduct, and sometimes, though but seldom, he betrayed so much real, hearty benevolence from beneath the ice of his exterior surface, that he commanded the respect of those who knew him. He took little notice of me, except by telling me, when first we met, that he remembered my aunt and mother when they were blooming girls. But he looked as awfully severe on me, as on any of his clerks, when ever I was noisy or inattentive in his presence.

I am sorry to say that the kindness I met with from my new friends had a bad effect on me. I became most insufferably opinionated and self-conceited. I put down the kindness and attention which I received as a homage paid to my own deserts. I talked incessantly when in the presence of Mrs. Arnold and her daughters, and talked on subjects which could not interest them. I might have seen that my conversation wearied my hearers, for Mrs. Arnold and Susan generally replied in monosyllables, though with their usual sweetness of manner; while Janet paid no attention whatever to me, but took up a book, and sometimes turned entirely away from me. The irregular habits of Janet continued, and Mr. Arnold often gave us lectures on the importance of regularity, and I, who happened to be an early riser, used to look up to him as he spoke with a feeling of great self-satisfaction. Sometimes I ventured a remark on the same subject, declared my conviction that nothing could be done without regularity, described to Mrs. Arnold the regular habits of our own household—in fact, I interfered when it would have become me to have attended to myself. I saw thatwhen I was speaking Janet often laughed to herself, or stared on me with rather a contemptuous astonishment; and her manner soon lost much of its warmth and friendliness towards me. On many other occasions I was equally impertinent.

My vanity, however, was soon well humbled. Thomas Arnold, the eldest son of my friends, came home. He had been many years at Eton, and was to go to Cambridge the following autumn. He seemed to be a favourite with every one in the house, and his return was hailed with one general feeling of delight.

We were sitting in the drawing-room when a loud knock was heard at the door, every one rose, for it was the day and the hour that Thomas Arnold was expected. The two girls rushed out of the room. Mrs. Arnold threw down her work, and Mr. Arnold put down the newspaper, and walked to the window. We soon distinguished the bounding tread of some one ascending the stairs, and the glad voices of Janet and Susan welcoming their brother. In another moment Thomas Arnold entered with his two delighted sisters clinging to each of his arms. He kissed his mother fondly, and even pressed his lips to the cheek of his father. All this time I stood unnoticed, till Susan observed me, and immediately led her brother towards me. He shook hands with me very heartily, and talked for a few moments with hearty good nature to me. Then he turned round again to his sisters and to his parents, and seemed as if he had entirely forgotten that

I was in the room. I now and then offered a few words in my new, presumptuous style of conversation, but even the gentle and well bred Susan stared at me, as if she had not heard a word I spoke, and was soon called back, even in looks, to attend only to the lively questions of her brother.

The easy and good-humoured manner of Thomas Arnold soon drew me to the same self-conceited familiarity with him as with the rest of his family. My good opinion of myself, my outward-self especially, now received a check. I came up one Wednesday afternoon into the drawing-room, and finding no one there, took up a book, and sat down near the window to read as long as I could by the dusky light. The door, leading from the room where I sat into another sitting-room, was open, and I soon heard by their voices that Thomas Arnold and his sisters were there. But my book was a volume of the Arabian Nights, and I did not care to leave the adventures of Aladdin. The dull light, however, grew more and more dull, and as my eyesight failed me, I suppose my sense of hearing became more acute. My own name first caught my attention. I did not wish to listen. I was just going to give notice of my near presence by a loud cough, when some words, spoken more loudly, stopped my cough, or rather turned it into a gape of surprise— "Oh! dont tell me," said Janet, with an indignant voice, "his self-conceit is intolerable! Yes, he was very well when he first came. I liked him, because

his manner was so natural. Good natured! Oh! yes!
and what should make him otherwise? But he always
seems best pleased with himself. How he does talk—
prose, I should say.   He goes on and on, never tired
with the same dull subject—self—When *I* was there!
when *I* said so! when *I* was asked! always I!! How
you can listen to him, Susan, surprises me, but how you
and mamma can answer him is perfectly astonishing!
Oh! Thomas," she cried out, but she could scarcely
continue speaking, for her voice seemed kept down by
irrepressible laughter, "Oh! my dear Thomas, if you
could have seen him to day, poor vain creature, as he
stood beside, or rather a little behind you, before the
large looking-glass between the windows. I saw such
a smile of self-satisfied admiration pass over his
face as he seemed to compare himself with you. He
passed his fingers so caressingly through his fine curls,
and then looked down with a sort of restless glancing
over his whole person, as if he could scarcely believe
that the glass was a faithful mirror to so charming a
figure. And then he turned with a smile of such
thorough self-satisfaction. I'm glad he did not meet
my countenance when he turned, for he must have seen
me laughing at him."

"Poor fellow," I heard Susan say, "how can you
abuse him so? He will grow out of these little faults.
I 'm sure he will. Really, Janet, I must tell you that
you are excessively rude to him."

"Oh, I do n't care," said she, in a laughing reckless

voice, " I wish him to see that I do n't particularly admire his ways. Then his insolence at breakfast—how he chimes in with papa, and looks upon me with such conscious superiority, because he is always down early with his shining morning face."

" Pray do n't speak so loudly, Janet," said Susan " or rather drop this subject. I never heard you speak so ill-naturedly of any one."

" I should like him to hear me," replied Janet, still more loudly, " he wants a little humbling.":

" But you would not hurt his or any one's feelings would you, Janet?"

" Feelings! do n't fear, his feelings are not so easily wounded, they are well covered by a shield of self-conceit ; one must pierce that first, which would be no very easy work to——

" Do stop, Janet," exclaimed her brother, " you are now getting unjust, very unjust, as well as unkind : poor fellow, I dare say his feelings are delicate enough; one might soon find out that, he has such a way of colouring. To tell you the truth, Miss Janet, I do n't quite admire your way of abusing a person behind his back, it 's not like you, Janet. You were always violent in your likes and dislikes, but I never remember this new accomplishment of yours—this back-biting. It is beneath you, Janet.

Janet replied loudly, and in anger to her brother; but I heard again Susan's sweet, beseeching voice, and when Janet spoke again her voice faltered, she confessed herself wrong, she spoke kindly about me, nay, the whole tide of her feelings towards me seemed to have been turned, for as she continued speaking, I felt the tears rush into my eyes, and I loved her the better for the lesson I had received, it now taught me, as all rebukes should teach; it made me feel the truth of the words, without being offended by the speaker. The two girls went up stairs together, and Thomas also left the room, but as they did not pass through the drawing-room, I was not discovered. In a few minutes after, I rose up, and treading lightly on the thickly carpeted staircase, I stole up to my own room.

I first met Janet again in the dining-room, and the moment she saw me, she said with an air of charming frankness, "You must shake hands with me, Mark, and forgive me, for though you did not hear me, I have been abusing you in a very shameful manner, and I am very sorry for it."

I could not resist, when I next stood near a large looking-glass with Thomas, I could not resist judging what truth there was in the remark of Janet. My vision seemed to have undergone a change, for I no longer thought my style of dress so superior; but I am sorry to say that my vanity was rather turned into a new channel than humbled. I was convinced that my appearance was not fashionable, but I was not convinced that my outward appearance ought to have been of inferior consideration to me. I became more anxious than I had ever been about my dress, and I did not feel well satisfied with myself till I had entirely, though gradually changed my whole style of apparel. I even thought of wearing a shade of powder in my hair, but the fear of being laughed at, if I did so at my age, stopped me.

But while I grew thus attentive to my outward appearance, I neglected more and more the state of my inward self. The Bible, my mother had given me, lay unopened week after week. My prayers, which had never been very long or very earnest, were always hurried through, and very often neglected altogether, God forbid that I should sit in judgment upon others, or condemn any one but myself; but I sometimes look back to the habits of Mr. Arnold's family, at that time, and grieve over the apparent forgetfulness of God, the apparent inattention to everything like religion among them, and I do not wonder that I thought and cared so little about the matter. They were upright, honourable, to all appearance strictly moral, kind and pleasing in their manners, bnt it seemed to me, that they could be all this without religious principles, or any acknowledgement of God. I do not say that I reasoned thus, for I was not concious of any reasoning about the thing; but it was too evident that religion was among them like something they were ashamed of. The family never once, that I remember, met together, children, servants and all, to ask for pardon, as repentant sinners, or to pray for God's help, or God's blessing through the Saviour who died for them. I know that religion is not ac-

cording to the new fashion of the present day, talking
about religion, or even knowing about religion; but it
is not only a reasonable duty of the creature, nay it is
according to the positive command of God, that His
children should unite together in the great congregation, or in the gathering together of even two or three,
from the highest to the lowest, from the eldest to the
youngest of the family, with confession, and with
prayer and praise, to seek His presence as a God of
grace, who is always present with them as a God of
providence. But alas! such is the way of the natural
man, and to use the words of a great living writer,
"Nature is in a state of exile from God, and such a
middle region, as the one we at present occupy, where
the creature *enjoys himself amid the gifts, and cares
not for the Giver*, makes him an anomaly on the face of
creation.

The Bridge over the Weare.

CHAPTER III.

I WAS now beginning to get accustomed to my London life as a merchant's clerk. The novelty of the change still excited and interested me; but my heart was often with the dear and loving faces, and the fresh and lovely haunts which I had left. London Bridge, and the broad waters of the lordly Thames, seemed to me but a poor exchange for the wooden bridge over the Weare, and the clear stream of the river Wey, winding along through the green meadows, or under the hanging woods of Tancred's Ford.

We had hitherto lived very quietly since my arrival in London.   I went once or twice with the Arnolds
to Drury Lane, and I was much amused and very much
wearied before the play was over.   Mr. and Mrs.
Arnold also gave a large dinner party, and I was
present.   They always lived, in what appeared to me,
a very good style, even when they saw no company ; but on this occasion two man-cooks were
added to the establishment, and were for two days
busily employed in preparing the dinner.   When the
dinner hour approached, and the company began to
assemble in the drawing-room, and as the servants
loudly announced them by name, I must confess I
looked up with some reverence on the grave and portly
gentlemen who were ushered up one after the other,
for many of them were men celebrated in the mercantile world.   While Mrs. Arnold conversed with their
wives, and Susan and Janet with their daughters, the
gentlemen gathered together in a group, where the
politics of the day, and state of the stocks, and the
arrivals at Lloyds, and such subjects were talked over
with quiet complacency.   Dinner was announced, and
we were all soon seated at the sumptuous table, and I
stared round in the brilliant lamp light upon the
rich feast.   Certainly nothing could be more dull than
the conversation of this party for some little time.
They had all excellent appetites, and I had observed that
some of the gentlemen looked anxiously impatient till
the very short grace was said, and every seat was taken.

Plates were quickly passed and quickly changed, and still, until the edge of the appetites was taken off, only a few ejaculations were uttered from time to time. I had heard much of the good appetites of city gentlemen, and I did not quite believe the account ; but really on that day I was convinced that the report was well grounded. There were, however, some gentlemen present from the west end of the town, who certainly shewed powers quite equal to those of their city friends. Before the second course was removed conversation became less abrupt, many persons looked up from their plates, and some began to converse very sensibly. Champagne and hock, and various other wines were handed round, all having been preceded by cold punch, as an accompaniment to the turtle, of which there was an abundance. At last every tongue seemed loosened, and the conversation became general and animated, at times full of sense and character, and everything was so new to me, that I could only look and listen, and forgot to eat or drink so much as I should otherwise have done. My attention was at one time quite engrossed by the conversation of a Mr. Standish, a young solicitor, who was giving a long and interesting account of a visit he had just made to France, to a very intelligent woman who sat next me.

When the ladies rose up to leave the room, I was surprised at the look of satisfaction which spread round the room, as the gentlemen quickly pushed away the chairs which their fair companions had so lately occu-,

pied, and drew nearer to each other. Mr. Arnold
went up to the head of the table, and as he passed,
stirred the fire into a brighter blaze, and the butler
brought in clean glasses, and cleared away much of
the rich desert, to my regret, that he might make a
free passage for the bottles.

How often one is told the old story of the Spartans
having made their slaves drunk, to disgust their children with drunkenness; but it has sometimes occurred
to me, that the dining-room of many an English gentleman, when the ladies have left it, might have a good
effect upon young persons in these days.* I shall be
told men do not drink now as they did some years
ago. No, they do not drink from glasses without feet
to stand on, till the drinkers are unable even to sit
round the table. No, men in these times only become
very heavy, or very silly, or over-poweringly friendly,
or uncommonly abusive, or disgustingly indecent; or,
in a word, anything but what they are at other times.
I had seen a drunken party before at Squire Burton's;
but there, I was not so much disgusted, or so much
astonished, as with the party in Mr. Arnold's dining-
room. To get drunk seemed a natural consequence of
the course of life at Squire Burton's. The company
talked, and eat, and drank eagerly, and roared with
laughter. But, here were decent, grave gentlemen
getting solemnly and stupidly drunk. I was quite

* The reader must remember that this was in the last century;
we hope generally speaking it is not in 1847 as it was in 17—.

surprised by the particular affection which one gentleman took for every one around him, he even leant
across the table to shake hands with me, as he told a
long and tedious story, in which every now and then
he quite forgot what he meant to say, and stared at me
with his mouth open; but he was interrupted by a
song, such a song! Love, and honour, and women,
were each eulogised, or, I should say, each insulted in
vile rhyme. The song ended, and the singer bowed
his head, as if affected by the sentiments which he had
himself expressed. "By Jove, how fine!" exclaimed
the young solicitor; and he was not alone in his
opinion; a sudden and rapturous enthusiasm seemed to
kindle in every countenance, and expressions of delight
burst forth all round the table. I was appealed to by
my neighbours on each side, as if the delight they felt
was too exuberant to be restrained. One old gentleman melted into tears, and sat speechless, either from
excess of wine or of feeling. I judged of the latter,
when I beheld the large tears roll out from his swim-
ming eyes; but a moment afterwards a long deep
hickup undeceived me. I must own that I now
began to feel indignant at the absurdities of those
about me. I knew that many of those very persons,
who in their sober senses would have laughed to scorn
the slightest expression of innocent, and I may even
say noble enthusiasm, were now lifted up by a mere
sensual excitement, to a state of idiotic rapture. I
soon became more and more heartily out of humour, as

my companions grew more and more drunk, particularly when about midnight the gentlemen stumbled
up to the drawing-room. All the ladies looked either
cross or grave, and Susan and her sister had already
retired to bed. I remember being struck with seeing
the young solicitor attempt to return to his former
conversation with the lady who had listened to him
before with so much interest and pleasure. He now
could scarcely balance himself as he stood before her,
and though she looked up with an expression of much
attention, he could not make himself understood, and
the end of his attempt to make himself understood, was
his emptying a cup of hot coffee over her delicately
white satin dress.

Of all the days in the week the Lord's Day was
always the dullest in Mr. Arnold's family. At that time
I scarcely knew why, I only knew that it was so. On
Sunday morning every one rose later than usual. We
went to morning service at a church where the prayers
were carelessly read, and the organ vilely played to
screaming charity children, and a short sermon preached, which was so utterly without interest, so dull, and
so heavy, that it was as tedious as a very long one.
The congregation consisted of a sprinkling of sober-
looking persons, who, instead of kneeling during the
service, generally lolled back in their pews, and seemed
to be glad when the time came for them to walk out
of the church again. After church we met at luncheon,
and then separated till dinner. The carriage rolled

away with Mrs. Arnold and one or both of her
daughters, either to pay visits, or to idle away the
hours in Hyde-park. Mr. Arnold walked off to the
West end of the town to call on some of his friends,
and Thomas Arnold gallopped off also by the New
Road to the Park. They returned home through the
dark and silent streets to dinner. In the evening a
sermon was read by Susan or Janet, to which Mrs.
Arnold alone attended. Thomas often got out of the
way, and Mr. Arnold yawned or fell asleep, and shook
himself as soon as the sermon was over, and then took
up the newspaper, as if heartily glad to have done with
so irksome a duty.

The Sunday before I removed to my lodgings, Mrs.
Arnold declared her intention of going, after church,
to pay a visit to an aunt of her's who resided in the
neighbourhood of London. I had heard but little of
Mrs. Aspen, and I soon found by the remarks of her
younger relations, that she must be a very repulsive
sort of personage. When the carriage came to the
door, Mrs. Arnold asked, in vain, who wished to accompany her? Susan was really unwell, and could
not go. Janet said she could go, if her mother desired
her, but that if the choice were given her, she would
certainly rather stay at home, dull as it was to do so,
than go to that gloomy house. Thomas would have
gone, but he had promised to meet his friend, Mr.
Tresham, in the Park, at three o'clock. Mr. Arnold
had already gone out. "Well, then, I suppose, I

must go alone," said Mrs. Arnold, "unless," turning
to me as she spoke, "you, Mark, will go with me."
I could not say "no," and I went. I remember
yawning as we stopped at the door of Mrs. Aspen's
house. Her abode was an old red brick mansion, with
a profusion of narrow casement windows. A small
court-yard paved with flag-stones, before which were
high iron gates, divided the house from the road. The
door was opened by a thin, tall old man, with a
peculiarly long solemn countenance. He made a low
bow on perceiving Mrs. Arnold, and we were soon
after ushered by him into the presence of Mrs. Aspen.
At the farther end of a large apartment, furnished just
as rooms were a century ago, sat the good old lady in
a high-backed ebony chair. A little girl was sitting
at her feet on a low stool, reading aloud from a small
quarto bible, which lay on her lap. "There, that will
do, little Miss," I heard the old lady say as we entered.
She took the bible very gently from the child, and
placing it on the table near her, took off her spectacles,
and laying them quietly on the open book before her,
she advanced to Mrs. Arnold. She curtseyed slightly,
and then leading her friend to a chair, kissed her cheek
and sat down beside her. "How do you do, my
love?" said Mrs. Arnold, to the little girl, and I could
not help smiling, when little Millicent made a low
curtsey. But I was pleased with the blush that spread
over her face, as she looked up, and with the sweet
but very mild voice, with which she enquired after

Susan and Janet. I was then introduced to the old lady, who received me with much form. Millicent, at Mrs. Aspen's desire, shook hands with me, and while the two ladies were conversing, she shewed me Calmet's Dictionary of the Bible, and some large books full of prints on scripture subjects. I was much struck by the appearance of this little girl, who seemed to have no companion but her grandmother. Her manner and her language were like those of a grown up and well educated person, and her dress was uncommon, and unlike that of most persons of her age; indeed it rather resembled one of the portraits of her grandmother or great aunts, painted in their childhood, which adorned the room, where I first saw her. With all her primness of dress, however, there was a total absence of personal affectation, the little girl seemed artless and good tempered, and was certainly very obliging. We remained nearly two hours with Mrs. Aspen, and I could not help frequently listening to her conversation with Mrs. Arnold. "I almost wonder to hear you speak of it as a dull day," the old lady exclaimed. "Pardon me, my dear Mrs. Arnold, but I must say, I did not suppose that you found the Sabbath so dull a day. You are not ignorant, I think, of the enjoyments of religion. I know that you have many hindrances in your family, too many, for though your husband is a great favourite with me, he thinks of little beyond this world. I have not scrupled to tell him so. I fear that religion in many families is rather known by a few unpleasant restrictions, than felt as the inspiring spirit of life, and joy, and peace. It has been said, that the way in which the Sabbath is kept, may be made the test of the real state of religion in a family. I am not surprised that with many it is the most irksome day of the week. What can be more tedious to a mind that has no holy dread of sin, no delight in prayer, or in the prospects of happiness beyond this world, than to be not only without employments, but without amusements. If the mind cannot find employment and delight in spiritual pursuits on the Sabbath, and has yet too strict a sense of the demands of the Most High, to give itself up to its usual worldly occupations, then indeed the Sabbath must be a weariness to it. I can only compare its state to that of a person, who has set his feet within the boundaries of a land of celestial enjoyments, but who turns away from the contemplation of them, who will not even taste and see how full of delight they are, but who stands looking back with anxiety, and sighing for the poor pleasures of the desert he has left. Depend on my words, my dear niece, you will not find the yoke of Christ easy till you try to wear it. You will not find the services of the Lord a joyous freedom till you seek to love Him with all your heart, with all your mind, and with all your soul. I would not have you make the Lord's day a dull and gloomy day. The countenance should be more cheerful, the heart more contented on that day than on any other. The day on which God rested from the work of the creation, and which He sanctified, should be a day of calm happiness. The day on which Jesus Christ rose from the dead, and triumphed over sin and the grave, should be a day of grateful adoration. The meaning of the word Sabbath, is rest; and we should endeavour to look upon the Sabbath as the figure, and its peace as the foretaste of the eternal rest which is reserved for the people of God. The temper and tone of mind must be acquired here, which begin the enjoyment of heaven, or there can be no fitness for heaven hereafter." I have since thought much of Mrs. Aspen's words.

I soon removed to my lodging at Kennington. The old widow lady and her daughters were very common-place characters, and have little to do with my narrative. I shall not say more of them, than that they were what I then called Methodists, and exceedingly vulgar. They were always leaving little tracts with strange titles about my room, which I was much annoyed at, and determined never to read. Sometimes too I heard their harsh voices united in a long hymn. They were really good persons. Their conduct towards me was dictated, I am now convinced, by true kindness of heart, and godly principle; but it had the very contrary effect from that which they intended on me. They felt some interest about me; for I was quiet and regular in my habits, and generally well-behaved. I treated every woman with politeness, and I was therefore a favourite with these new acquaintances. In the counting-house all went on well with me. I was always at my desk as the clock struck the appointed hour. My books were written up with the fairest exactness, and Mr. Brekelman looked upon me with favour; he even invited me with another of the clerks to his house one evening, and lent me a valuable meerschaum pipe to smoke with him, which I did, till I was half sick. He entertained us with long lectures on the necessity of correctness and regularity, and told us long stories on mercantile affairs.

I dined twice in the week, and usually on Sundays, with the Arnolds; on other days I was accustomed to adjourn with some of the clerks for dinner to one of the coffee-houses near the Exchange.

Among my companions I soon became most intimate with a young man about two years older than myself, named Stanley. I do not know that there was any similarity in our tastes or dispositions; but as he lodged in the same house with me, we usually walked and returned together to and from the counting-house. Stanley was well principled and steady, and his manners were pleasing, so that he was not only a pleasant, but a safe companion for me. He had certainly no talent, but he was uniformly cheerful and good tempered. "I know not how you like business," he said one day to me, "but for my part I am convinced I shall never learn to be a good merchant, unless I keep my head clear, and live a regular life. After all, there is a good deal of truth in old Mr. Brekelman's dry sayings; and see what a merchant he is." "A good merchant he may be," I replied, " but is he a man of general information? Has he any knowledge of the world? If he is the character you would point out as one's pattern; if one is to toil on year after year in his dull regular way, only to become a Mr. Brekelman, 'tis but a poor prospect one has." "You do not quite know Mr. Brekelman," said Stanley. "I will allow that his manner is repulsive enough, and that his conversation has no charm for the ears of young men like ourselves; he has, however, an abundance of strong sense, and he is a firm friend." "Well," I replied, "I dare say I shall like him by and bye—but do let us change this subject. How fond you are, Stanley, of prosing on about your old formal oracle! I really think you are growing like him. You are already as tall as he is, and tolerably thin—you only want a small brown wig, and a few wrinkles about your forehead, and a pair of huge spectacles, and a suit of his oddly cut clothes;—yes, I think you may entertain very reasonable hopes of becoming in due time rather like him." "Rather like whom?" cried Chillingworth, another of the clerks, who came up to us, smacking Stanley on the back with his open hand as he spoke; "like whom?" he said, as I repeated Mr. Brekelman in a low voice, "like whom?" and he thrust his face almost into mine with a sharp and inquisitive look. "Like old Brekelman? What, you, Wilton?

I hope not, my good fellow." "No, not me," I answered laughing, "not like me, but Stanley." "Ah, you're quite right there! I often call him old Brekel. Don't I, Stanley? But now, old Brekel, and young Wilton, I wanted to see you. What do you say to a beef steak and a pint of Port at the new Hummuns to-day, at half-past four; and we can go to the play, to see Macbeth afterwards." " I shall be delighted to go," I cried instantly. "And I," said Stanley, very calmly, " yes, I will go too." " I half wish that old Stanley had refused me," said Chillingworth, as Stanley turned away. "I like him well enough, but he is so terribly correct. He always rows the waiter if the dinner is not brought at the moment it is ordered; and he takes the half-pence in change when he pays the bill, and never gives the waiter more than sixpence; and he will only sit out the play, and go home before the after-piece begins, that he may not keep his old landlady up late!"

We went to the Hummuns, and I laughed as Stanley coolly put the half-pence he received in change into his pocket, and then put down sixpence for the waiter on the table. The man took up the money, looked at it, and with something like a smile, put it down again. " Very well, Sir," said Stanley, looking up in the waiter's face, and he put the sixpence after the half-pence into his pocket. We rose up immediately, and I felt ashamed, but half inclined to despise him.

As we crossed over the street to the Piazza, a poor half-naked wretched woman begged for money. Stanley gave more than the sixpence, for two pieces of silver slipped from the woman's hand, which he stopped to pick up for her out of the mud: I felt that I could not despise him. We entered the theatre, and walked straight to the pit door. "Oh, not to the pit, I hope," cried Chillingworth. "I wish to see Kemble in Macbeth, and the pit is the best place," replied Stanley. " I hate the pit; come, Wilton, let Stanley go to the pit. I am for the boxes; you'll go with me." "Or with me," said Stanley; and he put his arm within mine, and paying for two tickets, he drew me along with him, leaving Chillingworth staring after us. When the play was over, Stanley took out his watch, and asked if I had any objection to leave the house. "It's late," he said, holding up the watch; "do you wish to stay for the long noisy pantomime?" "No," I replied, "I do not much care about staying." He saw that I hesitated, and he instantly moved to depart. I followed him, and cast a longing and lingering look round the brilliant and crowded house as I entered the dark passage leading from the pit. "Button your coat well over your chest," said Stanley, turning round as we passed out into the open air; "it's a terribly cold night!" What with the noise of the carriages, and the roaring of the link boys, I hardly knew which way to turn.

I was staring about me, much bewildered, when a

link boy rushed past me with such violence, that he almost pushed me down, and half deafened me as he roared close to my ear, " Make way there; coach, coach !" The doors at the box entrance, near which I was standing, were flung widely open; and a little gentleman, arm in arm with two tall ladies, came quickly down the steps; I turned round as their loud laughter burst upon me, and recognised Chillingworth. He did not observe me, and I was looking for Stanley, whom I had just missed, when the same link boy came rushing back, hallooing, as he ran, to light them to their coach, " Ha, my boy; what, you 're here, are you?" cried Chillingworth, who now saw me; " and where 's Stanley? Oh! you 've lost him. All the better. Now I 'll tell you what you should do; we 'll give you a seat in our coach; we are going to supper at a friend's, and then with a party to the masquerade at the saloon. You 'll enjoy it, I promise you. Here Rosa," he said, turning to one of the ladies, " take Mr. Wilton's arm." " Who are these ladies," I whispered; " are they relations of your's?" " Oh, yes, relations, certainly." " Sisters of mine, allow me to introduce Mr. Wilton, my sister Caroline, Mrs. Painter, and Miss Rosa Chillingworth. I took off my hat to the two ladies, and Miss Rosa immediately seized my arm. We walked forward to the coach, I looking about me all the while for Stanley. The coach door was rattled open by the noisy link boy, and Chillingworth handing in his married sister, sprung in after her. Miss Rosa, accepting my assistance with a smile, followed, and my foot was on the step, when I felt myself dragged back. In an instant the door was firmly shut, and I heard Stanley's voice loudly commanding the coachman to drive off. Miss Rosa's neck was seen extended out of the window, and then Chillingworth's red face, as he roared out, "Stop, stop;" but Stanley hurried me on swiftly, and dashing through crowds of men and carriages, we were soon walking quietly along the left hand side of the Strand, on our way to Blackfriars Bridge. I now thought I should be able to make Stanley understand me, for I had tried in vain to do so before. He did not answer a word at first, but as I described Chillingworth's introduction of me to his sisters, and the invitation I had received, he replied only by a dry "Pshaw!" "But have I not been very rude? Will Miss Chillingworth forgive me?" I said, earnestly. "Oh yes, yes," he said; "pray do n't distress yourself. Miss Chillingworth is much more likely to do so than our old landlady would have been had you kept her sitting up till daylight." "But this meeting must have been a surprise," I continued; "for now I recollect it was but yesterday that I heard Chillingworth telling you that his mother and sisters were settled in a new house at Richmond, and I must have misunderstood him; I thought he said Richmond, in Yorkshire. He must have meant Surrey, not Yorkshire." "Well, never mind where they are settled, my dear fellow," said Stanley; "tell me how you like Kemble?"

F

Waverley Abbey.

CHAPTER IV.

THE winter passed away without my going again to the theatre. We were very busy, and often detained at the counting-house till late at night. Stanley and I were glad to hasten home to our warm comfortable lodging, where we sat till bed-time conversing and reading together, after our frugal supper had been sent up to us. On one of these evenings we agreed to read history together, and laid down a course which we followed up, with few interruptions, for many months. Stanley entertained a sincere esteem for me, and his quiet determined steadiness was for sometime a safeguard to me, from many dangers which I was scarcely aware of, but my very ignorance protected me.

Towards the end of the summer I went down to pay my relations in the country a visit. I felt myself a person of some importance, as I knew that my person and dress were considerably improved. To my astonishment, however, no one seemed surprised but myself. Nay, my aunt told me I had grown somewhat of a fop, and that she supposed I thought myself a very fine gentleman. My sister alone seemed to approve the change, though she did not say so. I had not been many days at home, however, before I returned to my old country ways. Again I walked with my good old grandfather round his farm, or accompanied him to Farnham, where he went to take his usual place among the magistrates on the bench-day. Again I rode with Alice through the beautiful grounds of Waverley, and explored the ruins of the old abbey, or made a round of visits to our pleasant neighbours, the ladies in the carriage, and I on horseback; and again Alice and I rambled away on our long delightful walks over the heaths, stopping to admire the broad blue expanse of our beautiful meres; or climbing to the tops of the wild fantastic hills, called, we knew not why, the Devil's Jumps; or resting in the deep shady lanes near the paper mills at Chert.

Often did I then wish, and often have I since wished, that I had lived a country life, and never left the peaceful seclusion of Tancred's Ford for London, and the prospect of wealth. Ah! it had been better for me had I been only a poor day-labourer on my grandfather's estate, than to have come back ruined as I now am in health and character. But no—it is wrong to speak thus! It was not the circumstances of my past life which have made me what I am; the man is the same man, let the circumstances by which he is surrounded be what they may. They may influence and affect him, but if he has not strength of principle—high principle before God, to rise superior to the circumstances around him, he will be but a poor worthless creature, whoever he may be! As for me, I was always unstable as water, and should have still remained so, had I not been made, as I trust I now am, by the goodness and the grace of God, an altered man—humbled and broken in heart— that I might be made by the same transforming grace a new creature.

With no little regret, I left the fresh and beautiful country for the smoky streets of London in hot weather. The Arnolds—I mean the female part of the family— had left town during my absence for Ramsgate. Who does not know, that has been obliged to pass the summer in London, what a dull and weary time it is! For my part I must own that for the few first years of my residence in London, I used to grow low-spirited as soon as the hot summer came on, which I had enjoyed so heartily in the country.

I received frequent invitations from Chillingworth, but something had always prevented my passing an evening at his lodgings. I did not feel much esteem for him, but I began to find him a far pleasanter companion than Stanley. Stanley wearied me with his correct and methodical ways, and with his common-place conversation. There was no want of head, but, if I may so discriminate, a want of mind about him, which made his society distasteful to me. I knew not how to find fault with anything he said or did; all seemed right, but all was dull—oh! most oppressively dull. If he tried to be sprightly, for such natures will have their frisky moods, the heaviness of his gambols made one yawn. It was just at the time that I began to decide on the fact that Stanley was too common-place to be always an agreeable companion, that I made two new acquaintances.

One Saturday morning on my coming into the counting-house a note was put into my hands by the porter, who told me that Mr. Maxwell had himself called with it, and that he should expect me to join him, if convenient, at his office in Old Broad Street, at two o'clock. I carried the note at once to Mr. Arnold, for it contained an invitation for me to accompany Mr. Maxwell to his house at Hampstead. "I know all about it, Mark," was Mr. Arnold's pleasant reply; "Mr. Maxwell joined us at breakfast this morning. And as there is little for you to do this morning, shut up your books in an hour's time, and go back to your lodgings, and pack up a couple of shirts and a night-cap, and take care to be at his door in Old Broad Street as the clock strikes two, and you will find my worthy friend, John Maxwell, ready to start, and to give you, as he says in his note, a seat in his coach. And now I think of it, lad, perhaps I can help you to something which you will find very handy when you have to pay these short visits. Here, come with me," he added, opening the door and leading the way to his dressing-room. "You are the youngest, so stoop down and open that cupboard," and he pointed to one of the doors of a range of mahogany cupboards, beneath the long and well filled book-case, which extended along one side of the room. "There," he said, "pull out that little valise; it will just do for you, and let me see, here's the key for you. Now do you want anything else. By the by, have you a bible and prayer-book? Yes, so I supposed. Well, you will want them there, for you will have plenty of praying and psalm-singing." I met the significant glance which accompanied these words with a smile. But as I was going away, Mr. Arnold called me back. "Stop, young man," he said; "I was wrong to treat with anything like ridicule the religious practices of Mr. Maxwell's house. In all the circle of my friends, and that circle is very large, I cannot name a friend whom I value and respect as I do John Maxwell. For plain manly consistency, for genuine truth, and for hearty unaffected kindness, I know not his equal. You may look as narrowly as you will into his own ways and the ways of his household, and you will find, as I have found, that if he aims high, his life has always the same high direction. He carries out into temper and active duties the profession he makes. He does not merely put up a sail, but he carries ballast. His wife too, God bless her! is just what John Maxwell's wife ought to be.

The clock of the Royal Exchange wanted a quarter to two when I entered Old Broad Street; and I had not been long pacing up and down before Mr. Maxwell's door, when a plain, but handsome coach, drawn by two very strong fine horses, came somewhat slowly into the street. I saw the coachman take out his watch as he approached Mr. Maxwell's house; but he did not stop; he passed along to the end of New Broad Street, and there turned, and then came back; and having thus passed and re-passed several times, just as the clock struck two, he drew up before the door. At the same time Mr. Maxwell and two young men came out: I was waiting with my little valise in my hand. Mr. Maxwell smiled when he saw me, and shook me heartily by the hand, and then introduced me to his two sons; and, in another minute, the footman had opened the coach door, let down the steps, taken my valise from me, and we were driving off.

Mr. Maxwell had taken a house at Hampstead for a few months in the summer, for the sake of one of his younger children, whose health had been in a declining state, and required a fresh bracing air. I must own, that with all my respect for the character of Mr. Maxwell, and with all my personal liking for himself, I felt a kind of mysterious dread come over me on entering his house—a dread of their religion. However, this dread soon passed away: the Maxwells were much like other people in many respects, only there was more of the reality of kindness and good temper about them.

Nothing struck me so much as the manners of the elder children towards their parents; there seemed to be the happiest understanding between them, the most perfect confidence, the most tender affection. I took a walk with some of the party after dinner, but Mr. Maxwell did not accompany; us he expected the arrival of a young relation from Scotland that evening, and wished to be at home to welcome him. He was, I afterwards found, a poor relation, almost friendless, and an orphan; but he was received, from that evening, as a son into the bosom of that excellent family. Mr. Maxwell then told me, as he introduced us to one another, that he hoped Angus Murray and I would be good friends, as we were likely to pass some years together. " I particularly wished you to meet for the first time," he added, " under my roof, and I hope you may both feel inclined to come to us often, and to look upon us all as old friends. Angus is to become what you are, a clerk in Mr. Arnold's counting-house, and will, if it please God, accompany you thither on Monday morning." I must own, that the very first sight of Angus Murray, the first sound of his voice, made me think well of him. There was a fire and a sweetness, and yet an ingenuousness about his sun-burnt countenance, such as I had seldom or never seen before. He was tall and rather slight, but his frame was evidently strong and muscular from healthy exercise; but what drew me to him more than anything, was his extraordinary likeness to the friend of my boyhood, Charles Halsted. There was every now and then a look, a manner, which made me feel almost as if Halsted had been present. He was dressed in very deep mourning, for his father had died suddenly, only a few weeks before he left Scotland.

I confess, with shame, that until I became Mr. Maxwell's guest, I had never been the inmate of a house where family prayer was offered up. So strange did the practice at first appear to me, and so careless was I even to give it common consideration, that I looked upon it as a methodistical observance, and thought that it was only to be met with in the families of the over-religious, or, I ought rather to say, the ultra-religious. Alas! where God is not worshipped by a family, God is not really acknowledged in that family. I was much struck by the reverend and devout manner in which Mr. Maxwell read a short portion of the Holy Bible, and then offered up a plain but fervent prayer, and I thought I had never heard such sweet singing as when that whole family stood up to sing a fine but very solemn hymn. My time passed so agreeably, that I felt heavy at heart when I found myself returning to town on Monday morning. Murray accompanied me to the counting-house. Mr. Maxwell told me that he should put him under my care, as he had an engagement which prevented his going with us. I could not help remarking the manly yet modest ease of my young companion in a situation altogether new and strange to him. Young as he was, humble as he was, I think I never saw in any one such deep unaffected humility; still he had learned to respect himself. I have often felt that when a man has learned both to know himself, and to respect himself, he has learned much of the secret of true wisdom. When I speak thus of Angus, I do not mean that I came to this conclusion about his character, or that I thought so highly of him, or even did him justice, at first. On the contrary, I often took offence at his plain speaking in what he said, and his godly decision in what he did ; but I was always touched and soften- ed towards him by his likeness to Charles Halsted. I now bear this testimony to his character and conduct, that of all the men I ever met with, young or old, no one seemed to have so clear a knowledge of the differ- ence between right and wrong on every subject; and no one was ever so resolute to do the right, and to have nothing to do with the wrong. A very different charac- ter was he whose acquaintance I also made about this time.

Angus Murray, notwithstanding his strict notions, had some very agreeable qualities. He was open- hearted and sweet-tempered, and always ready to do a kindness. We were thrown much together, and I was beginning unconsciously to feel the influence of his principles and example, when I made the other acquaintance of whom I spoke. Some of my fellow clerks, and several other young men, clerks in other counting-houses, were accustomed to meet together in boating parties on the river. During the long summer evenings we found the coolness of the fresh winds which played over the broad current of the Thames delightful, and the manly and bracing exercise of rowing was a pleasant change after the enervating confinement of narrow streets and heated offices. Angus often made one of our parties, and he was perhaps the best and most elegant rower among us. His active habits from his earliest youth among the mountains and lochs of his native highlands, had given unusual strength to his slight frame, and a well-poised share of muscular vigour to all his limbs. He enjoyed the recreation as much as any of us, and was so unpretending and obliging that he was a general favourite.

Occasionally we were able by turns to have a whole day to ourselves, and we then made a party to Kew or to Richmond, or some other place on the banks of the Thames. On these occasions, however, Angus was never present but once. Upon that excursion Chillingworth and another of our clerks named Hanson got intoxicated in a tavern at Richmond; and behaved in a very riotous and disgraceful way. It was on that day that a young man who had been absent for some months, rejoined the boating party. Neither Angus nor I had ever seen him, though his name had been repeated often enough in our ears, and some of our companions had been constantly expressing their wish that Desmond Smith would come among us again. I thought then, and I think still, that I never saw any one so handsome as that young man. He had been ill, and was then only just regaining his strength, and was therefore very pale and thin; but his features and his figure were like those of some fine Grecian statue; and there was a noble and manly grace about his every gesture which it was impossible not to admire. The expression of his smile, when he did smile, had a kind of fascination about it; and his voice, though deep and manly, had a sweetness in its mellowed tones, which made it fall like music on the ear.

We had rowed up from Queenhithe Stairs, but he came on board our boat at Whitehall. We were almost tired of waiting for him, and were just returning to the boat (I should have said that most of the party were lounging about on the shore), when Desmond Smith made his appearance; he came on horseback cantering slowly, and his servant, a slight stripling of a boy, running by his side. As soon as he entered the boat, he threw off his coat and insisted on taking an oar, but we soon saw that the exertion was too great for him. At first the colour came so brightly into his pale cheeks that it looked like the glow of health, but after a little time he became more pallid than before. "My dear fellows," he said at last, "I am afraid I must ask one of you to take my oar. I find that it is too much for me to-day." As he said this he laughed, but in another minute he fell back in a fainting-fit. He soon recovered, and though he seemed ill and exhausted, he would not hear of our turning back on his account; he wrapped himself in his large roquelaure, and leaning back on the cushions which we placed behind him, the fresh air and the rest soon revived him. We dined, I remember, in our boat on the Twickenham side of Richmond Bridge, and Desmond Smith and some of the party sauntered about in Twickenham meadows, or threw themselves down upon the soft dry grass, while Murray and I started off to see the view from the top of Richmond Hill. As we came back we met Chillingworth and Hanson at the door of a low tavern, and in a loud and angry dispute with the keeper of the house. They had accused him of trying to cheat them, and Hanson had struck him; and he was sending off a pot-boy for a constable just as we came up. I was astonished at the calm and simple manner in which Angus interposed, and succeeded in restoring something like order, and a good understanding between the parties. With gentle authority he quieted our two drunken companions, and called back the pot-boy; and then taking the landlord aside, in a few words, full of good sense and feeling, and spoken with great kindness, he appealed to his head and his heart, giving him at the same time a mild rebuke for allowing the young men to drink as they had done. He offered his own money instead of the money which they would not pay, and he made the apology which they would not make for the blow which Hanson had given, and he even prevailed with the man to assist us in getting them down to the boat. We had a good deal of trouble with Hanson on our way back; he was violent even to fierceness, and he so nearly overset the boat more than once, that at last we all agreed to tie him hand and foot till we got to town. He then poured forth his abuse of us in no measured terms, and swore frightfully, till he tired himself out and went to sleep. We had but little trouble with Chillingworth, for he was stupified and heavy with sleep from the time he took his seat in the boat.

"I have quite done with those water-parties," said Angus Murray, to me, in reply to a question which I put to him, a few days after that excursion to Richmond; "I shall be glad to go out with you or with Stanley on the river, but not with the others." "O! I will allow," I said, "that Hanson and Chillingworth made their society as unpleasant as it was disgraceful; but do n't you like Desmond Smith, Angus?" He made no reply, and I thought at first he had not heard me, for he began to talk on another subject. I repeated my question, and then he said at once, "I do not like Desmond Smith; first impressions may be wrong, but you know we have seen him since. I hope my judgment may not be a correct one, but I fear that such an associate would be as dangerous as he is agreeable. I have little to judge by; but trying his words, and the spirit of what he said and did, by the plain rule of right and wrong, I found enough to make me dread any further intercourse with him. The danger of such companions as Hanson and Chillingworth is, that habitual intercourse with men of violent temper and of intemperate and profligate habits may by degrees wear away the aversion which we must at first feel to their vices. The danger of intimacy with such a man as Desmond Smith is, that there is something to captivate the taste and blind the judgment. I may be wrong about him, I hope I am; but I would have you keep on your guard, as I intend to do. I feel when in his presence as one does in an atmosphere where one cannot breathe freely."

Angus here alluded to a visit which he and I had paid to Desmond Smith one evening after the party to Richmond. We were on our way to execute a commission for Mr. Arnold at the west end of the town, and we overtook Desmond Smith, who was also walking thither from the city. He pressed us so earnestly, and with so much kindness of manner, to come to his lodgings and take coffee with him, that I willingly and at once accepted the invitation. "You forget," said Angus quietly, turning to me, " that we have to go to the further end of Piccadilly for Mr. Arnold, and that we promised to deliver the packet to Lady Sussex before six o'clock." " Well, my dear fellow," replied Desmond Smith, putting his hand on Angus's hand, " that arrangement will just suit me; I could not give you coffee much before seven, for I have one or two calls to make. You will find Jermyn Street quite in your way as you return; and so good bye," he added shaking the hand of Angus, which he still grasped— "you both promise to come?" I said, "Yes;" but Angus hesitated. Afterwards, however, he also promised, and we parted, Desmond Smith calling out "You walk too fast for me, for I am not quite the man I was before my illness, even yet."

It was before seven that we entered the room of our new acquaintance. I almost started back at the elegance and luxury of everything before me, and foolishly expressed my admiration of what I saw. Angus said nothing, and there was a coldness about his manner—usually so hearty—that I had never seen before. "You must excuse my getting up to shake hands with you both," said Desmond Smith, "glad as I am to see you, and admiring as I do your more than mercantile punctuality; but I thought this would be over before you came. I am going, to tell you the truth, to Lady Sussex's masquerade to-night, and I sent for Achille to dress my hair at half-past six, that I might be able to pass the rest of the evening with you. I hate powder and never wear it, but I don't wish to be known this evening; and I am going in the character of a French gentleman of the ancient regime, a sort of gentleman that I hate as heartily as I hate powder. A better reign of things has commenced in that 'beau pays de France; n'est ce pas, Achille?'"* Monsieur Achille shrugged his great

* Fine land of France; is it not so, Achille?

shoulders, and made a sort of grimace, which was intended for a smile, as he said, " Pour moi je deteste la poudre, et les petits maîtres; et je dis á bas l'un et l'antre."*

All this time Desmond Smith was reclining carelessly in a large arm chair, with a loose dressing-gown of rich brocaded silk thrown round him, and Monsieur Achille, a gaunt ferocious-looking puppy of a hairdresser, was frizzing and powdering his hair. " Vraiment," said Monsieur Achille, as he lifted up one of the fine dark curls, and looked at Angus, "quel dommage de souiller une chevelure si magnifique avec cette vile poudre de farine, et cette detestable graisse."† " It is unnatural enough," said Angus, " but many whom I love wear powder." " That man," said Desmond Smith, as the hair-dresser quitted the room, "is a remarkable person, he is a great politician. He came to me as a favour this evening, for he is about to return to his own country in a few days; you would not think it, but he has been recalled." " Ah, well," said Angus bluntly, " perhaps he will be no great loss, and will lose little in leaving our island. His trade is a more flourishing one there, I hope." " He does not return to any trade," replied Desmond Smith, gravely. It has been intimated to him that there are open-

* For my part I detest powder, and fine gentlemen, and cry, 'down with them both.'

† "Truly," said Monsieur Achille, "it is a pity to defile such a magnificent head of hair with this vile flour, and this detestable grease."

ings at present for political advancement to men o
talent and enterprise at Paris. A wonderful era has
lately commenced there." Angus smiled. "Do you
really mean what you say, Mr. Smith?" he said. "I
should be sorry to speak uncharitably of any one; and
a hair-dresser, if a good and wise man, is a credit to
his country; but, is that grinning, ill-looking man a
wise man, letting alone his being a good one?" "To
say the truth," replied Desmond Smith, "I may tell
you with confidence that Achille is not the very best
of characters; it has been said that he left his own
country because he was branded for some crime or
other, and could not show his face there.   However,
he has been unrivalled here, and they do say that he has
not left his equal even in Paris. I could not have gone
to-night to that masquerade, that is, I mean in the
character I have chosen, if Achille had been unable to
dress my hair." As he spoke Angus rose up. "You
are going out," he said, "and we must only be in the
way, so good night to you." "I can't hear of your
going," replied the other. "Why, my good friends,
my evening will not begin till you are both in bed and
fast asleep; now do sit down. Rush will be here in one
moment with the coffee, and I wish you to taste it; no
less a person than Achille himself taught the boy to
make it." He rang the bell, and Rush, his young
servant boy, immediately made his appearance with the
steaming coffee, and biscuits, and a little bottle of
liqueur on a silver waiter. "You told us that you

were to be at Lady Sussex's to-night," I now remarked, "how odd; we have just taken a packet to her from Mr. Arnold." "Why," he replied, colouring slightly, and hesitating, "it is a most mysterious circumstance that a ticket was sent to me, and I can't tell by whom. However, here it is," he added, carelessly tossing it to me; "for, on these occasions, every one must have a ticket, and so I mean to go. I think that my friend Achille may have had something to do with that ticket, he knew I wished to go. I have met Lady Sussex often, but I have never been introduced to her."

"And do you mean," said Angus, with a glow of honest warmth, "to put a mask upon your face, and go among your betters, when you have not been even asked. Surely you will do up the ticket in paper and seal it, and send it back to her Ladyship, and explain that a mistake has been made." Desmond Smith threw himself back at the risk of discomposing his dress and powdered head, and laughed aloud. "My dear fellow," he said, "I love your honesty, indeed I do, quite admire it," and here again he laughed, as if unable to suppress his laughter. "I wish I had the same inimitable simplicity, but I know the world, and you do not. What you say about my betters, however, I don't exactly understand—a mere title does not make any man or woman my betters; and I rejoice to think that the new era, which has already commenced in France, will soon dawn upon our own country, an era of glorious independence and equality, when the rights of

man will be not only understood but allowed.—Here,"
he added, handing to Angus a pamphlet which he had
laid down as we entered, "here is a new play by
Monti, full of the bold and new-born freedom which
I adore."

I do not forget the countenance of Angus, the look,
calm, noble, but searching, which he fixed on Desmond,—"You are but a youth," he said solemnly,
"and I am no more; but I should be false to my God,
and to you, if I did not tell you to your face that you
have entered upon ways, smooth and pleasant as they
are perhaps to you now, which, unless you turn from
them at once, and for ever, must end in eternal misery.
As for the world, I know that we are both pledged to
renounce it, and if I had not understood its dangers before, I have heard and seen enough this night to do so."

"Here is a note of invitation for us both," said
Angus Murray, as I passed his desk one morning;
"shall I answer it, and say Yes or No?" The invitation was from Mr. Maxwell, and we accepted it. He
had returned to his town house in Great Ormond
Street, for it was there he resided, his counting-house
only being in Old Broad Street. Our invitation was to
dine with the Maxwells at four o'clock on Saturday,
and so remain with them till the Monday morning.

We were a large party of young men. Besides
Angus and myself, and the two sons of Mr. Maxwell,
whom I had met in the summer, there was another
son, who had just returned from college, and with him

was Thomas Arnold, whom I have mentioned before, his college friend and companion. The evening passed very pleasantly in the society of this excellent family. I did not feel much relish for the religion of those around me, but it was impossible not to be struck with the manly good sense for which their conversation was distinguished, and the enlarged views which they took on every subject. I have since learned to understand this,—Religion, true religion, puts little and trifling things in their right place; it not only enlarges the mind, but causes it to be occupied by what is really noble and great, or at least forbids it to feel satisfied with what is not.

"I hope," said Mr. Maxwell, as we were walking together to church, "that you will listen to the sermon which will be preached this morning. When I say listen, I mean more than that sort of careless, passive hearing with which sermons are received by some persons. I would call ' listen' a verb active, and 'hear' a verb passive ; and I would urge it upon you, that if we do no more than let the sound of the preacher's words enter into our ears, without any care whatever to attend to the sense of them, they cannot possibly be words of influence and power in our minds. It was thus with me for many years, when I was a youth," he continued; "I went a passive, careless hearer into the earthly sanctuary of God. However earnest, however interested I might feel elsewhere, there I sat like one who had sunk down wearied into a heavy slumber, and I heard, as one who hears not. For many years I was, with my father and mother, the regular attendant on the ministry of one of the most persuasive preachers I have ever heard—one whom I should now listen to with a deep and absorbing interest. It may seem strange to you, but it is true, that I have not the faintest recollection of a single word which then proceeded from his lips. I remember his youthful countenance, and firm and powerful voice, (he is now an elderly man, much broken in health,) but everything else, all that might have profited me to eternity, is gone for ever. I was pleased, at least I had a kind of undefined pleasure in hearing him, because I saw that he was kind and pleasing, and I knew that he was good; but my mind had acquired an habitual exercise for my thoughts on other topics, when my ears were unconsciously hearing the words of the sermon. And thus, Sabbath after Sabbath, and year after year, found my spirit sealed under a deeper slumber. Glory be to that grace which at length awakened the sleeper." We were entering the outer doors of the church, as Mr. Maxwell said this. He just added, in a whisper, as we turned into the aisle, pressing my hand for a moment, as he disengaged his arm from mine, " Don't let it be so with yourself to-day. Watch and pray."

It was impossible not to be struck with the countenance of the preacher who occupied the pulpit that morning. It was full of expression, of energy, of fire.

His voice and manner seemed to say, " I must have attention! I have you here for a certain time, and I am resolved to make the most of that time." I was interested in the first part of his sermon, but I have forgotten it. I only know that he spoke of his abhorrence of hypocrisy; and he said, that not only did the word of God bear its testimony against all that is false and hypocritical, but that His work in the heart of every godly man would stand as His witness against false characters at the great day. He spoke of Ezra, and held him forth as an example to men of business; he described him as placed in circumstances as difficult as can be well conceived, as having to contend with the scorn and the opposition of the Pagans, and the corruption of the Jews, and as bearing up with an undaunted spirit under his diffi_ culties, and labouring through them in a full dependence upon God, the unseen God—upon him alone. He spoke of him as a truly humble man; and of humility, as the real ground of all that is great and noble. He spoke of him as a man of faith, as going up to Jerusalem with an implicit trust in God, confident that he should succeed in the great work before him, if God were with him; but quite careless to attempt it without God. " If Thy Spirit go not with us, carry us not up hence." He spoke of Ezra as a man of prayer; and the true man of business, he said, was the man of prayer. " No men seem to have been more engaged in business," said he, '' or more qualified for business, than Ezra, Nehemiah, and Daniel—men in high offices, and men of eminent abilities. But where should we find men who looked more entirely to God? For instance, Nehemiah seems to say, ' I set myself to the work—my heart was in it —my plan was laid; but before I spoke to the king on the business, I spoke to God: I said, O Lord, touch this man's heart, before he gives me the answer; that it may be Thy answer, though spoken by his lips.' So, in the case of Daniel, his heart was set on the honour of his God; and you will find him treating with God continually, and carrying all his concerns to God; so that the transaction from beginning to end, was a transaction with God. Now these were men of the highest eminence, and of first-rate abilities; but above all, they were men of prayer."

His look seemed to search one through and through, as he addressed himself to every separate hearer. "Are you a man of business?—perhaps you say, 'I am; and so much a man of business that I have no time for prayer.' You do not understand your business,—you know not how to transact your affairs. Instead of pleading business as the reason why you do not pray, the more business you have to get through the more you ought to trust and to pray. It is the grand secret of a pious man, in conducting all his affairs, that he first treats with God about them; he thinks not of crafty management, or artful expedients, which are the subterfuges and the miserable contrivances of an unbelieving heart—he is a man of prayer."

There was another part of his sermon that struck

me. He described Ezra looking with holy courage to God alone as his safeguard. "'I sought of the Lord a right way for us, and for our little ones, and for all our substance. For I was ashamed.' He expected to meet robbers in the way, and might by asking have obtained a band of soldiers of the king; but, he adds, 'I was ashamed! I would not have the king suppose, while I professed to trust in God, and to teach others to trust in Him, that I wanted this confidence myself. Should such a man as I flee!' It was right," he said, "to use all reasonable prudence and all means of safety; but situated as Ezra then was, he chose rather to expose himself to danger, than to have the honour of God, and His cause, called in question; especially as he had to do with those who did not see things as he did, nor believe in God, nor trust in His promises." These were the parts of the sermon that I remembered. Of course I cannot be exact as to the words, but there was a reality about the preacher, and a reality about the subject on which he spoke, which I felt it, at the time, impossible to resist.

He seemed to touch a spring in my heart which opened it at once, and forced me to feel the unprofitable and senseless folly of my whole course. Would to God that I had paused at that stage of my journey, that I had followed up the convictions of that morning; but there is a sentence in one of our Lord's Parables which exactly describes the effect of that sermon on my heart. "The seed is the word of God. And some fell on stony ground, where it had not much earth; and immediately it sprung up, because it had no depth of earth: And these are they which are sown on stony ground; who, when they have heard the word, immediately receive it with gladness; and have no root in themselves, and so endure but for a time."

I heard Mr. Cecil again on that same day, and I heard him with increased interest. It has been well said of him that he dealt with the business and bosoms of men. An energy of truth prevailed in his ministry which roused the conscience; and a benevolence reigned in his spirit, which seized the heart. I felt the thrilling power of his words, and I said to myself, " Surely he knows that I am present, and he knows what a weak and despicable wretch I am. He has been speaking of me; for I, and no other, am the character he describes: and yet how deep a sympathy he feels with me ! How kind he is! He cannot spare the sin; but he would spare the sinner: he would not hurt a hair of his head !"

I was full of admiration for the preacher on our return home. None of the party spoke in higher terms than I did of his power and eloquence; but I could not help feeling a little mortified on perceiving that there was a slightly distrustful manner in those around me. They were as kind as ever; they agreed with what I said: but there was something in their manner which I could not well define, which made me feel as if they did not exactly care to take me at my word.

No; it was not quite this, but it was something of the sort. I was left alone with Mr. Maxwell for a short time, when all the rest of the party had gone up stairs to bed, and I asked him the reason of the feeling of mistrust, which, however slight it might have been, was evident to me in the manner of himself and his family. " I was not aware of it," he answered, "no, nor were the others, I should think; but I dare say you are right; and if you ask the reason," he added, "with respect to myself, I will tell you at once. I cannot trust you as yet—I do not know that you mean half what you have said, nor do you know yourself. 'The heart is deceitful above all things,'—such is the description which God himself has given of our hearts. I suspect that you have not learned the truth of this in the experience of your own heart. I hope I need not assure you, my dear young friend, of the sincere interest I feel in your well-doing. Nor would I say a word to discourage you, if you are beginning in right earnest to seek and to serve God, and to make principle to God the foundation of your future life. If such is the case, I am really sorry that we have seemed even slightly mistrustful in our manner towards you; but if it is otherwise, then I must be allowed to say, as our Lord and Saviour would Himself have said to you, I cannot help you to build your house on the sand. Good night! God bless you! Remember what Mr. Cecil said to-day of Ezra and the man of business, and remember this in the counting-house, and among

your young friends, for there is the place where your
religion is to be acted out.   Alas! it was always thus
with me; I took the tone of the company with whom
I was. I acted on the impulse of the present feeling—
I had no stability—no manly decision; above all, I had
no godly principle.

On Sunday night I had been one of Mr. Cecil's
hearers.   On Monday night—the very next night,
I was at Vauxhall, one of a party of thoughtless and
profligate young men.   I was alone, and I had just
taken up a book which Angus had lent me, and was
quietly pouring out a cup of tea, when a loud ring at
the gate drew me to the window. A little servant-boy
stood at the gate, and a gentleman sprang out of the
gig, which had just drawn up, as I made my appearance at the window. It was Desmond Smith—and in
another minute he was in the room with me. " There
is no time to be lost, my dear fellow," he said, " you
must dress instantly, and come with me."—" No time
to be lost," I repeated, " why, what has happened? and
I *am* dressed." He laughed, and threw himself into
my arm-chair, taking up the open volume which I
had put down, and while he was quietly running his
eye over the leaves, he said as quietly, " I am come to
carry you off to Vauxhall. Hanson says you have
never been there, so go and get ready; you cannot be
seen there in a morning dress—but first ring the bell
for another cup, and put some green tea in the tea-pot,
and leave me to read your book and drink your tea,

while you are making an Adonis of yourself."—"But I do not know that I can go," I replied; for I was thinking of Angus Murray, and a conversation which had taken place between him and me, as we walked into the city that morning from Mr. Maxwell's house; and I felt that Mr. Maxwell and his family, and Mr. Cecil, would all have disapproved of my going with Desmond Smith. For my own part, I did not like going; not so much because I felt any strong objections, but because it was so soon after having been in such different company. "Why, what's the matter?" said Desmond, "ar'nt you well? or has your visit to Great Ormond Street put you out of conceit with the pleasures of the world? At any rate, there can be no great harm in a garden and a few lamps, and a concert and cold chickens." I still hesitated, but Desmond Smith said coldly, "You can go this once, and if you disapprove the thing, you need not go again. I would advise you to go." This was the reasoning to which I yielded, because I liked to yield, and because I could not summon the courage to say, as I knew I ought to say, No! I went up to dress. When I came down, I found Desmond Smith sitting in deep abstraction of thought, and when I spoke, he sighed heavily; but he started up, and began to talk in a loud, cheerful voice, and continued talking till his gig stopped before the door opening into the lamp-lighted gardens of Vauxhall. "That book of yours has made me feel rather queer," he said, as he passed his arm within mine, and hurried into the gardens; "but here is a place which will soon make us forget it. Hanson and Chillingworth, and some other fellows, friends of mine, promised to come by water—I wonder if they have arrived yet." We soon after met them.

I was amused and excited by the novelty of the scene, and by the gaiety and splendour of everything around me. Desmond pointed out to me many of the leaders of the world of fashion, whose names I had often heard, and who were much talked of at that time. The Prince of Wales and Lord Essex, Mr. Fox, the Duchess of Devonshire, and the Duchess of Rutland, Mrs. Crewe, and others. I was much entertained, and the evening passed rapidly away. I should probably have stayed till a late hour, had not my companion met with a foreign gentleman, the Marquis De Mirabel. They spoke together in French for some time. "You hear how anxious he is to take me with him to-night," said Desmond, turning to me, "and I have promised to sup with him." "Is it very late?" I asked. "Near midnight," he replied; "and if you wish to be at home in any reasonable time, I would warn you not to join Hanson and the rest of them. They have ordered supper, and will be here later than any one else. One or two of the party are half drunk already. If you like to get away at once, the Marquis tells me he has a coach waiting at the door, and we can give you a seat as far as we shall go in your direction." It was beginning to rain hard, and this decided me. I accepted the seat in the coach, was set down by them, and reached home just at midnight; but with my thin shoes wet through, and my coat in the same state. "You are out very late, sir," said my good landlady, as she opened the door herself; and she looked cross and spoke sharply. " I have sent the servant-girl to bed, and I have been sitting up and waiting for you above an hour; it's on the stroke of twelve. But, dear me," said Mrs. Thompson, "why, you are wringing wet;" and all her crossness gave way to motherly compassion. She insisted on taking my coat to the kitchen fire, and she bustled up stairs for my slippers; and before I could get to bed, I heard her kind voice at my door, and received a cup of hot gruel well spiced, from her kind hands, with many entreaties that I would be sure to take it at once while it was hot.

I had seen nothing that appeared to me objectionable on my first visit to Vauxhall; but I went again, and then the party was not broken up by the departure of Desmond Smith, and myself, nor did it rain. We were among the last of the company to leave the gardens, and we all remained long after the more respectable portion of the people had departed. We remained to sup in the king's box, and to drink and to dance— but there is no occasion to describe minutely the proceedings of that evening, or of any other such evening. Alas! I soon became accustomed to scenes and practices which had at first made me feel uneasy. My conscience began to upbraid me less frequently — my judgment being continually overpowered by my will and inclination. Often and often was I out till long after midnight. Mrs. Thompson became at length wearied out by my irregularities. On her coming up to speak to me, one evening, just as I was going out, I begged her to allow me to have a key made to her house door, by which I might admit myself at any hour, without disturbing the rest of the family. To my astonishment, she told me plainly that I must look out for lodgings elsewhere. I expostulated with her, but to no purpose.

"Many of the young gentlemen," she said, "in Mr. Arnold's counting-house, and in the other great merchants' houses, had occupied her lodgings; but she had never had cause to complain of any one of them, except it was of poor Mr. Vining, who had run just such a course as I had begun, and who, I might have heard, was taken up and tried for his life, and hanged for forgery. She should never forget the night when the Bow Street officers came after him. He had been dressing to go out, and when she went up stairs, to the very room where I was then sitting, to tell him he was wanted, one of the strange, rough-looking men followed close at her heels, and was in the room, looking over her shoulder before she had done speaking; and the poor young man knew the face of the Bow Street officer the instant he saw him, and made a rush into the bed-room—the very bed-room where I had been dressing—and he had managed to bolt the door, and to throw himself out of the window into the back garden; and would probably have escaped, had not the other Bow Street officer been on the look out for him, and seized upon him almost as he dropped from the window." The good woman was in tears while she told me this, and her manner was more than usually kind; but I found her quite decided as to my leaving her house. This was anything but pleasing to me; and I could not help shuddering when she spoke of the merchant's clerk who had been hung for forgery, and who had occupied my rooms, and whose irregularities had been so like my own.

On other accounts I was glad to go. I felt that Stanley's correct and steady habits were a reflection and a restraint upon me. He said little; he had left off speaking, for he found that I only took offence, and still followed my own ways. Indeed, a coolness had arisen between us, and we seldom met or spoke except at the counting-house, and on business. But, as I said before, Stanley was too common-place; and, as I assured myself, too cold-hearted to suit me. "Why does he not speak out and tell me that he disapproves of my ways?" I said to myself, "instead of putting on that cool, careless look, and speaking with that dry, heartless voice? How very different from Angus! How kindly, and yet how faithfully he spoke to me only yesterday; how his colour came and went; and how his voice trembled with emotion when he said the severest things! How his heart seemed to speak even in the most cutting words (and they were indeed cutting words) which he spoke!"

I might have added—" but the expostulating words of Angus had no more effect upon me than the phlegmatic silence of Stanley."

I had now begun to feel a craving for constant amusement. I had formed a habit of going continually to some place of entertainment. I could not bear to pass an evening by myself, and I seldom did so. Lodgings I had easily found, not on the southern side of the Thames, in the outskirts of London, as before, but at the West-end of the town, though in a dark narrow street, and at a higher price.

And now I soon began to find that my new mode of life was a very expensive one: I could not, indeed, go to one place of amusement after another, without paying away my money; but, added to this, I could not frequent such places without dressing more finely and fashionably than I had been accustomed to do; and expensive dressing required more money than I had ever been accustomed to spend upon my person. I stood aghast one afternoon, on returning to my lodgings from the city, when I opened the large folds of what seemed to be a long double letter—it was my tailor's bill. I glanced my eye at the amount; it was double the sum that I expected to receive during the whole of the next year. How it was to be paid I could not tell. Moodily I paced up and down the room, thinking over first one plan, and then another. I would have written to my aunt, or to my mother, confessing my profligacy and extravagance, and intreated them to forgive me, and to enable me to extricate myself from my difficulties; but I had not the heart to do this, for I recollected that my aunt had just lost a large sum of money by the stoppage of one of the Sussex Banks; and only the week before, in answering a letter—an application of mine for money—that dear kind aunt had sent me twenty pounds, telling me at the same time of the loss of her money; and adding, that they had been obliged to discharge one of their servants, and that they meant to live as economically as possible for the next two years, if they should all be spared so long. I thought of Angus, but he had spoken to me so often and so earnestly, warning me of what had now come to pass (the difficulties in which I had involved myself), that I felt I could not bear to speak to him on the subject. Besides, I said to myself, he is as poor as I am, and could not help me if he would; and I murmured to myself something about Scotch nearness and love of money. In the midst of these perplexing thoughts, a hand was laid on my shoulder. I started, for I had not heard any one enter the room; but when I looked round I saw the handsome and smiling face of Desmond Smith, now my frequent visitor—indeed, my favourite companion. "What is the matter?" said he; "for I am sure something is the matter. Why, I never saw you so woe-begone before.

If you could but see yourself in that glass, you would agree with me that you might go to the masquerade at the opera-house to-night without a mask, as the knight of the rueful countenance?"

" Is that all?" he said, when I had put my tailor's bill in his hand, and he laughed. " Why, what a novice you still are! " But do you see the amount?" I said, pointing to the bottom of a long list of charges.

"To be sure I do, man; and all I have to say is, that I am glad I see it to-day, for had I seen it to-morrow, I could have done nothing to assist you; but I have been so successful, that to-day I can help you out of your difficulties at once. Will that do?" he added, taking a single note from a small pocket-book of embroidered satin; " you see there are plenty of them;" and he put the note-case, which was filled with bank notes, into my hands. " Do admire the note-case," he said; " it was poor Lisette's work just before she left England." I looked at the note-case, and said it was pretty; but when I looked at the large amount of that single note which I was to keep, I began to pour out my thanks. " There, there," he said, " put it away safely, and say no more about it: when you can pay it you will; and, perhaps, some day or other you may have it in your power to help me. And now come along at once and dine with me, and dress at my rooms for the masquerade. Hanson will be waiting for us. I have chosen three witches' dresses for us. Come with me and witch away your troubles."

CHAPTER V.

THE sight of my tailor's bill had filled me with dismay, but as Desmond Smith had said, I was but a novice then. Other bills came in from time to time, and when I thought about them, I was very wretched; but I did not think about them more than I could help. I did not even look at them, except just at first, when they were put into my hands. I thrust one after the other into a drawer, which I always kept locked, and said to myself, that some day or other I would look them all over, and think of some way of settling them. I cannot say that any possible way had yet appeared, but I suppose I felt that I must take my chance about them.

Alas! it is thus that we often reason about concerns of the very highest importance. It is thus that we leave the debtor and the creditor account with our God unexamined into. We are sometimes startled into reflection, but while we tremble we turn away, and oppose ourselves to all serious consideration. The time will come, we promise ourselves, when we will consider our ways. But while we are thus deliberating, thus resolving, we are perhaps called to give in our account at the great day of reckoning, and it is then found, not only that the account which stands against us is beyond all calculation, but that we have failed to apply in time to the only Being who could have given us a full discharge of the debt, having paid it by His precious blood. Thus it is that we go on deceiving ourselves—forgetting the amount of our offences before God, and saying to ourselves, I will take my chance with others.

Remember, my reader, that the man who thus addresses you, though he gives you the account of what he has himself been, writes as a penitent but wretched offender, and hopes and trusts that the warning of his life may not be lost upon you.

My debts increased in number and in amount—it could not be otherwise, for my extravagance was fast settling itself into a habit; and it was becoming also a habit with me not to think about bills, or debts, or duns, but to harden my heart and my conscience against them. "For the sake of peace," I said to myself, " I must do this." I ought rather to have said, for the sake of mere self-indulgence, at once criminal and inexcusable. I was constantly with Desmond Smith. I found that, with the exception of Angus, he was much the most agreeable person I had ever met with. He was remarkably good tempered, and overflowing with talent of a certain kind—the talent of bringing forward all the information he had ever gained. He had, in fact, been more highly educated than any of us, except Angus, and he was able to speak (and it seemed to me to speak well) on any subject. He was also an accomplished man. He spoke French almost as well as his native language; played on several instruments; had a voice of great sweetness and power, and sang finely. He rode, danced, and fenced elegantly, and was reckoned a capital whip; added to all this, his face and figure, his style of dress and manners, generally drew the attention of all eyes upon him wherever he appeared. Alas! I have often thought upon poor Desmond Smith, that he had everything to recommend him but principle. He was utterly without principle, and never seemed to think of acting from any motive but that of seeking what was most agreeable to himself; but as he was evidently pleased to be admired, he took some pains to please others that he might be admired, and having naturally no bad tempers to struggle against, he did not find it difficult to make himself popular among those with whom he usually associated.

" Pray, Mr. Wilton, who is your friend, that drives so elegant a curricle," said grave Mr. Dawson to me. "I think I saw you, Mr. Wilton, in his curricle this morning. It was standing before the bank." " Yes, it was my friend's curricle," I replied. " And who may this friend be," said Hanson, for Mr. Dawson was suddenly called away by Angus Murray, to answer some question about which Mr. Arnold was waiting to see him in his private room. "It was Desmond Smith's curricle," I replied. " I must own it is a mystery to me how Mr. Smith manages to live in the expensive style he does," said Angus. "It is a mystery easily explained," replied Stanley, who had overheard the remark, and who now joined us. "You don't mean to say, Wilton, that you have been all this time ignorant of Desmond's ways of getting money," cried Hanson. "Indeed I have," I replied; "but I have often thought of asking him; for from one or two remarks of his, I have half suspected—" "what I have long known," continued Hanson, "that he plays—gambles, you would say; but it is one thing to tell you that he does this, and another thing to tell you how he does it—how he manages to be always successful! I am sure, I wish I could succeed as he does. But the fact is, Desmond Smith is an extraordinarily clever fellow. With him, gambling, in all its branches, has been made a study, and reduced to a system. I have tried in vain, and over and over again, and I have repeatedly given the thing over as a bad job. I can make nothing of it. I always lose." "I am heartily glad of it; I wish you may always lose," said Angus. "Thank you for that wish of yours, Mister Scot," cried Hanson, scowlingly; "but I don't exactly understand why you should wish me ill." "I wish you well, with all my heart," replied Angus, with a voice of unaffected kindness, and looking Hanson full in the face; "and therefore I rejoice to hear that you never succeed when you gamble." "Murray is quite right," said Stanley; "gambling is bad in itself, and never brings any permanent advantage to a man."

" There you are mistaken, Squire Stanley," said Hanson. " I know a man who has gambled for the last twenty years, chiefly on the turf, and he has succeeded in making a large fortune. He has bought a fine place down in Suffolk, and has got into parliament." " But he has not come to the end of his course," replied Stanley. " I have heard Mr. Brekelman speak of a case very like your friend's (if he is a friend of yours), who made a fortune, and even broke off his gambling habits, and married, and retired into the country, to a beautiful seat, which he had bought near Reading. He was the son of a good old clergyman, and he made a promise to his father, when the old man lay on his death-bed, that he would never gamble in any way again. I forget how it happened, that many years after he broke his promise; but having done so, he rushed back to his former ways with eagerness. The tide of fortune, as they call it, set against him. He lost everything, and he died in Bedlam only a week or two ago."

" Ah! I know what I wish," said Angus, and he seemed about to make some remark; but he checked himself and turned away, and I heard him draw a deep sigh as he did so. " Come, let us hear your wish, for once," said Hanson, in his strong, brutal voice, for he had, at times, a way of saying things that was quite brutal. " Come, my little preacher, let us hear what you have to say." He put his leg out so as almost to trip up Angus as he passed. " Don't be a brute, Hanson," said Stanley, quietly, " and let Murray pass; you know he has the finest temper in the world, or you would never taunt him as you do. You take advantage of his temper, but I won't allow it." " Come, come, Mr. Steady—you are in a rage, are you? Leave the little preacher and me to fight our own battles, and don't be coming old Brekel over us." " *Little* preacher," repeated Stanley, with the same quiet, imperturbable manner; " why, man, he's a head and shoulders taller than you, and though he has not so much bone, he has more muscle about him." " That's a lie," cried Hanson, turning scarlet; " and the first man that says so shall try the force of my bone and muscle. Do you see this?" he added, speaking between his closed teeth, and thrusting his doubled fist almost in Stanley's face.

But now Angus came forward, and put an end to the whole affair at once. I can't describe his manner—I can't repeat his exact words; but I felt, and so did the others, the power of both, and the quiet dignity of his manliness, though he spoke, as he always did, with such real kindness. He would fight, he said, his own battles, as he came between Stanley and his opponent, and, with a hand as strong as Hanson's, gently put down his uplifted arm. " Our weapons are not the same," he said firmly; " mine have nothing to do with violence or anger: but I shall not *say* more about them," he added, with the same dignified seriousness of manner. " Stanley," he said, " you are kind to me, and just—you always are, but the cold and cutting scorn with which you treat Hanson, is as unkind as it is unchristian. Hanson, you may say whatever you please to me, and you may or may not, as it suits your mood, put out your foot to stop me, or to trip me up —pray do so, if it is any amusement to you; though I must own, I think you may find a more sensible and gentlemanly way of employing yourself. But I do entreat you to curb this dreadful violence of temper— it may lead you to lengths which you do not dream of at present. If you trifle with such passions, they may so overpower you at last, that they may bring you to dye your hands with a fellow-creature's blood." He passed his arm within Hanson's as he spoke, and drew him aside. I was astonished to see the influence which he exercised over the hard nature of Hanson, and I could not help looking at them, as they stood together at some distance, and observing the abashed and down-cast looks of Hanson, while the countenance of Angus, as he pleaded with him, reminded me of the description given of that faithful and devoted servant of our Lord, the holy Stephen—"and all that steadfastly looked on him, saw his face, as it had been the face of an angel." I marvelled within myself at the wondrous power which godly principle, when accompanied by a consistent course of life, possesses even over those who are most opposed to it.

"Tell me," I afterwards inquired of Angus, "what you were going to say, when you said, 'I know what I wish,' and then checked yourself, just before that

quarrel began between Hanson and Stanley ?" "I was
going to say," replied Angus, " when you were all
talking about gambling, that I wished you would not
argue about the expediency of any line of conduct
from the success which may or may not attend it, but
that you would ask, before the thing is done, whether
it is right or whether it is wrong.   I was going to say
no more than this; there is no kind of principle so plain
as this, and this is the only principle on which a
Christian can act."

CHAPTER VI.

A FALL from the curricle of Desmond Smith put a stop, for a time, to my career of folly. I was taken up to all appearance dead: and for many weeks it was feared that a concussion of the brain had taken place. But it pleased God to spare my life. My dear mother came up to nurse me at my lodgings: and as soon as I was able to bear the motion of a carriage, she carried me back with her to Tancred's Ford.

I had full time during my quiet sojourn at home to think over my misspent time, and to make many good resolutions for the future. Of my thoughtless associates I heard nothing; but I received one or two affectionate letters from Angus Murray, and a few lines of kind but dry remonstrance from Stanley. My mother had been so pleased with Angus, during her stay at my lodgings, and had said so much about him, that my good old grandfather wrote him a pressing invitation to pay us a week's visit at Tancred's Ford. The invitation was accepted, and I was sufficiently well to go over in the old chariot, and meet him on his arrival in the coach at Farnham. He saw with surprise, when we came out upon the summit of the Fox Hill, the picturesque character of our wild heathy country. The hills of purple heather; the dark woods of Scotch firs; the wild-looking sheep browzing on the close green herbage; the straggling houses of the Bourne Hamlet; the little stream itself; the fresh elastic air fragrant with turf smoke — everything around him reminded him of his own northern land; and the nearer we approached to Tancred's Ford the more his delight increased. The journey at that time, though little more than three miles, generally took the old horses almost an hour to accomplish, on account of the deep sandy road, and the long winding hills which we had to pass over.

"You have never said half enough of this delightful place, Wilton," he said, as we left the heath, and drove along through the grounds. "What a noble grove of old fir-trees that is rising above the sweep of the river, and forming a kind of amphitheatre round the stream, and the broad green plain below!" "That hanger of pines is much admired," I replied. "You call a hanging wood, then, a hanger," said Angus; "and now I remember I have seen the word in a charming book which is just published by the clergyman of Selborne, which must be somewhere in this neighbourhood." "When I am stronger," I replied, "we will pay a visit to Selbourne; it is but a pleasant ride of seven miles across the heath."

Our road through the grounds drew forth fresh exclamations from my friend, as it wound along through the fragrant shade of the old Scotch firs, following the course of the river which flowed beneath, and coming at length to the pleasant spot where our modest mansion stands.

"There," he said, "I suppose, is the village church, raising its old grey tower above the trees of that green woodland. And there the river is seen again, broad and shallow, with that fine old bridge crossing its shining waters." "And there," I continued, "your favourite hills of purple heather are still a striking feature of the landscape; you may see their shadowy sides through that old fir-grove. Welcome, dear Angus, to Tancred's Ford."

He met with a hearty welcome from all our party, and soon became a favourite with every member of my family, from my venerable grandfather to my sister Alice, then a girl of sixteen. My health improved rapidly from the time of my friend's arrival, and he was enabled to prolong his stay for nearly three weeks. We were constantly together, and found much enjoyment in our rides over the wild and hilly heaths which extend through a broad tract of this part of England. I have often wondered that this country is so little known, and so seldom visited; for the landscape is beautifully diversified, and few parts of England combine so lovely a country with a climate so bracing and salubrious; space and grandeur in the hills and heaths, and lakes of water; and softness and smiling verdure in the lanes and pastures. Towards the north, the fine old forest of Alice Holt, a royal domain;* to the south, the dark and lofty ridge of Hind Head, the highest spot in the south of England; to the east, the pine woods of Waverley; and to the west, the romantic and sequestered woodlands extend to the beautiful villages of Hedley and Selborne. No high road passes through this part of the country, the point where the three counties of Surrey, Hampshire, and Sussex meet, well termed the wilds of those three counties. Perhaps early associations have caused me to regard them with a partial eye, but be this as it may, I have seldom known a stranger to come for the first time into this wild, lovely region, without hearing exclamations of surprise and delight from his lips. Angus, especially, was never tired of pouring forth his tribute of admiration, as we cantered together over the breezy hills and slopes of heather. " Here is Scotland," he often said, "within forty miles of London; and by all you tell me, as unknown and unvisited a

* It was at that time a magnificent forest of stately oaks, with herds of deer scattered over its lovely glades. The trees have since been cut down, and the forest replanted.

tract of country as my own native Scottish county, four hundred miles away to the north." We stopped our horses on mounting a lofty ridge which crossed the heath towards Chert, and I called his attention to the lakes of clear water on either side, not inferior in beauty and extent to some of the northern lakes. "This," I said, "is at least three miles in circumference, and the other, which is the most picturesque of the two, is of almost the same extent." "And those dark hills," said Angus, "rising from its shores, have quite a mountainous character about them. And how like the cottages on my native moors, those that I see scattered here and there over the broad heath, with their bright green fields, and an old Scotch fir or two, and a few graceful birches forming a little island of verdure in the wilderness. And then again that grassy level, that strip of emerald pasture, stretching away for miles, unseen till you drop suddenly down upon it, with a clear stream flowing through the midst, and herds of ragged colts grazing upon the short soft herbage, and the heron standing in the stream, or rising slowly on its broad wings at our approach.

A change had taken place in our neighbourhood. The parish had been much neglected, and had been without a resident clergyman: the service had been hurried over by a curate, who resided in another parish, and of whom it is unnecessary to say more, than that he made it too evident to all that his heart was not in his calling. Mr. Trafford, the vicar, had now come to reside among his people. Illness had before prevented his doing any duty, and he had been living in London, in order to be near the celebrated Dr. B——. It had pleased God to restore him to health, and during his illness a far more wonderful change than that of his bodily health had been wrought within him. He came back after his long absence an altered man, and his preaching and his living were—as I am now enabled to see—those of a true minister of our Lord Jesus Christ. The influence of his ministry had begun to tell in various ways upon the household at Tancred's Ford. My grandfather's chief feeling was that of gratification at the return of an old friend, whom he highly valued; but he spoke rather slightingly of his new views, and often said he could not imagine what Mr. Trafford was driving at, and that he required impossibilities; that he liked him as well as ever out of the pulpit, but when in the pulpit he was too often up in the clouds to suit him. My aunt was extremely angry at what she called his intolerable interference, and hesitated not to say that she considered his kind of preaching very dangerous; that he might be a good man himself—she supposed he was, but that when he said so much about faith, she had often a mind to tell him that he was forgetting morality; and yet with the inconsistency of such critics of God's faithful ministers, she complained that she could not endure such strait-laced ways as those which he evidently expected his flock to follow. My dear mother said little, but I saw that she was of a different mind from her father and sister, by the look of approval which she gave to Angus Murray, when, on his return from church, he spoke in high terms of the sermon which we had heard from Mr. Trafford.

Trensham Mere.

CHAPTER VII.

IT was on our return from church the second Sunday
of Murray's sojourn with us, that I was astonished
to meet some of my London acquaintances on our wild
heaths. The day was warm, but there was a fresh
breeze, and I proposed to Angus that he and I should
take a circuitous walk home. Our parish had long
been celebrated for the finest hollies in England; and
I led the way through the narrow lane opposite the
church, which was then bordered on either side by
rows of those magnificent hollies. Their green and
shining branches meeting overhead, formed a bower of
grateful shade on that sultry day. Just at the end of
the lane where it opens out upon the heath, we
saw, as it seemed to us, a well-dressed stranger saun-

tering slowly before us: we were passing him, when
the loud, well-known voice of Hanson called after
us, "What in the name of wonder brought you
here?" he said; "I thought no one had discovered
this out-of-the-way spot but Desmond and myself."
"We might ask you the same question," I replied; "at
least I might do so, for this is the place where my
family have long been settled, and I am sure I thought
you were a stranger to it." "I was so till a day or two
ago," said he; "but Desmond, Chilly, and I have been
making a little tour on the southern coast, and on our
way back to town, we heard at an inn on the high
road, that there was capital fishing in the piece of
water which lies before us, and we made up our minds
to have a day's sport there." "You are coming from
church now, are you not?" I said; "though I did not
see you there." "Church!" he repeated, with a loud
hoarse laugh, "not I. Why, man, I should have
thought you knew that church-going is not in my
way. I'm but just up, and should have slept longer,
had it not been for your church bells, which woke me
with their plaguy din; but I was so tired that I fell
asleep again. We were up late last night. We lost
our way on your dismal heaths, and had an overturn,
owing to your abominable roads, with their deep ruts;
and knocked up the people in the alehouse, at the
head of the lake, who took us at first, I do believe,
for robbers. They had only two beds to give us, and
so they got one for me in the house opposite your

church. Come along, old fellow," he continued, passing his arm through mine, and scarcely noticing Angus. "You'll find Desmond and Chilly at yonder little inn—a pleasant little place enough. I must have some breakfast, for this air has made me as hungry as a hunter. It is just the day for fishing, for the sun is clouding over." "It is Sunday," I replied, disengaging my arm, and looking round towards Angus, who was quietly walking away. "Sunday! yes, I suppose it is; and I know that as well as you. Is that your news? Why, Mark, you are not going to be squeamish, and to tell me that there's any harm in a little fishing on a Sunday. Hang that fellow, he's a Methodist," he added, catching up a stone, and aiming it at Angus. "I wish it had hit him," he said, as the stone passed over the head of my friend; "I should like to pick a quarrel with him, and have a fight. I hate your Methodists, and I shall hate you, if he infects you with his puritanical cant. I say, Murray, Methodist Murray, that stone was aimed at you, and I wish it had knocked your hat off, and your head with it. Aye, turn round and be in a rage," he added, with a brutal oath. "Come along, come along, I'm ready to fight you." "And I am ready," said Murray, coming back, and meeting his insolent look with a calm, open, sweet-tempered smile, "I am ready to shake hands with you, Hanson, for I have not yet done so. We don't fight on Sundays, or any other days." "Well, well, you are a good fellow, Murray," he re-

plied doggedly, but wringing his offered hand; "upon
my soul you are, and this is the way you always get
the better of me. I hate you, and I wish to hate you,
and yet I can't do it, for you force me to love you."
"Hanson," said Angus gravely, still holding his hand,
"leave off swearing, and don't say, 'upon my soul!' it is
an awful way of speaking." Hanson looked at him
steadfastly. "Leave go my hand, you canting fool," he
said fiercely; and violently jerking away his hand,
with a perfect volley of oaths he left us. Angus
gazed in silence upon him as he went, and sighed
deeply. "Poor fellow," he said at length, as he took
my arm; "he is not himself. How strongly he smells
of brandy." "It is an old habit of his," I replied;
"he always declares that he is fit for nothing without
a glass of brandy before breakfast." Just when we
came to a point where the mere was shut out from our
view by the high heather banks, I looked round,
and saw a boat upon the water. "Angus," I said,
"they are beckoning to us." "Well, Mark," he replied, "what of that! Come on, and don't let them see
that you have noticed their signals. Don't look back;
remember what Mr. Cecil said the last Sunday when
we were together at St. John's Chapel, 'Looking back
is more than we can bear without going back.'" I did
not reply to his remarks; but said, "Don't you think
we ought to ask them to Tancred's Ford? shall I ask
my grandfather to invite them?" "No," he replied
decidedly; "it may seem ill-natured to say so, but I

say at once, do not invite them. I do not think they are
the kind of guests that ought to be admitted there.
Your family would be annoyed by their sentiments
and manners, unless, indeed, they disguised them, and
surely that would be still worse."

The next day, however, without waiting for an
invitation, Desmond Smith and Hanson made their
appearance, just as we were sitting down to our early
dinner. I went out immediately to them, and my
grandfather, with his usual hospitality, followed me,
and courteously invited them to come in and join our
party at dinner. They readily accepted the invitation.

Desmond Smith made himself very agreeable, and
Hanson appeared at first to be on his best behaviour,
speaking little, praising the home-brewed ale, and
drinking so much of it that he soon became rather
noisy. After the ladies quitted the room he drank
still more largely of the wine. My grandfather looked
astonished, but said nothing. Angus, however, glanced
at me, and rising up, said, " I am sure, sir, we have
all had enough wine; may we not join the ladies."
" Unless," said my grandfather, " you would allow me
to order another bottle of wine." Hanson, who was
draining a decanter, muttered something about never
refusing good wine; but Desmond also rose up, and
we all left the table. On entering the drawing-room,
the conversation turned on the amusements of London;
and my country relations appeared to be much entertained by the accounts which Desmond Smith gave

them of the favourite actors and actresses of the day. Hanson said that the best actor he had ever seen on any stage, was Desmond Smith himself: and, turning to me, he added, "I wish you had seen him the other night, in Captain Macheath." My aunt spoke of the beautiful music in the Beggar's Opera; and then Hanson told her, that if she wished to hear it well sung, she should ask his friend there to sing to them. Desmond Smith was easily persuaded to open the harpsichord and sing several songs, which he did with a voice of great power and sweetness.

Angus sat without making a remark; and when a question was now and then addressed to him by one or other of the party, his replies were short, and his look unusually grave. After one of the songs, which was warmly applauded, Hanson clapped Angus on the back, crying out as he did so, "Come, my little Puritan, beat that if you can. Ask Murray to give you a song, ladies; he has a singing face, has n't he?" Angus, of course, was asked to sing, but he said very quietly, "If I have a singing face, I 've not a singing voice," and declined doing so. "Oh! don't tell us that you can't sing," said my aunt, "for I heard your voice in church; and I dare say you can remember some of your sweet Scotch songs." "Now I 'll lay a wager," said Hanson, "that Murray thinks it sinful to sing anything but psalms and hymns. He never goes to a play; do you, Murray?" "Never," said Angus, calmly. "But surely," said my aunt, "you don't see

any harm in a good play, Mr. Murray!" "I fear," he
replied, " that there are few plays that can be called
good; but perhaps I am no judge on the subject, for
I have been brought up among those who disapprove
of such things, and I value their opinion so much, that
out of respect to their wishes, if from no higher motive,
I should never go to a play." All this was said with
perfect ease and much modesty of manner. " Here is
one, however," added Angus, as Mr. Trafford at that
moment made his appearance, " who can speak to you
better on this subject than I am able;" and quietly
turning to the clergyman, he said, with a slight Scotch
accent, which sometimes betrayed itself when he was
much in earnest, " Will you, reverend sir, tell us what
you think of plays and playhouses?" " Oh, there is
no occasion to trouble Mr. Trafford," said my aunt,
smiling. " We can tell beforehand what his opinion
will be, and I dare say he knows as little about
them as you do, Mr. Murray." " You are mistaken,
madam," said the clergyman, mildly. " I know too
well, from my own experience, the evil of plays, and
the danger of playhouses. I cannot call to mind
a single play, in which, if there is not something irre-
verent towards God, and offensive to morality, there
are certainly false views of human nature, and pictures
of society presented, which are anything but edifying
to those who profess to be followers of our blessed
Lord." " I can't agree with you," said my aunt.
" I thought it was generally acknowledged that one

may go to the play and hear many a lesson of morality there as likely to profit one as the opinions of those who would throw a wet blanket upon all innocent amusements." Mr. Trafford laughed, and said with much good-nature, " My dear friend, you are becoming quite personal, for I see plainly that I am the person intended by your remarks. Your father and I used to go to the play together years ago, before you or your sister were born, and we have seen Garrick; and as I tell you again, I know what I am talking about; and I thank God that he has opened my eyes to the evil of such things, and I pray God he may open yours also. I have learnt to hate everything false, and I think it's an evil, and a great one, when men and women who might be serving God and their country in some useful profession, or noble calling, come forth upon a platform, dressed up and painted to look like kings and princes, and heroes and heroines, just to amuse the immortal creatures who are gathered together on the occasion. Such exhibitions could only be justified if every sentiment and every scene were to teach what is truly grand and virtuous; but I say again, such is not the case. False views are given by these false heroes and heroines; and all the accompaniments of play-houses are demoralizing and bad. Young men, I would have you think of these things. I am old and grey-headed, and I speak plainly, and at the risk of giving offence. An uncle of mine was ruined in body and soul by a play that was once in great vogue in

London. It was at the time that that pleasant poet Gay, little dreaming of the mischief he was doing, produced the Beggar's Opera, which was acted for sixty-two nights running, and all the world went mad at the acting of Miss Fenton, afterwards Duchess of Bolton. To cut the story short, the poor lad, who had learnt to look upon Captain Mackeath as the model of a hero, fell into bad courses, became a highwayman, and was hanged at Tyburn! I was a boy at the time, but I remember the agony of grief which made our home a house of mourning on the day of his execution. My good old friend Shirley," continued he, putting his hand upon my grandfather's arm, and looking him in the face with great earnestness, " you remember my uncle Harry, one of the finest, handsomest young fellows of his day?" "I do, I do," said my grandfather; " and I remember also, what you perhaps have forgotten, that a sweet, modest girl, who was a relation of my mother's, and whose picture hangs up in the chintz room, died of a broken heart, in consequence of your uncle Harry's untimely fate! They had been engaged to be married, but she was a girl of principle, and refused to have anything to say to him a year before his death; but she never held up her head again!" A dead silence followed this conversation, for all present seemed to feel uncomfortable. The colour rose in the cheek of Desmond Smith, and Hanson walked to the window with his hands in his pockets, and stood there whistling, though not for want of thought, as his future career will show. Mr. Trafford was the first to speak, and seeing the harpsichord stand open, he asked my sister Alice if she had been singing much lately, and told her that his grand-daughter had sent her a message by him, which he had forgotten till then, asking her to come and practise with her, unless she was otherwise engaged, the next morning. And here Hanson turned from the window with a flushed face and a bold look, the effect, I doubt not, of the ale and wine that he had drunk, and said, with a coarse oath, "We had some capital singing before you came in, old gentleman, and my friend, Desmond, there, will sing you one of Captain Macheath's songs in rare style, if you wish it; and by Jove I'll say in the face of any man that Macheath was a prime fellow, and I had rather live a jolly life like his, and die game, than be a milksop, like that smock-faced Angus there."

Here Desmond Smith and I interfered. We both were shocked and disgusted, and by force—and no little force it required—we got our half-drunken companion out of the room. The ladies were deeply distressed, and my grandfather so angry that I think if Angus had not restrained him he would himself have turned Hanson out of the room. My aunt's eyes flashed, and yet tears stood in them, as turning to Mr. Trafford, she said, "It is best to speak out, and own oneself in the wrong, which I do with all my heart. You have preached a sermon to me this day which I shall never forget. It has done more to convince me

of my own ignorance, and my own prejudices, than all
the sermons I have ever heard from your lips in the
pulpit. I ask your pardon, dear, true friend, for all
my unworthy thoughts, and all my hard speeches
against you and your new doctrines. And mind my
words, Mark," she added, turning to me, " that young
man will come to no good, and you had better beware
how you keep up your acquaintance with him; and
what's more, nephew, if I can read character, and I
think I am sharpsighted enough to do so, you'll get as
little good from his smooth-spoken, handsome companion. God forgive me for saying so," she said,
very solemnly, " if I'm wrong! but he seems to me
as bad as the other, though much deeper!" " You're
quite right, Kate," said my grandfather, still trembling
with angry agitation; " and mind you, Mark, neither
that scoundrel or his friend enter these doors again.
What brought them here, I can't tell." " My dear
father," said my mother in her usual gentle way, " it
was yourself, if you remember, and not Mark, that
invited them in." " Well, well, Mary, and what if I
did? But I should like to know how Mark became
acquainted with them?" " Oh, sir, that is easily explained," I replied. " Hanson is one of Mr. Arnold's
clerks as well as myself; is he not, Angus? and Desmond Smith is in Simon's house. They came, it
seems, to fish in these meres, and we were astonished to
meet them yesterday as we came home from church by
the heath. I gave them no invitation, though I think

I should have done so, had it not been that Angus cautioned me against asking them."

"Who is that young man?" said Mr. Trafford to my aunt, as Angus quitted the room. "I also think I can read character, and if ever I saw a noble spirit, I should say from his countenance and bearing that he is such an one."

"Mr. Murray is Mark's chosen friend," said my dear mother. "He is also a clerk in our cousin Arnold's house, and from all that I have heard and seen of him, I should say that you were right in your judgment. There are few young men at all like him."

Tilford Green and Oak.

CHAPTER VIII.

WE heard no more of Hanson and his companion till the return of Angus and myself to London, about a week after the scene which I have just described; but on entering the counting-house the morning after my arrival, and looking round me, I saw that Hanson was not there. His place was occupied by another, and in answer to my inquiries, Stanley told me, with a grave countenance, that some circumstances had occurred of a very disgraceful nature, and that Hanson had been dismissed by Mr. Brekelman. Chillingworth, as Stanley told me, was the only one who kept up any intercourse with Hanson, though they had often quarrelled when together. Their pursuits, however, and their tastes were similar, and they

had heard from him that Hanson was about to. enter
into business on his own account, as partner with a
Mr. Wallis, a wholesale woollen-draper, in Wood-street,
Cheapside. This Mr. Wallis I afterwards heard was
a man of disreputable character, who had more than
once failed in business, and defrauded his creditors,
but who had managed to commence the world again,
and, to the astonishment of every one, to carry on a
flourishing business. Chillingworth told me that Mr.
Wallis had a charming cottage at Finchley, where he
had met Hanson one Sunday, and he talked much of
Mrs. Wallis and her sister, Miss Flower, as being
very pleasing and agreeable women.

Angus generally called on me on Sunday mornings
as he passed my door, and we walked together to Mr.
Cecil's church. Since my return to London he had
gained a kind of half promise from me that I would
go constantly to St. John's Chapel, and that I would
not allow myself to desecrate the day, as I had too
often done before. I was just sitting down to breakfast
one Sunday morning, when a gig drove up to the door,
and a few minutes after I heard Chillingworth's voice
and step on the stairs. "I am come for you, old
fellow," he said, as he entered the room. "I have a
new turn-out below, and I have set my heart on taking
you to spend the day with some friends of mine." I
made several excuses, but in an awkward manner,
instead of plainly saying "No, I cannot go." "Ah,
what have we here?" he said, taking up my bible and

prayer-book which lay on the table, where I had just
put them, that I might have them at hand when
Angus called. "Very neat this binding, and very
handsome too: a present, I suppose," and he opened
the bible. "Mark Wilton, from his affectionate friend
Angus Murray." I was annoyed with myself for
colouring; but I did so, and my look and my manner
betrayed my fear of being laughed at; but Chillingworth did not laugh. Slightly shrugging his shoulders,
he walked to the window, and said soon after, "I suppose then, Wilton, you can't go?" "Not very well,"
I answered, hesitatingly. "You *must not*," he added,
turning round with an arch glance, and something like
a sneer slightly curling his lip. "*Must not*," I repeated, sharply. "I don't know what you mean by
must not. I suppose I can do as I please, and go where
I please?" "Oh, of course," he replied; "only that we
have all seen lately how Murray manages to lead you by
the nose; and I do wonder that a man of spirit like yourself can submit to be led by that canting Scotchman. I
don't like him, Wilton, and so I'd tell him to his face;
and I do like you. None of us like him; we see what
he is aiming at, with his correctness and his regularity,
and his respectful attention to the heads of the house.
He hopes to curry favour with them, and so he may for
what I care. For my part I make no profession, and
when I see a profession I suspect something; and
perhaps one of these days Master Murray will be
caught tripping." I was beginning to get very angry,

but my visitor changed his mode of attack. "I am a plain-spoken fellow," he said, " and you see the worst of me. I may be mistaken about Murray—perhaps I am; but I am always afraid of your high professors. I hope I've a bible and prayer-book as well as yourself; and perhaps I may go to church, though I can't say I go every Sunday. I must have a little relaxation, and a little fresh air, after being cooped up all the week in a counting-house, breaking one's back over a desk. I feel a pain in my chest when I talk of it; and I thought for once in a way you might enjoy a quiet drive in the country, and so I called for you."

Just then the servant of the house entered the room, and brought me a message. " Mr. Murray's servant is below, sir," she said. " He sends his kind regards, and told him to say that he is too unwell to leave the house this morning, and cannot call for you, and he hopes you will not wait for him." " Call for you," said Chillingworth, as she left the room. " So the secret is out; Murray calls to take you to church. But forgive me, Wilton, for returning to my idle banter;" and looking graver, he added, " you are quite right in going to church. But really, my good fellow, for once in a way you might break your rule, especially as by obliging one friend you 'll not disoblige the other. Come, finish that dish of tea, and take your place in my gig. You may bring your bible and your prayer-book, if you like, and go to church in the country; and that, you know, would satisfy the keeper of your conscience, the incomparable Murray. But seriously, Wilton, if you'll let me lead you off to-day perhaps another day you'll find me as willing to be led by you, as you are to be led by Murray. I should like to hear this Mr. Cecil whom Murray talks about, and I'm sure he is better worth hearing than that dull prosy old gentleman whom Stanley goes to hear, who is as stupid in the pulpit as Stanley is out of it. I often wondered why Stanley could tell us nothing of his sermons at second-hand, till I went to hear him myself, and found that at first-hand it was utterly impossible to discover what he was driving at, or to make head or tail of his incomprehensible stupidity. 'Pshaw, nonsense, Wilton!" he continued, as he saw me take up my books; " leave your bible and prayer-book behind. I was only joking when I asked you to take them. Do you think there are none to be found in the country? Though I should be *rather* surprised," he said, staring me full in the face, as we drove off, " if you find either bible or prayer-book in any room in Wallis's house." " You are not going there, I trust," was my astonished exclamation. " What in the world should you take me there for? I don't want to know those people, Chillingworth." " But they want to know you, my fine fellow," he replied; " and so I in my good nature promised to bring you down some Sunday. Now, just tell me, why don't you like them?" " Because," said I, " I have formed my judgment from your description of them, and from nothing else." "Then I have not done them justice," he replied, "or you have galloped off with a false impression; but I must have done you more justice, for it is from my description of you that they are wishing to know you. But no, you have had another trumpeter in that rough, hearty fellow, Hanson; and he wants to see you, to beg your pardon for getting drunk at your grandfather's, and for some scene that followed there, of which he says he has no very clear recollection." "Well, Hanson is a good fellow after all," I said; though I felt that I was forcing myself to say so, contrary to my own conviction. "I say, Wilton," continued Chillingworth, after a pause, "tell us about that place of your grandfather's? Hanson liked the place and the people vastly, and says that you have a pretty sister down there. I suppose you'll be heir to the estate when the old fellow makes his exit? How much has he a-year, do you think?" "Indeed I can tell you very little about it," I replied, gravely; and, to say the truth, I did not feel much inclined to continue the conversation; but my vulgar-minded companion was not to be put off by my reserve. "The thing must be plain enough," he said. "Have you a brother, Wilton, or rather has your grandfather any grandchildren besides you and your sister? Is there any one in the way?" "My sister and I," I replied, "are his only grandchildren." "Then, my dear fellow," he said, "you make yourself easy, for the place must be yours: and I'll tell you what, Wilton, I should have no objection to drive you down there some Saturday. This little tit of mine will trot the whole of the way, if we bait at Virginia Water. I hear that Murray has been there, and I think it monstrous hard that others, who like you quite as well as Murray does, should get no invitation to see your sister and your grandfather. Hanson says he is as hearty an old chap as he ever met with. It is near Tilford, I hear, where I often went when a boy to see a poor little sick brother of mine. He was put out to nurse with an old servant of my mother's, who had married and settled in a cottage there. My mother, you know, came from Godalming. I should like to see Tilford Green again, and the old oak tree; and one of these days I must, and will, drive you down."

All this disgusted me exceedingly, but I was obliged to hear it; at least so I thought, for I wanted self-possession and self-respect to put a stop to it, as Angus would have done, had he been in my place.

I turned the conversation, however, and nothing more was said on the subject till we stopped at Mr. Wallis's garden gate.

Mr. Wallis and Hanson were walking together up and down the lawn, in front of the house, in close conversation; and whatever the subject might be which occupied them, they were so engrossed by it, that it was not till Chillingworth had shouted twice or thrice at the top of his voice that they came forward to greet us. The first sight of Mr. Wallis prejudiced me against him;

and though he overwhelmed me with civilities, which made me endeavour to like him, I could never quite get over the effect of that first impression. He was a tall, heavy man, and of an athletic figure; quiet, and even sheepish in his manner, but there was a winking in his eye, and a drawing in of his under lip, and a sort of uneasy hesitating manner about him, which formed a strange contrast to the bold, bullying coarseness of his friend and partner, Hanson.

"What can have become of your groom, Wallis?" Hanson said, after his greetings were over. "But if you will take Wilton to the ladies, I'll go with Chillingworth to the stable, and I dare say we shall find Weasel there." But as he spoke Weasel made his appearance, and we all four proceeded to the house. It was an ill-built, comfortless-looking villa, or rather cottage, with windows down to the ground, by one of which windows we entered, and found the ladies still sitting at the breakfast-table, and a young man with a handsome, but vacant countenance, and flashily dressed, in the extreme of fashion, lounging on a sofa, with a newspaper in his hand. We met with a very smiling reception from Mrs. Wallis and her sister. They were both pretty—the unmarried sister more than commonly so. Neither of them wore powder, and Mrs. Wallis reminded me of one of the French caricatures of the ladies of the revolutionary circles— a sort of ill-dressed statue, with a short waist, a little train depending from her very scanty gown, and a profusion of long dark corkscrew ringlets hanging on each side of her face, considerably below her chin. She had very high arched eyebrows, and was much rouged, so that she had succeeded in making herself look very like a Frenchwoman of the style she admired. Her sister had evidently better taste, and the eye was more attracted to herself than to her dress. Her long, beautiful hair was dressed *à la victime*, and tied behind with a green riband. I soon saw that the one lady passed for a *bel esprit*, and that the other affected a kind of childish simplicity; but I ceased to exercise my judgment, and began to think them both very agreeable when they paid me marked attention, and listened and replied to several common-place remarks that I made.

I can hardly say how the day was passed, except that every now and then I felt that the conversation was most unprofitable, and that I had an uneasy sense of being among a set of persons very unlike those with whom I had before associated. There was a licence of tongue, and a freedom of manner, not exactly exceeding the bounds of decorum, but certainly approaching very near the line. Both the married and unmarried sister seemed to flirt, without hesitation, with all the gentlemen. Mr. Elrington, the good-looking, and good-natured stranger, had eyes and ears only for Miss Flower, who appeared, so my vanity told me, rather better pleased with myself than with him. Mr. Wallis seemed a mere cypher, and said little, and even that little no one seemed to attend to. There was much eating and drinking during the day; a great deal of wine was drunk; and Hanson and Wallis called for pipes, and brandy and water in the evening.

This was the first day of my introduction among a set of persons of whom I afterwards saw too much. The uneasiness of which I had at first felt in their society very soon passed away, and the constraint which I was conscious of showing left me. I became as free and easy among them as any of the party; in fact, I sunk to their level, and became one of them.

Before many weeks were over I had become a frequent visitor at Finchley, and my scruples had so far worn away, that when a card-table was opened on Sunday evening, I sat down as readily to it as any of them, and played till long after midnight.

But where was Angus all this time? and how was it that his influence had not been exerted to restrain me from mixing with bad company? He had questioned me more closely than I liked, and on my giving him some account of my first Sunday at Finchley, had shown such marked disapprobation, that he had made me more vexed with myself than I had been before he spoke, and as I could not justify myself, I chose to be angry with him. We quarreled, or rather I quarreled, for his sweetness of temper was as undisturbed as his sense of right and high principle was inflexible. On the following Sunday he came in as usual with his

smiling, open countenance, and with as friendly a
manner as if nothing had happened; and we went together to St. John's; but that Sunday was the last
day that we past together for a long time. I found
him on the Monday morning overwhelmed with
sorrow, weeping like a child, with an open letter in
his hand. The post had brought the news of the
death of one of his sisters, and he left town that night
by the mail for Scotland. There he was laid up by a
dangerous illness, having caught the fever, of which
his sister died, from her husband, a clergyman of the
Scotch church.

I know not whether I should have seen so much of
my new acquaintances, had it not been for my daily
intercourse with Chillingworth in the counting-house,
and that, owing to his lodging being at the same end
of the town as my own, we often walked home together
in the evening. I wondered at the time why the
whole party cared for my acquaintance, and was vain
and foolish enough to imagine that there must be
something peculiarly agreeable about me; but I
have since been led to conclude that they thought
I had money either in possession or expectancy, and
that they had found out that I was weak and easily led,
and might become an easy prey; and thus they taught
me to gamble, and after they had allowed me to win,
and given me a taste for the excitement of play, on
more than one occasion, they won from me large sums
of money, so that I was not only prevented from

paying any portion of my debts, but involved myself in fresh difficulties. Sometimes the Wallises called at my door in a hackney-coach, and insisted on carrying me off to the play or the opera with them, and from thence we generally went to Vauxhall, or some other place of entertainment to sup. We went also together not only to Epsom races, but to Ascot, and Egham.

I had plunged deeper and deeper into various excesses, and became more and more perplexed by my thoughtless extravagances, when Angus Murray returned from Scotland. His recovery had been slow, and his absence very long. I rejoiced, and yet I was ashamed to see him. I was indeed more struck than ever by his superiority to all the young men I had ever met with; and while I saw that with regard to steadiness and sobriety of spirit, his character had ripened since we had parted, I also found that for gentleness and winning sweetness he was more distinguished than ever.

About two months after his return, he begged me to pass the evening with him. "I would come to you," he said, "but as I wish to have some conversation with you on a subject of much importance, I would guard against interruptions of any kind. Some of your new acquaintance might come in and disturb us." I must own I dreaded what was coming, and yet I knew that he had but a slight acquaintance with my goings on during his absence in Scotland.

I was scarcely seated in his room than he closed the

door, and said, "I claim the right of a friend—your most attached friend, dear Wilton, in putting to you some close questions. And first, let me tell you, I know more than you think I do. I have been narrowly observing you since my return to London, and I see you are ill at ease. You have now and then dropped expressions which betrayed a familiarity with things and persons to which till lately you were almost a stranger. Once or twice I have heard an oath from your lips. Your frank and open expression of countenance is much changed. You have had more than one visit, if I am not mistaken, from creditors, who pressed you for money, which you could not pay; and the only one of your fellow-clerks with whom you seem to associate is Chillingworth; with him you appear to be on terms of intimacy, and yet I have heard you say, not long before I left, that you disliked and disapproved of him. Now, tell me, Wilton, what is the reason of all this? I know that such plain speaking—such direct questioning, may be offensive to you, but I think that the plainest way is the best, and my sincere affection for you forces me to speak thus plainly. Answer me two questions. Do you not, in your heart, disapprove of the society which you are now keeping; for I am sure you are keeping the company of ungodly and unprincipled persons? Will you first answer this question?" I drew myself haughtily up, and staring him in the face, with an assumed boldness, I asked him, in a dry, frigid tone, what right he had to ask such questions? "I have told you the right," he replied, with great mildness; "the right of a friend who loves you, but does not love your sins; and, I may add, the right of a friend who would make any sacrifice in his power to save you! No, no, Wilton, don't put on that look! I am not deceived—you are not angry—you are not offended. Come, come, own that you love me for this plain speaking, though you may not love the plain speaking itself? Answer or not, however, as you please, to this question. I need not words to tell me that you value my friendship. But to my second question, I must have a plain and full reply. How much money do you owe? for I am certain that you do owe more than you can pay; and tell me in what manner you think to extricate yourself?" "I could not resist his kind, but manly appeal. There was now no look of offended dignity on my face, but there were evasions on my tongue. For a long time I could not; and I would not tell him anything, or give him more than vague and general answers. He fixed on me a searching look, and said, "Have you seen much of Desmond Smith lately?" "I have not seen him," I replied, "since we both saw him at Tancred's Ford." "I am glad of it, very glad," he replied. "But now, dear Mark, do tell me—give me a plain, explicit answer?" "Really, Angus," I said, with an awkward smile, "you are treating me like a child. What possible good can it do for me to make you as unhappy as myself, for, my dear friend, I appreciate your noble affection, and I am quite sure, if you were to know all, your grief would be as deep as it would be useless;" and as I spoke, my emotion choked me, and I gave way to a burst of weeping. Angus appeared almost as calm as usual, but the colour forsook his face, and I saw him brush away a tear or two with the back of his hand. " My dear Mark," he said, with a low and tremulous voice, " I should have asked for your confidence, even had I possessed no power to help you. But I have the power: I have a certain sum of money—a larger amount than you suppose. The whole of it, if necessary, shall be yours. You shall repay it when you can, or never, if inconvenient. But I must know the truth, and I must have a sacred promise, made in the strength of God, and kept in the strength of God, to give up entirely, and for ever, the company of the people who have led you astray. If this decided step is not taken without another hour's delay, mark my word! you are a ruined man, in time and eternity. You have neither strength of principle, nor moral courage as yet; but you must seek both; and unless this step is taken, you will be putting the attainment of them more and more out of your reach. Promise, dear friend, to hide nothing from me. Indeed I won't reproach you." I said nothing, but clasping my hand, he continued, " Just one word, Mark: is it not as I thought? Do you not need the help I offer?" I was quite overcome, and told him everything—described to him the society I had been keeping, their habits and their conversation—gave him an account of the sums I had lost, and the debts I had contracted—in short, I kept nothing back from this true and faithful friend. But when I had told him all, and had seen his look of sorrow and astonishment, I covered my face with my hands, and felt, for the first time, the degradation and the wretchedness to which I had reduced myself. "There is one thing now to be done," said Angus; and as I looked up at the sound of his voice, the expression of his countenance seemed almost heavenly. "We must pray !" he said. "We must kneel down together, and ask His help who has been the unseen witness of this interview between us, who has heard every word that we have spoken, and who knows in what deep earnest I desire to prove my friendship for you, and my sense of all His goodness to us both. We must kneel down and ask His forgiveness also for all the past. You have not sinned, dear Mark, in ignorance; you have resisted His spirit, and you have outraged your own conscience. You cannot altogether have forgotten that last sermon that we heard from His faithful minister, the day before I was called away from you."

At another time I might have felt ashamed of kneeling down in the presence of another; and I was now taken by surprise. I had never done so before; I had never heard of any one having done so; but I did kneel, and while he prayed the tears flowed fast down my face, and I caught something of the spirit which breathed in every word of that noble, true, and godly friend, who stood by me in my hour of peril, almost like a guardian angel! If, from that hour, I did not love God—and alas! I did not—I *did* love that true friend, that child of God, with my whole heart!

The next evening I brought all my bills at an early hour to my friend, Angus Murray, and we were occupied till late in the night arranging them, and summing up the amount of my debts. As is commonly the case, they proved to be much greater than I had suspected, and we found that notwithstanding the sacrifice which Angus had agreed to make, a considerable sum would still remain unpaid. It was determined, however, that the most pressing claims should be discharged immediately, and we were to think over the subject, and then to determine whether it would not be advisable for me to lay my difficulties before my grandfather, and to ask for his assistance.

An event occurred shortly after, which unexpectedly relieved me from every perplexity. Mr. Brekleman died suddenly, and when his will was opened, it was found that he had left me a thousand pounds, in token of respect, as it was stated, to my reverend grandfather. The will was dated about the time that I entered the counting-house of the firm of Arnold and Brekleman. The money was directed to be paid immediately, free of duty. And thus it was, in God's good providence, that I was enabled not only to clear the whole of my remaining debts, but to repay to Angus the sum which he had so nobly advanced. Ah, who cannot recal some such periods as these in his course! some occasion when the opportunity is given him, by the wise and gracious Disposer of all events, of emancipating himself from the chains and fetters with which his sins have bound him, and of again starting fair in the race that is set before him? But, alas! how few there are who have turned such opportunities to good account! As this narrative, to my shame and sorrow be it spoken, will testify, I was not one of them. I do not mean to say that the effect of my friend's counsel and conduct had not a temporary influence upon me. A reformation took place, and the house was swept and garnished; but so far as any vital principle of godly life was concerned, it stood empty. Will it be believed, that the fact, that I no longer owed a mere debt of money to Angus, did, in some sense, cause me to feel less deeply the far greater debt of gratitude which could never be cancelled; and that, though I did not own it to myself, my feeling of obligation was lessened. I may assure my reader that it is not without a pang that I make this confession. I not only feel the humiliation of the confession, but I acknowledge with shame the proof that it gave of the deep corruption and depravity of my heart. I have set before me, however, the galling task of keeping back nothing which may be a useful warning to others. I did act well on the impulse of the moment, but who does not? I had yet to experience and to exhibit the

difference between those actions which spring from
impulse, and those which proceed from deep-rooted
principle.   It might have been said of me, as it was of
the first-born of Jacob—my whole course has been an
illustration of that sentence—" Unstable as water, thou
shalt not succeed !"

It was not till after some length of time that I
began to fall away and to return to my former courses.
I received a shock which sobered me more effectually
than any circumstance which had yet occurred, and
kept me steady for a longer period than I think I should
otherwise have been.   One morning, on entering the
counting-house, I found Chillingworth muttering with
ill-suppressed rage at Stanley, who had a newspaper in
his hand, from which he was reading aloud, with a dry
sententious voice, the account of a transaction, which,
as he said in the running commentary with which he
garnished the account, covered some of his acquaintances with infamy.   " It was but last Sunday that I
met you, Chillingworth," said he, " in company with
a very strange set of people, as I was walking over
Westminster Bridge, after church, to visit my aunt at
Chelsea.   You were on the box of an open carriage:
you did not see me, for you were lolling back to talk
to a lady, whose flashy dress, and painted face, made
me think that she and her companions were no better
than they ought to be.   I saw Hanson's bold eyes
staring out, and at your side was seated a man who,
if my memory does not deceive me, was no other than

his new partner, Wallis, as great a scoundrel as ever lived. Our house had some dealings with him when he was a sugar broker, about ten years ago, till Mr. Arnold all but turned him out of the counting-house for his gross dishonesty. You know, my good friend, that I warned you against this intimacy several times, and now you see what your two precious friends have been about. The warehouse in Friday Street burnt to the ground, and poor Fennings' premises, which were only partially insured, burnt too; and what is worse, two lives lost; and all this done, as it clearly appears, on purpose to defraud the fire-office, and extort twice as large a sum as the property was worth. Well, I don't want to be uncharitable, but I should be glad to see those two knaves stand in the pillory; and if I know anything of law, I suspect that will be part of their punishment. Here, Wilton," he added, "you may wish to read the account; and I think you will say with me, when you have read it, that it's a bad piece of business! bad, very bad! There's an attempt at an alibi put in by both the partners; and in Hanson's case, all I can say is, that if he were occupied elsewhere, in the manner he contends to have been, his conduct was as disgraceful in the one place as in the other."

Angus had been seated at his desk while Stanley was speaking, with his pen suspended in his hand, though once he had raised his expressive eyes, and fixed them on me. "Let us do Chillingworth the

common justice," he said, when Stanley had ceased
speaking, " of believing that he deplores the conduct
of those persons as much as we do. He never knew
them in their true character, or I feel persuaded he
would have shunned their society. But, remember,
Stanley, that Hanson was Chillingworth's friend when
he was here with us; and at any rate it was kind in
him not to turn his back on his friend when discharged
in disgrace. This exposure shows us all the danger
of such company.—Really, my dear Stanley," he
added, " I cannot but regret the spirit in which
you speak. You read your bible, and you know
that it tells us to look upon a fallen brother with pity,
and to consider ourselves, lest we also be tempted. I
felt sorry for Hanson before this, but I never felt so
very sorry for him as I now do. I shudder to think of
what may be the end of his course; but as for Chillingworth, you know as well as I do, that he has
always been honourable and upright, and is as little
likely to justify the ways of Hanson as any of us."
" Well, Murray," said Chillingworth, " you are really
a good fellow. I did not like you, and I think you
are a Methodist now, and I hate Methodists; but I not
only like you now, I only wish that I could be as kind-
hearted and good-tempered as you are. But as for
you, Stanley, you old crabbed cynic—you old formal
square-toes, all I can say for you is, that, preach and
prose as much as you choose, your dry lectures will
have no effect upon me. There's an old saying, and

I wish you would profit by it; 'a drop of honey will catch more flies than a gallon of vinegar.'"

I was glad to be alone with Angus afterwards, and to talk over with him the escape which I had had from a closer intimacy with Hanson and his companions. I shuddered when I recalled many circumstances of which I have said nothing, and shall say nothing in these pages. To Angus everything was known, and among other facts, how nearly I had committed myself by a clandestine engagement with the sister of Mrs. Wallis, whose great beauty and apparent simplicity had so captivated me, that I was about to propose to her, when all intercourse had been so abruptly terminated between us. I afterwards learnt from Chillingworth, whose eyes were opened after the affair of the fire, that the unfortunate girl was made a kind of bait to attract other young men besides ourselves to the house of her unprincipled brother-in-law. They were duped by the attentions they received, and then fleeced of their money. One, alas! became, in every sense, the victim of the snares by which he was entangled! I little thought, when I saw the vacant countenance of the good-natured young man, whom I met at my first visit to Finchley, how fatal and frightful the conclusion of his story would be!

At the time of Mr. Brekleman's death, the elder Miss Arnold was about to be married to a Mr. Tresham. The marriage, however, was put off for some months, and Mr. Tresham became a partner in the firm. It had been at one time the custom of some of the chief London merchants to receive a certain number of young men into their houses, not exactly as clerks, but in order that they might become acquainted with business, and be fitted to undertake in time the management of a firm themselves. Some of them were the younger sons of noblemen, or the sons of rich foreign merchants, who came to England, their places being supplied, for a time, in their father's houses, by the sons of English merchants. Mr. Tresham was the second son of the great Dutch East India house of that name, at Amsterdam. His father, the brother of the late Lord M——, had been placed, when a young man, in the house of Mr. Vander Vanderluyht, and had married the only daughter and heiress of the rich Dutch merchant; from which time the Tresham family become settled and naturalized in Holland. The younger Mr. Tresham had been the inmate of Mr. Arnold's house, and had returned to Holland the very year that I entered the counting-house. Such a person as Mr. Tresham was much needed after Mr. Brekleman's death, as the business of the house was so extensive, that otherwise it might have proved too burdensome for Mr. Arnold. It was impossible not to be pleased with Mr. Tresham, whose high and honour-able character, and pleasing manners, won upon all of us. He was peculiarly kind to Angus Murray and myself; and after his marriage we were often with him at the pleasant house which he had purchased on

Wimbledon Common. Mr. Arnold's country-seat was at Thames Ditton, and both Angus and I had been occasional visitors there, but now we became more intimate with him. We had been mere youths on our first coming to London, and, owing to the difference of age between ourselves and Mr. Arnold, there were not many subjects in common between us. Such was not the case with regard to Mr. Tresham; and we had now also grown up to manhood. He sought our society, and our acquaintance ripened into confidence and friendship. He felt, perhaps, that he could not take a better way of attaching us to the interests of his house than by treating us as his equals, which, in fact, we were, though not so highly connected in point of family as himself. Angus, I believe, was nearly related to some of the noblest noblemen in his own country, but he was one of the few Scotchmen who said nothing on the subject; indeed he thought little of such distinctions. The only elevation of birth or rank which he had learnt to prize, was that of a spiritual nature; and he would have thought the highest nobleman in the realm—if an ungodly man—low and mean, compared with the the poorest child of God's grace and adoption. This was the secret of that lovely humility, which, amid the many graces of his noble character, shone forth the brightest, and shed its pure lustre upon them all. This imparted to him in every society that remarkable and graceful calmness which distinguished him above all

other young men whom I have met with. But notwithstanding his great superiority to myself in every way,
it was evident that I was rather the favourite of the
two with the Arnolds and the Treshams. There was
a godly singularity on some points about Angus, which
could never be understood or appreciated except by
those who—to use the words of Scripture—were, like
himself, " transformed by the renewing of their mind."
He was not singular in trifles—there was no narrow-
.mindedness about him—there was neither harshness
nor unkindness in his judgment of others, but on all
points where principle was concerned, his inflexible
adhesion to the high standard of God's word, caused
his conduct to appear like a reflection upon the principles and practice not only of myself, but, I fear, of
all those with whom he was associated, who acknowledged no higher standard than that set up by the
honourable and excellent of this present evil world.
It was, alas! too true with regard to the Arnold family,
as it is with many other families as distinguished as
themselves for all that is amiable and honourable, that
there was no reference to God, either by word or
action. In their daily life there seemed to be no sense
of His presence, no acknowledgment of His authority,
no reverential mention of His name. God, the Crea-
tor, the Redeemer, the Sanctifier, was as much forgotten as if He had been never heard of; and it might
have been said of all that kind and excellent family, with
the exception of Mrs. Arnold, "there is none that under-

standeth, there is none that seeketh after God!"   In-
difference with regard to God, neglect of His revealed
will, and no return of grateful praise for more than
ordinary blessings—was the state of this peculiarly
amiable family.   A spiritual discernment was needed
to perceive this; and I, at that time, had no spiritual
discernment, and did not perceive it.   And now that
God has opened my eyes to see everything in His
light, it is not for a poor, broken-hearted wretch like
myself to make these remarks in an uncharitable
spirit.   I rejoice indeed to know that few would now
agree more entirely with me in the opinion I have
given of them than the members of that very family,
who have been brought, by the mercy of God, to
a vital knowledge of truths which before they misunderstood and despised.   It was the character and
conduct of Angus Murray, as they have since told me,
at once so perplexing, and yet so admirable, which
first excited a doubt within their minds as to their
own views, and their own practice, and led them to
inquire, to read, and to think, with the earnest and
anxious desire to know the truth, which God never
fails to bless.

I had neither seen nor heard anything of Desmond
Smith since I had called on him to repay the money
he had lent me.   I remember remarking to myself
that he was then in an unusually low spirits, though
much gratified by my bringing him the sum that
I owed him.   I heard from Chillingworth soon after

that he had left his lodgings, and that the people of the house either could not, or would not say where he was gone. It was about two years after this time that Chillingworth told me that he had again met with him, but in such altered circumstances, that he could hardly believe the gay and elegant Desmond Smith stood before him. Whether he had been dismissed or not from the office of Simon, French, and Co., we could not learn; but Chillingworth was told by a friend of his in the same house, that after a longer interview with one of the firm, he had resigned his situation. Chillingworth had been playing billiards at a house in D—— Street, and there he had found our former companion filling the place of a billiard-marker. He could hardly help smiling when he told me that Desmond—for he was convinced it was he—had stared at him with a calm effrontery, which at the time almost staggered him, and had assured him that he was certainly mistaken in supposing that they had ever met before; and that, notwithstanding all that he could say, he persisted in refusing to recognise him.

We agreed to go together to the billiard-room, determined to make him acknowledge us, and prepared to offer him every assistance in our power. We did so, but were told that the person we inquired for was no longer there. On our asking his name, they said that they believed it was Smith, but that they knew nothing of the name of Desmond.

" Wonders will never cease!" said Chillingworth

to me, one Sunday afternoon, when we met in the park. I was walking, and he stopped his horse to speak to me. " Whom do you think I saw last night? but let me first tell you where and in what company I saw him. I was at the Opera last night, and while looking round the house, and pointing out to a friend—a country cousin, who was with me—some of the great people, whose names he had seen in the newspapers — among the highest in rank or the leaders of fashion, or the belles of the season—my eye was caught by a gentleman who was standing in Lady M.'s box, talking to herself and Lord M. They were evidently listening to him with that pleased look and manner which showed that he stood well in their opinion. There was something in his countenance which fixed my gaze upon him — it was for a moment—for my eyes was turned away to the next box, into which the Prince of Wales had just entered, accompanied by Lord Essex. The following conversation between two gentlemen behind me, drew my attention to him again. " His name is Desmond, and he has only lately come to London." " Where does he come from?" " From the north of Ireland— his uncle or cousin died lately. You see he is in deep mourning—he was the heir." " He is rich, then?" " No, not what we should call rich. I should say some two or three thousand a-year." " Well, he is one of the handsomest fellows I ever saw!" " I agree with you there." " Are you acquainted with him?" " Slightly. I met him at Lord M.'s the other day at dinner. He is a capital judge of a horse, and has the neatest turn-out in town. M. took me to see a horse of his which is to run for the Derby. Perhaps you have heard of young Sly?" " Why, you do n't mean that he is the man that bought young Sly?" " Yes, but he is! I like Desmond, he is a quiet, gentlemanly fellow—no humbug about him!" The name had caught my ear, and recalled my attention to his face. And the man in Lord M.'s box—the possessor of young Sly—the quiet, gentlemanly fellow, with no humbug about him, turns out to be Desmond Smith, of old Simon's counting-house, alias the billiard-marker— Smith, of Lorimer's billiard-rooms." Here, however, I interrupted Chillingworth. " Look behind you," I said, " and you will see the very man you are speaking of." A groom, with two horses, mounted on the one, while he led the other, had been pacing up and down before a house near the Grosvenor Gate, not far from the spot where we then were. The door of this house had opened, and a servant, out of livery, stood within, receiving his master's orders with an air of great deference. The master stood on the steps, turning his head occasionally while addressing the servant within, and pulling on his gloves. He was about to mount his horse, which the groom had brought up to the steps, when his eye caught mine. A look of surprise and perplexity suddenly passed over his countenance, but as suddenly passed away, and, coming forward, with perfect self-possession, he greeted us both, apparently with real pleasure. Chillingworth was taken aback, and so was I. Before we could recover ourselves, he had dismissed his servant with the horses, and passing his arm within mine, he was walking with me along the pathway within the park. " This is a pleasant meeting, my dear Wilton," he said; " and you and Chillingworth are two of the friends that I was wishing to see. You find me in somewhat altered circumstances. I have lately come into possession, as you may have heard, of my uncle Desmond's little property. I always looked for it. You remember, I dare say, or Chillingworth will," he added, turning his head to Chillingworth, who was riding beside us, "my speaking of an uncle in Ireland?" (of which, by-the-bye, I had not the slightest recollection, nor, I suspect, had Chillingworth.) " I have dropped the plebeian name which I formerly carried—in obedience to the requirements of his will, and you will know me now only as Algernon Desmond."

Here Chillingworth interposed. " Upon my word, Desmond, 1 congratulate you; but I must own I am almost as much astonished as I was the other day, when I thought that I had found you at Lorimer's billiard-rooms. You must not be offended at my saying so, but I mistook a billiard-marker for you, whose name, it seems, was Smith. A strange coincidence, was it not?" " Very strange!" replied Desmond, with imperturbable calmness, and a faint smile. " But such coincidences are not uncommon. At any rate, my dear fellows, I see that my servant is bringing back my horse, as I desired him to do in ten minutes;" and taking out his watch, he added, " I have an engagement for this morning; but we must not part without my knowing when we can meet again. Let me see, to-day—to-morrow—no—on both these days I dine out; but on Tuesday—yes, I can give you Tuesday. Now consider yourselves engaged to me for Tuesday. I shall give you a very quiet dinner, and have, perhaps, but one or two friends to meet you. On Wednesday I leave town for a few days—but more of this on Wednesday. Adieu! adieu! Remember six o'clock on Tuesday."

Chillingworth and I remained fixed to the spot where he left us, staring at one another for a full minute in mute amazement, till I burst into a loud laugh. And when I could find my voice—for I tried in vain to speak, being choked with laughing—I cried, " Is it a hoax, Chillingworth? Is all this story a hoax, or is it true? Which is it? What do you think?" " Think!" said Chillingworth; " I neither think nor care whether it is or is not true; but this I know, that if Desmond can give one a good dinner, I shall be as ready to swallow his story as his wine. On Tuesday, at six, remember, Wilton, you and I will return to this pleasant quarter of the town, and then we shall see with our own eyes, and hear with our own ears, more of this marvellous affair. True! why should it not be true? Is Desmond the only man who has ever come in for the fortune of an old uncle? For my part, I must say, that when he was a merchant's clerk in the City, he was tiptop the primest fellow for enter_taining his friends I ever met with. Wilton, I believe it all! and as for the billiard-marker, I am now quite sure I was mistaken there! Did you see how cool he was when I told him of my mistake? Why, he merely shrugged his shoulders, and smiled at my stupidity."

We parted, but I had not walked far, when Chillingworth returned. "What do you do with yourself to-day, Wilton?" he said. "Where do you dine?" "At my lodgings," I replied. "You shall do no such thing," said he. "You shall get a horse at Prescott's, and let me carry you off into the country to dinner." "What, to your friends, Messrs. Wallis and Hanson's?" I replied. "No," he said, "not to Wallis's nor Hanson's—they are no friends of mine— I 've done with them. I cut Hanson dead the last time I saw him; and don't talk to me of Wallis and his painted lady—they are a bad set, take my word for it. No, I dine with a few friends at the Castle, at Richmond, and they will be glad to see you. Will you come?" "And have to do what Angus did, I suppose—to separate you and a Richmond pot-boy?" "'Pshaw!" he replied. "Don't be so witty at a friend's expense, Master Wilton. As for that pot-boy

affray, that brute Hanson got me into that row—but
there was always a row when he was present. I'll
engage to be on my best behaviour, if you'll come.
Say yes or no, old fellow, for we have no time to lose?
I was on my way to Richmond when I met you."
"Thank you," I replied; "I do n't think I can go with
you." But I hesitated. He took advantage of my
hesitation, and said, "But I am sure you shall go.
Come with me, and get yourself mounted, and we'll
canter quietly to Richmond, and get an appetite as we
go, for a good dinner."

The party at the Richmond dinner were a set of
foolish noisy young men, among whom I was one of
the most foolish and noisy. We sat long and drank
deep, and were in a very unfit state to ride home; but
notwithstanding our intoxicated condition, we arrived
safely in town. My horse stumbled with me and
broke his knees, for which I had afterwards a tolerable
sum to pay. When I awoke the next morning, my
aching head and uneasy conscience reminded me that
I had begun again to break through my good resolutions. My unwholesome sleep had been heavy, and I
found that I should not have time for breakfast if I
would reach the counting-house at the appointed hour.
Angus was there, as bright and cheerful as ever. He
was coming up to speak to me, but Mr. Tresham
called him away, and a minute after, he went out with
a packet of letters in his hand. Perhaps, had he been
there, I should have told him of the Richmond party,

for I was in a penitential mood, and had at that time no reserves with him. But he did not come in till the afternoon, just after Chillingworth and I had returned from dining together at the same chop-house. I had had no appetite for dinner; and Chillingworth had bantered me on my dismal looks. "You are vexed with me, old fellow, eh! for drawing you away to the Richmond dinner; but I assure you, I thought we should have had a very quiet party. Between ourselves, however, you were one of the most riotous." "I know it, I know it, Chillingworth, and I 'm not vexed with you, but with myself." "Well, don't be such a noodle as to lament over what is done, and can't be undone. Why, really, Wilton, one would think you were just fresh from the country, and knew nothing of life. The fact is, and you know it, that that sanctified dolt, Murray, has got you into his leading-strings, and you are not half the man you were. Where is the harm, as I often say, of a little innocent pleasure? and what 's the use of setting yourself up for being better than everybody else? it does not sit well upon you, and you are too knowing a chap for that sort of thing. Come, come, take a glass or two of this port, and you 'll be all right again. By-the-bye, Wilton," he said, gravely, "I think we might as well agree to say nothing about Desmond, till after our dinner with him." I was secretly of the same opinion, but I replied by asking him his reason. "Oh! as for reason," he said, "I 've none to give you; it is rather an impression than a reason that makes me say this. I don't distrust Desmond's account of himself. You know I believe it: but I shall be better satisfied after I have seen him again, and when we have really dined at his table, and met his friends." I made no reply, but I determined in my own mind to say nothing to Angus.

Soon after six on the following day, I was at Desmond's door, and was ushered by the respectable-looking servant into a small and elegant drawing-room. Chillingworth had already arrived, and was standing near a window, talking to an elderly man of very gentlemanly appearance. Desmond held out his hand, and shook mine with much cordiality, but then turned away, and never noticed me again till he asked me to take wine with him at dinner. The party was evidently a select one, and all seemed well acquainted with each other. Chillingworth and myself were, apparently, the only strangers present. Desmond was kind, but slightly distant in his manners; and the consequence was, that Chillingworth and I, who were seated at opposite ends of the table, had but little share in the conversation. I saw that he was unusually constrained in his manner, and I felt that the same was the case with myself. We gathered, however, from what was said, that the cause of Desmond's intended absence from town was, that he was to be returned on the Thursday following as member for one of Lord M.'s close boroughs in Somersetshire. And after dinner some arrangements were talked of by Desmond and Lord M., who was present, and the elderly gentleman before mentioned, whom I found to be a lawyer and the agent of Lord M.

As the evening advanced, Chillingworth and I did nothing but stare at one another; and, as if by mutual consent, took our departure at an early hour. Just as we were leaving the room, Desmond, who had returned to the sofa, where he was sitting with Lord M., re-called me, and said, " I don't know, Wilton, what your engagements may be for this evening; but my friend, Lord M., has begged me to offer to Chilling-worth and yourself some opera tickets, if you like to take them. His lordship's box will be empty to-night." " And I am sure," continued Lord M., with a very courteous manner, " if you and your friend like to occupy it, you are most welcome." " Mara sings to-night," said Desmond, smiling, " and perhaps you will be glad of such an opportunity of hearing her." We took the tickets, and bowed our thanks.

As we walked away together, we both agreed in words, but I 'm sure, so far as I was concerned, only in words, that we had passed a very pleasant evening. " What a very gentlemanly fellow," said Chilling-worth, " Desmond is! He always had an aristocratic manner. And a capital dinner, was n't it? I say, Wilton, did you hear them talking of the French cook. I wished to get a peep at the bill of fare, which he kept by his own side, but he only handed it to

Lord M. Did you taste the quails? I never tasted quails before." "He is a very quiet, gentlemanly fellow," I replied; "and it was just like his old good-natured way to think of asking Lord M. for these opera tickets." "Rather fine, though," said Chillingworth; "I think he might have talked a little more to his old friends!" We walked on in silence, and in a subdued mood, which we only lost when seated in the front of Lord M.'s box. There we assumed to ourselves, from our position, a free and easy air, and made ourselves vulgarly conspicuous to those who were near us, and heard our loud conversation during some of Mara's finest passages; for, more than once a hissing "Hush" was directed towards our box.

A few days after, the papers contained the address of Algernon Desmond, Esq., to the electors of B.; Chillingworth pointed it out to Stanley, who was poring over the paper, and then gave him an account of Desmond's change of fortune, and of the dinner-party in Park Lane. At first Stanley shook his head, and muttered something to himself which we could not catch; and I afterwards heard him ask Mr. Tresham if he knew anything of Lord M.'s new member, the Mr. Desmond whose speech was in the paper. Mr. Tresham replied that he did know him, and had met him frequently at Lord M.'s. Nay, more, to Stanley's astonishment, for I saw him raise his eyebrows at the information, he said that he had been more than once at Wimbledon. "I believe, Mr. Stanley, he was for a short time in Simon's house, and was glad to accept the situation; but he is of a high family, one of the Desmonds of Antrim, Mr. Stanley, and a very quiet, gentlemanly man." "You told me nothing of this," said Angus, as he overtook me in the street, when I left the counting-house that evening. "I have no right to claim your confidence, and perhaps I am wrong in feeling as I do; but your reserve makes me rather uneasy, not about Desmond Smith, or Mr. Desmond, as I hear we must call him, but about yourself. His story is natural enough; but if the man is not changed, Wilton, he may still be a dangerous companion for you, and the more so from his altered position. If I know anything of character, he is the most dangerous associate you have ever met with." "Well," I replied, "you need not be under much apprehension about my intimacy with him; for, to tell you the truth, Angus, though he was kind and courteous, and invited us to his house, he took pretty good care to keep both Chillingworth and myself at a distance." "Beware of him," said Angus; "time will show, I only hope he is what he seems. You remember telling me about the billiard-marker. I say it only to yourself; but that billiard-room was at a notorious gambling-house, and Desmond is a consummate actor. Is it quite impossible that he is a successful gambler? Keep to yourself what I say. It may be uncharitable, and I hope I am mistaken; but be on your guard." "But Mr. Tresham, is he likely to be taken in?" I replied. " He is not," said Angus. " Mr. Tresham is a clear-sighted, sensible man; but his cousin, Lord M., whom I have met more than once at Wimbledon, is weak and unprincipled, and, I believe, is not a stranger at gambling-houses. I don't know that Mr. Tresham is aware of this; and I only heard it a few days since, at the house of a friend, whose name I had rather not mention. But you must remember that Desmond owes his introduction at Wimbledon to Mr. Tresham's cousin, Lord M., and is so specious and pleasing in his manners, that I can easily account for his speaking of him as a very quiet, gentlemanly man, perhaps a better specimen of Lord M.'s friends than others whom Mr. Tresham may have met with him." " I don't agree with one word that you have said, Angus," I replied; "and if I did not know you to be the best and kindest fellow in the world, and the truest friend I ever met with, I should tell you that your speech savours of a harsh Scotch presbyterian sourness; and I should remind you that, from the very first, you took a prejudice against Desmond; and, really, you do him injustice. Let me tell you also, that, though you dislike and abuse him, he has never said an unkind word of you; and I can't say as much for some others of my companions—" "Who are not, as I told you before," said Angus, " half such dangerous companions for you. Keep to yourself my suspicions; forgive, I repeat, my seeming want of charity; but be on your guard; time will unveil the truth."

The Arnolds had frequently invited my grandfather to pay them a visit, and to bring the ladies of my family with him; but he had as often pleaded his age and the state of his health, as a reason for his not leaving Tancred's Ford. Alice, however, was now grown up, and Mrs. Arnold and her daughters renewed their invitation in so kind and pressing a manner, and expressed so earnest a wish to become acquainted with my sister, that, as my aunt wrote to me, it was agreed that she and Alice should come up and divide the time during their stay between the Arnolds and Treshams, and pass a-week with the Maxwells before they returned home. Nothing unusual occurred during their stay. My dear sister was much admired and became a general favourite. Her modest ease and the sweetness of her manners in the society of those who had been personally strangers to her till that visit, took me by surprise. Scarcely a day now passed in which I was not either at Ditton or Wimbledon; and before they left I had seen so much of Miss Arnold, that I began to think very seriously that she was the most charming person I had ever met. She and my sister had become great friends; and my aunt had obtained a promise from Mr. and Mrs. Arnold, that on their return to Tancred's Ford, they should take Miss Arnold with them. Lord and Lady M., and their friend Mr. Desmond, often joined the party. The first day that they came I was not a little curious to discover the impression that Desmond would make on my aunt, for I remembered the circumstances under which she had seen him at Tancred's Ford.

He was introduced to her by Mrs. Tresham, and the coldness of her manner almost amounted to rudeness, as she bowed haughtily. But the next morning, as she and I were walking together on the lawn, she said, " I must tell you, Mark, that I am convinced it is not always right to consider one's first impressions the correct ones. You know I rather pride myself on my discernment of character, and I certainly had taken a great prejudice against Mr. Desmond; but I have quite changed my opinion. I was not a little annoyed, I assure you, when Mrs. Tresham desired him to take me in to dinner; but I was agreeably disappointed. Nothing could be more rational and sensible than his conversation—indeed, I found his remarks quite instructive. Almost the first word that he said was to apologize for the scene that took place at Tancred's Ford; and he laid much of the blame of it on himself, and regretted the low company with which he was associated. He has been wild and foolish, I dare say, in his time; but he is, evidently, a reformed man."

Angus was present, and I could not resist asking him afterwards if he had had any reason to deem that his suspicions were well founded with regard to Desmond. " I have seen no reason to change them," he replied; " but indeed I've no wish to speak on the subject, nor would I be so unkind as to breathe a word to any one but yourself. It is a strange elevation, I allow, if he were indeed a billiard-marker six months ago, to be a member of parliament now. We should not believe such things if we were told them, but seeing is believing." "I observed him in close conversation with you, Angus," I said, "and you did not repulse him." "I had neither right nor reason to be rude," he replied; "but if I did not repulse him, I repulsed as civilly as I could a pressing invitation to dine with him to-morrow." "But you have no engagement," I remarked; "for both I and Desmond heard you tell my aunt that you had not been invited to the Arnolds to-morrow." "Yes," said Angus; "and he made that the ground of his invitation, and offered to take me to the House if I would dine quietly with him first." "And you had been saying at dinner," said I, "that you should much like to hear the debate to-morrow evening; and yet you refused?" "I did indeed," said Angus. "Well," I replied, "your coolness and frankness astonish me." "It was one of those occasions," said Angus, "when it is as necessary as it is difficult to say, No. I did not like to associate with Mr. Desmond when he was a city clerk, because I thoroughly disapproved his principles. I see him now under different circumstances, but I see the same man; and, believe me, Mark, one is saved a great deal of trouble, and spared running the risk of much evasive shuffling, by speaking plainly, and doing at first what our judgment tells us is right." "But one would not willingly give offence," I answered. "Not if one can help it," said he; "and I hope I did not offend. Mr. Desmond could not complain of any want of courtesy in my manner. I thanked him, though I declined his invitation." "And gave no excuse?" I inquired. "I had none to give," returned Angus, "and so I gave none."

I met Desmond but once or twice after this, either at Mr. Tresham's, or Mr. Arnold's. His visits were suddenly broken off, and I could not discover the reason till some time after, when I learned that he had proposed for Miss Arnold, and had been refused both by the lady and her parents. My acquaintance with him, however, did not cease; but more of this in the proper place.

I had always been an especial favourite with my aunt, and had been accustomed to make her my confidant, and consult her in all my difficulties from my earliest childhood. I much wished to find an opportunity of being with her alone, that I might ask her advice, and soon found one. She led to the subject, without knowing it, by her high commendation of Miss Arnold; and I then told her of my attachment, and asked if she saw any prospect of my being accepted in the event of my proposing for her. "I am glad you have asked my opinion," she said; "for, to say the truth, since I have seen her, I have secretly set my heart on her becoming your wife; and I may tell you, in strict confidence, that I think it very likely you may not be rejected— at all events by my cousin Arnold. In point of family, you are about equal: the whole of my little fortune will be yours, and the greater part of my father's also, together with Tancred's Ford. And you do not know, perhaps, that we look to your being taken, some time hence, as a junior partner into my cousin's house. This was partly agreed upon when you entered the counting-house as a clerk; though Mr. Arnold said plainly at the time that he would make no promises, and that everything would depend on your own steadiness and good conduct. I hear an excellent character of you from Mr. Arnold; and you are a great favourite with Mr. Tresham, who has more than once told me, that since Thomas Arnold has entirely relinquished the thought of being a merchant, he hopes that they may be able to give you a better situation than that of a clerk. In fact, Mark, I have talked the subject over with them, as I promised my father to do; and I am at liberty to tell you all this—but we must keep the matter secret for the present." I had not interrupted my aunt with a single remark, for I feared to lose a word of the information she gave me; not, as I told her, that I cared much about having any share in the business, except that I now saw a dawning of hope that my suit to Miss Arnold might not be discouraged; for I had feared that, as a clerk in her father's house, I should have had but little chance of succeeding.

My aunt and Alice met with a hearty welcome at the Maxwells'. Many years had passed away since my aunt had seen them; but in their early life she and

Mr. Maxwell had been much thrown together, and they had a sincere respect and regard for each other.

Of late years I have often looked back to the contrast presented between the household of Mr. Maxwell and that of Mr. Arnold. At the time that I was so much with them both, I was not capable of understanding the difference of principle which influenced the spring of action in those two families. I have been lately reading a volume by a master-mind of the present day;* and I owe much of my clearness of apprehension, under God, to the lucid statements of that original and powerful writer. How earnestly I wish that his book had its allotted place in every counting-house of this professedly Christianized country. His arguments have this distinguishing peculiarity, that if they are but thoughtfully weighed, it is impossible for any man to get over them. He describes the state of Mr. Arnold's house, and the pervading spirit which influenced the heads of the firm in all their foreign correspondence, and in all their social intercourse, in the passage that follows. Though he wrote long after the period now referred to, I could almost imagine that he had been the unseen spectator of all that was going on in the bosoms and in the daily habits of the Arnolds and the Maxwells. "It is very noble," he writes, "when the simple utterance of his word" (read here Mr. Arnold's word) "carries as

* Dr. Chalmers on "The Application of Christianity to the Commercial and Ordinary Affairs of Life."

much security along with it, as if he had accompanied that utterance by the signatures and the securities, and the legal obligations, which are required of other men. It might tempt one to be proud of his species, when he looks at the faith that is put in him by a distant correspondent, who without one other hold of him than his honour, consigns to him the wealth of a whole flotilla, and sleeps in confidence that it is safe. It is indeed an animating thought, amid the gloom of this world's depravity, when we behold the credit which one man puts in another, though separated by oceans and by continents,—when he fixes the anchor of a sure and steady dependence on the reported honesty of one whom he never saw,—when, with all his fears for the treachery of the varied elements through which his property has to pass, he knows, that should it only arrive at the door of its destined agent, all his fears and all his suspicions may be at an end. We know nothing finer than such an act of homage from one human being to another, when perhaps the diameter of the globe is between them; nor do we think that either the renown of her victories, or the wisdom of her councils, so signalizes the country in which we live, as does the honourable dealing of her merchants; that all the glories of British policy and British valour are far eclipsed by the moral splendour which British faith has thrown over the name and the character of our nation ; nor has she gathered so proud a distinction from all the tributaries of her power, as she has done from the awarded confidence of those men of all tribes, and colours, and languages, who look to our agency, for the most faithful of all management; and to our keeping, for the most inviolable of all custody. There is no denying them the very extended prevalence of a principle of integrity in the commercial world. But he, of whom it may be said, that he has such a principle of integrity within him, *may not have one duteous feeling of reverence which points upwards to God,*—he may not have *one wish* or *one anticipation which points forward to eternity,*—he may not have *any sense of dependence on the Being who sustains him,* and who gave him his very principle of honour, as part of that interior furniture which he has put into his bosom; and who surrounded him with the theatre on which he has come forward with the finest and most illustrious displays of it; and who set the whole machinery of his sentiment and action a-going, and can, by a single word of his power, bid it cease from the variety and gracefulness of its movements. In other words, *he is a man of integrity, and yet he is a man of ungodliness.* He is a man born for the confidence and admiration of his fellows; and yet a man whom his *Maker* can charge with *utter defection from all the principles of a spiritual obedience.* He is a man whose virtues have blazoned his own character in time, and have upheld the interests of society; and yet, a man who has not by *one movement of principle* brought himself *nearer to the kingdom of heaven* than the *most profligate of his species*. *The condemnation* that he is *an alien from God*, rests upon him in all the weight of its unmitigated severity."

Such a description, alas! agrees well with the class of character of which Mr. Arnold was then a bright illustration, seeking his reward on earth, and finding it; conscious of his own rectitude; gratified by the homage of society—a homage always paid to those virtues which support the interests of society; enjoying the prosperity which is the general accompaniment of that credit which every man of undeviating justice is sure to draw around him; *influenced in everything* by a *refined selfishness*, and sustained by the *thorough understanding* of the principles of *self-interest* between himself and others.

At the time I refer to, it would have been impossible to point out any want of honourable feeling or amiable conduct in Mr. Arnold or his family. But there was *no recognition whatever of God as He is revealed in His own Word*. Our Heavenly Father, our Blessed Redeemer, our Divine Sanctifier, were as entirely unheeded, and to all intents and purposes as much forgotten, with the exception of a formal Sunday attendance at the parish church, as if they had been inhabitants of Rome or Athens before the dawn of the Christian faith. Ah! how shall the question of Him, who we believe shall come to be our judge, be answered by such members of a *professedly Christian society*, on the great day of account: " *What hast thou done unto me ?*" And here let me plainly declare that I could not have written down these remarks, and given any application of them to the Arnold family, had it not been that I can now also bear witness to the marvellous change which it has pleased God to effect in all the members of that excellent family, particularly in Mr. Arnold himself, of whom it may be said, that whatever he did at all times, both before and after the above-mentioned change, he did it heartily.

But I spoke of the contrast which was then presented by Mr. Maxwell—whom I may bring forward also as a type of the class (alas! never a numerous one) to which he belonged. Religious principle, that which is in fact alone worthy of the name of principle, animated, in him and in his family, all those virtues which are admirable in the eyes of man with a new spirit; and gave a religious character and importance to all such things as are " pure, and lovely, and just, and true, and honest, and of good report." Simplicity and godly sincerity gave a peculiar grace to his intercourse with all his foreign correspondents, as well as with every child and servant of his family. The Kingdom of God had its faithful subjects beneath his roof; and its pervading spirit was the leaven which leavened that which would otherwise have been still in all the corruption of a fallen nature, and an ungodly world. There was nothing of cant or of religious display in Mr. Maxwell's circle; but there was at the same time a direct and constant recognition of the

Divine presence, and the Divine authority. The mention of that Name which is above every name too often imparts a chill, and spreads a gloom when brought forward in some companies; and His professed disciples are ashamed to own the master by whose name they are called: but here it was not so. Vital religion spread its brightening and freshening influence over every occurrence; and the language of every heart seemed to be, "all my fresh springs are in Thee."

I was frequently one of the party at Mr. Maxwell's during the stay of my aunt and sister there; and I well remember many of the striking remarks which occurred, even in common conversation. One evening Mr. Cecil and his friend Mr. Bacon were present; and I could not help observing the effect of some of their sayings upon my aunt, who, though she had lost many of her prejudices since Mr. Trafford had returned to the charge of his parish, was still disposed to maintain stoutly some of her old views and opinions. The conversation had assumed a directly religious character; and Mr. Bacon, who was sitting next her, had made a remark that rather grated upon her notions on such points. "As to that, Mr. Bacon," said she, "my religion is to fear God, and keep his commandments; so we will talk no more of such matters." I could not help saying to myself, "Here is my dear aunt's old maxim in a new dress, that religion is a thing of the heart, and is too sacred a subject to be brought forward in conversation." But Mr. Bacon had an admirable reply ready. "You will remember, madam, that it is said, 'They that feared the Lord, *spake* often one to another.'" My worthy aunt did not attempt another encounter, and, I trust, on that evening heard many things which, I have reason to believe, produced a deep impression on her, though the effect did not immediately appear. It was well said of Mr. Bacon, by his friend Mr. Cecil, that, "elegant in his manners, and rational in his mind, without any affected singularity, he dared to differ from the world so far as the world dared to differ from its God." There was always something to be learnt in the society of these men, and it was to such society that Mr. Maxwell delighted to introduce his guests. It was impossible not to take knowledge of such men, "that they had been with Jesus!" At the time I am speaking of, infidel opinions were beginning to be fashionable in the world. Many persons were led astray by their admiration of the French philosophers, and the Revolution that was taking place in France, the frightful consequences of which had not yet manifested themselves. The excellent Mr. Cecil took pains to lay bare the fallacies of the specious opinions which were gaining credit with the ignorant and inexperienced. "Young men," he said, turning to myself and Angus—after the ladies had withdrawn from the dinner-table—"mark my words. The nurse of infidelity is sensuality. Youth are sensual; the Bible stands in their way; it prohibits the indulgence of the lusts of the flesh, the lust of the eye, and the pride of life. But the young mind loves these things, and, therefore, it hates the Bible which prohibits them. It is prepared to say, if any man will bring me arguments against the Bible I will thank him; if not, I will invent them. But remember what I tell you—and I have sounded the depths of infidelity—there is no weight in infidel arguments; they are *jejeune*, and have often been refuted. Why, infidels themselves are not convinced by them. I would give you this advice. When you meet with infidels, observe them; they are loose, fierce, overbearing men; there is nothing in them like sober and serious inquiry; they are the wildest fanatics on earth; nor have they ever agreed among themselves on any scheme of truth and felicity." These were strong and startling statements. Their abruptness gave them additional force. It was during a quiet, general conversation, that the speaker, who had till then said little, suddenly roused himself, and addressed them to us. They set me thinking. Would to God I had done more than think! It was the practice of Angus not only to think upon such statements, but to act upon them. Alas! I have often recalled, with all the bitterness of self-accusation and self-abhorrence, the many opportunities I enjoyed, and the many more I might have enjoyed, in the holy, happy circles of Mr. Maxwell's family and friends, and felt how solemn an account I should have to render of such opportunities, not only wasted, but in a manner despised! "My dear youths," continued Mr. Cecil,

" he that has worn the fetters, and smarted under the
lash, is best fitted to speak of the horrors of slavery;
and when I speak to you of this slavery of the evil
one, I speak as one who is but too well acquainted
with the galling bondage. I was once an infidel, and
I have read all the most acute, and learned, and serious
infidel writers; and while under the controul of those
wretched principles, I gave way to licentiousness of
life. I was suffered to go great lengths, and, to a very
awful degree, to believe my own lie; and yet I had a
pious mother. There were few like her, and I had
opportunities and advantages such as many children
never possessed. My father had a religious servant;
I frequently cursed and reviled him, but he only met
my insults with a pitying smile. He drew me once to
hear Mr. Whitefield, but his preaching had no sort of
religious effect upon me; nor had the preaching of any
man in my unconverted state. Yet I conceived a high
reverence for Mr. Whitefield. I no longer thought of
him as the Dr. Squintum we were accustomed to
buffoon at school. I saw a commanding and irresis-
tible effect, and he made me feel my own insignifi-
cance. It was one of the first things that struck my
mind in a profligate state, that in spite of all the folly,
and hypocrisy, and fanaticism, which may be seen
among religious professors, there was a mind after Christ
—a holiness—a heavenliness among real Christians;
and my first convictions on the subject of religion were
confirmed, from observing that really religious persons

had some solid happiness among them, which I had felt that the vanities of the world could not give.

"I feel it a duty, an imperative duty—nay, it is a consolation to me," he added, turning to Mr. Maxwell, and his whole countenance beamed with an expression of benevolence, while the tears rose to his bright, pene-trating eyes, "to speak a word in season to these young men. I owe it to the class to which they belong. I have made converts," he said—and the crimson colour suffused his whole face—"converts to infidelity. It was only yesterday that I met one of them, and he laughed at all my affectionate and earnest attempts to pull down the fabric erected, alas, too much by my own hands!"

Alas! with what feelings of shame and sorrow do I write down the above conversation, of which I have now as vivid a recollection as if I still saw that re-markable man, and as if his powerful words were still sounding in my ears. But I may say of him as he said of Mr. Whitefield, "That neither his preaching nor his conversation had any abiding effect upon me. It was not by the experience or admonitions of other men that I was to be brought back from that career of vanity and sin, which I was still, with some interruption, pursuing. I was preparing the fetters and scourge for myself, and when I had smarted and suffered, and been brought to feed on the husks of the swine-trough, then, and not till then, did I come to myself, and arise, to go to my Father's house."

The Bridge and River at Tancred's Ford.

CHAPTER IX.

THE visit of my aunt and sister had come to its close. It would still have been prolonged at the earnest entreaties of their friends, among others of Mrs. Arden, who was then in great grief from the death of her charming little grandchild, and who had been one of my grandfather's earliest friends; but we were alarmed by a letter from my mother, who mentioned that my grandfather had had a slight attack of paralysis. This was only to be expected at his advanced age, but the news filled my dear affectionate aunt with grief and anxiety. She could not rest till she had returned to him. The three ladies set out a later hour than they had intended. This was owing to my aunt's taking her departure a day earlier than that which had

been fixed upon. In those days travelling was not
what it is now. A journey of forty miles was a serious
undertaking, and many of the high roads were infested
by highwaymen. My aunt's friends and myself were
not easy at the thought of the ladies going without
the escort of some of the gentlemen of the family; but
my aunt laughed at the idea of any danger, and said
that our old man-servant, Thomas Frost, was as
good a safeguard as any of the gentlemen, "and as for
myself," she added, smiling, " I think I could act on an
emergency with as much nerve as a man." They had,
however, to pass two notorious spots—Hounslow Heath
at the commencement of their journey, and Bagshot
Heath towards the end. My sister's letter to Mrs.
Tresham will give the best account of the fright
which they met with on that journey, and my readers
must remember that such events were far from being
uncommon at the time I refer to.

" It was a foolish speech of mine, dear Susan, to
say when I left you, that I hoped we should meet with
some adventure on our journey home. I assure
you we have met with one, that will satisfy me for
many a year to come; indeed I hope never to meet
with such another. The road was new to me, as on
our journey up we went by the other road, passing
through Guildford and Cobham to your house at
Ditton. But as we started from your father's house in
London, and as my dear aunt had always travelled by
the Bagshot road to Farnham, she preferred going

by the way where our family are well known at the various inns along the road. I could see nothing to alarm one on Hounslow Heath, but its ugly flatness, and one or two frightful gibbets, which made me, who was after all the only coward of the party, feel rather nervous. When we stopped at Bedfont, the civil landlord of the inn there, told us that no less than two robberies had taken place during the last week; one on Hounslow Heath, and the other in the hollow between the two hills on the road near Virginia Water. But my aunt said that as both the robberies occurred after dusk, she could see no danger to us in broad daylight; and she scolded the landlord—who is always, she says, very talkative—for mentioning the subject before Janet and myself. We reached Bagshot in safety, though we were somewhat suspicious, at least I was, from observing a man on horseback, who rode at a short distance from the carriage; sometimes ahead of us, sometimes dropping behind. I begged my aunt, who had on a habit and hat, to look as much like a man as she could; and as I saw that Thomas Frost had his eye upon him, I must own I was more curious than frightened, particularly as, from his countenance, so far as one could judge, he seemed to be a harmless-looking young man. When we arrived at Bagshot no horses were to be had, but the landlord told us that the first pair that came in should, after baiting for a short time, be put to our carriage. We ordered dinner, and made up our minds to wait with as much patience as we could. Here, however, we found that there was some serious cause for alarm on the road, for many stories were told us of a daring fellow who has committed several robberies, and whose brutal manner have been particularly noticed. I became so frightened that my dear aunt had made up her mind to order beds, and pass the night where we were; but just as I rose to ring the bell, the carriage came round to the door, and as I saw my aunt's anxiety to reach Tancred's Ford that night was very great, I was the first to propose our setting off without loss of time. The afternoon was dull, but we knew that we could calculate on daylight till we reached Hale; and so it would have been, had not our horses been too tired to get on as fast as a fresh pair would have done. You may imagine my dismay when, just as we began to ascend the hill by the Golden Farmer—a well known spot, so named after the robbery of a rich farmer at that very place—the young man who had been riding beside us before we came to Bagshot, suddenly made his appearance from a cross-road, and rode on at a short distance from the carriage as before. We had passed Farnborough, and came out upon the wide, open heath, soon leaving every house far behind us, when I saw, on looking through the little round window at the back of the carriage, that there were two horsemen instead of one, close to the carriage; and I had scarcely whispered my fearful news to my companions, when we heard a coarse loud voice calling upon the post-boy to stop. My aunt thrust her head out of the front window, and ordered the post-boy to drive on as fast as he could, and he made an effort to do so, but the poor jaded horses were spurred and flogged in vain. Good old Thomas Frost looked and spoke most fiercely; but many minutes had not passed, before the post-boy was dragged from his horse, and one of the horsemen stood at our horses' heads, while the other, who had a black crape over his face, came up to the side of the carriage. He knocked at the glass with a pistol, and my aunt, with an untrembling hand, let down the glass, and with a firm voice, asked him what he wanted; laying her commands on Thomas Frost, almost in the same breath, to sit still and make no resistance. 'Oh! the old story,' was his reply; 'your money, and everything else worth having, that you have about you; and be as quick as you can, or I may ask for your lives as well as your money.' 'Put down your pistol, sir, and give us time,' said my aunt; 'for if you frighten my two young companions, you will only cause delay. Give all that you have,' she said to us both; and our three purses were produced. 'That's not all,' said the fellow. 'It is not,' replied my aunt, coolly; 'I had forgotten my watch; but these young ladies have nothing else to give you.' 'What more?' he cried. 'Nothing,' she said; 'and yet I remember there is this,' and she drew forth the miniature of her father, which she always wears, and which is set in large pearls. 'The picture I will not give you—the pearls you may take.—Break the glass with your pistol!—Thomas Frost, sit still!' she cried; observing, with a glance, that the good old man, who had been motionless till now, could restrain himself no longer. 'My command is, that you do not stir a finger!' 'What more, my brave madam?' said the fellow. 'Nothing whatever,' she replied. 'Will you swear it?' said he. 'I will not swear,' she said, calmly; 'but, on my word, we have given you everything. You may drag us from the carriage, and search us, if you please; you may add insult to robbery, but you will find I have spoken the truth; and, what is more to your purpose, you will be losing time. Take the money, and be gone. I pity you, from my soul! I rather think that you have been brought up to better things.' 'You're a brave one,' said the man, with a horrible oath; 'and I take you at your word.' 'Stop! stop!' she cried, as he was turning away; and, doubtless, astonished at such a request, the man turned round, with his pistol still presented. 'Hear me,' she said; 'my voice may be the last voice of friendly warning which you may ever hear,' and that kind voice now shook with emotion as she spoke. 'You are known, but your secret' . . Before the words, which she would have added, could be spoken, his pistol was discharged—but with a quickness and a courage equal to my aunt's, Janet Arnold had anticipated the danger, and knocked aside the muzzle of the weapon. The report was terrific, and we were half stifled with smoke, but the bullet had passed through the opposite glass, and at the same moment a tremendous blow had fallen on the ruffian's head, from the stout cudgel of Thomas Frost. The fellow staggered back, and had nearly fallen from his horse. His hat, however, was knocked off, the crape slipped aside, and though he quickly turned away, I caught a glimpse of his face. By this time Thomas Frost had drawn out the pistols, and fired at the villain, who, on his part, again fired. How the contest would have ended I tremble to think, but at this moment both the fellows suddenly galloped off, and the reason was soon obvious. A troop of Dragoons, on their way from Windsor to Southampton, was close behind us. They had seen, as they advanced, the carriage standing still, and had heard the pistol shots, and they came forward at full charge. Some of the soldiers pursued the two ruffians, the remainder drew up round our carriage, and the Officer in command came forward. We needed assistance, for my poor aunt—as we now discovered—had fainted away, and lay as one dead. Her courage had inspired us with a presence of mind which had astonished us, but now the danger was past we could only weep and tremble till we became ashamed of ourselves.

" The whole adventure passed in a shorter time than it has taken me to relate it; and our bold assailant had gained but little booty in the encounter, for two of our purses and the miniature had been dropped by him in the scuffle, and were picked up, and restored to us by the soldiers, among whom my aunt divided the contents of the purses.

" The troop rode by our side till we entered Farnham, and Captain Grant, the officer in command, begged to send some of his men on with us to Tancred's Ford; an offer which my aunt gladly accepted. We found the coachman and horses waiting for us at the Bush; and we arrived here without any further adventure. We were rejoiced to find my dear grandfather almost himself again. Our fears had magnified his attack, which appears to have been a very slight one. We have not yet told him of our adventure. My dear mother seems really more terrified by our account of it than we were by the attack itself. The quiet and freshness of this sequestered place, the exquisite greenness, the trees and meadows, and the morning sunshine, form a delightful contrast to the gloom and the terrors of last night. Janet and I were walking before breakfast in one of my favourite haunts, and I insisted on her sending you the sketch which she has made of the old bridge, and the sparkling river, and the smiling landscape around. It will give you some idea of the place with which all my happiest and earliest associations are connected."

I also received a letter from my sister by the same post, in which she entered fully into the account of their attack on Bagshot Heath. It would be needless to repeat it here ; but she adds, " My aunt wishes me to mention a circumstance we have kept secret from every one at present. She recognised the voice, and I saw the face of the highwayman; and that voice and face were those of no other than your former acquaintance, Mr. Hanson—the same coarse, brutal man who came to this house with Mr. Desmond, when Mr. Murray and yourself were staying here after your illness. We dread your holding any communication with him; but if you could possibly seek him out, and warn him of the perils of the course which he is evidently pursuing, surely it would be well to do so. Is it not dreadful to think that one of your associates should have entered upon such an awful career! Where can it end, if persisted in? my aunt says, ' surely nowhere, but at the gallows,' for murder was nearly committed last night! We conclude that he was not taken. His secret, too, is safe, for he was unknown to every one else, and we would willingly conceal his shame."

The letter dropt from my hands when I came to the name of Hanson: I felt horror-struck to find how rapid had been his downward course! I shuddered when I considered how lately he had been almost my daily companion! Yet ought I to have been surprised? Like myself, at that time, he had no right principle of any kind to actuate him. His temper was under no control, and he never would bear contradiction, or opposition of any kind. He had followed blindly every impulse of his unbridled passions, and stooped lower and lower to procure the means of his brutal self-

indulgence! Such an outbreak was not extraordinary
in such a character. But he had not yet reached the
termination of his frightful career! I made some inquiries after Hanson, that I might write a few words
of warning to him; and I sent a letter at a venture to
the address given me. I never heard if he received it.

Soon after the return of Miss Arnold from Tancred's
Ford, I was induced, by the encouragement my aunt
gave me, to ask her father's consent to pay my
addresses to her; and I was as much delighted as
astonished by the way in which he received my pro-
posal. "If my child prefers you," he said, "so far
from making any objection, I may promise you the
hearty concurrence of her mother and myself. I tell
you frankly, Mark, that I expected she would make
a higher marriage. Her large fortune, and her
personal attractions, naturally led me to expect this;
and she has already had several opportunities of making what would be considered a better match. But
you have my consent to propose to her, and perhaps
you may not be so indifferent to her as all others have
hitherto been. Still I must tell you with the same
plainness," he continued, "that if she should accept
you, though I dislike long engagements, I should
wish your marriage to be deferred for two years. You
are both young, and though you have always been a
great favourite with us all, I must see more decided
proofs of steadiness of character about you. I could
not consent to entrust my daughter's happiness to any

man whom I could not fully depend upon. And now, my dear Mark, I leave it to you to find out Janet's mind on the subject. You will not be long in doubt, for, if I am not mistaken, she is as fond of plain dealing as her father, and will be above concealing from you her preference, if anything of the kind exists."

As my reader may suppose, I was not long in finding the opportunity I desired; and I felt that the happiest day of my life had arrived when Janet Arnold, with a modest sweetness entirely devoid of anything like affectation or prudery, allowed me to look upon her from that day as my future wife. Nothing could be kinder than the behaviour of all the Arnold family to me. I had never seen a more united and domestic circle than theirs; and that which gave happiness to one seemed to be a source of joy to all. Though no secret was made of our engagement among our own families, it was Mr. Arnold's wish that, with the exception of Angus—whom I regarded as my dearest friend—it should not be generally spoken of. I applied myself with more than common interest and diligence to business, and, I am sorry to say, was more than commonly satisfied with myself, and consequently more than ever off my guard. Few temptations for some time tried me, but I was ill prepared to resist them. Yet, though I was unaltered, and still the same weak, vain, unstable character that I had ever been, all the circumstances by which I was surrounded were at this time favourable to me. It was, as it were, the summer season, and the house built upon the sand, and without a foundation, was assailed by no beating storm, or violent winds, or rushing waters, and, therefore, it continued to stand for a season. I saw but little now of those associates whose influence could in any way have injured me. Chillingworth had availed himself of an opening which he had been long seeking, to enter a foreign house of business at Frankfort, where he intended to remain some years; and we met no more. With Stanley my former intimacy had long subsided into a very cool and commonplace acquaintance, and though he was still as kind and friendly to me as usual, I had not the least desire to be on more familiar terms with him; but had such been the case, his influence would always have been on the side of what was highly moral and equitable. Angus was more pleasing and more affectionate towards me than ever, but, strange to tell, I began to be somewhat estranged from him, simply because I was now in a manner identified with the Arnolds, and secretly preferred their ways of thinking and acting to those of Angus, and, I may add, of the Maxwells. All that was highly esteemed among men was to be found in the amiable circle of the Arnold family. But as the gentlest and wisest of beings, He who came to bear witness of the truth, and was Himself the incarnation of the truth, has said, " That which is highly esteemed among men is abomination in the sight of God!" This is strong language, I am well aware. It may be offensive to some of my readers—it was once so to me; but when there is no recognition of Him, whose name they bear, by the amiable and upright of His professed disciples, it is as fearfully true as when applied to the immoral and profane. Angus Murray, though in the world, was not of the world! He was unwilling to censure others; he was ready to make allowances for the faults and inconsistencies of others, but he was at the same time inflexible with reference to his own walk, and careful to abstain from everything that was even questionable in the ways of this ungodly world. He was one of those whose constant inquiry is not, "How far may I lawfully go with the multitude? how near may I venture to approach, without risk, to the broad way?" but, "How can I give glory to God? how can I best serve and please Him in everything?" The one thing needful was the one thing chosen by him; and not only because it was the one thing needful, but because in every point of view he regarded it as the good part, as the only solid and eternal happiness of the child of God. He had some sharp trials to undergo, and I have often wondered at the firmness and the gentleness with which he met them.

I never saw Mr. Arnold intoxicated, but the scene which follows is one which some of my readers may know, as I do, to be a faithful picture, of no unusual occurrence, at the table of a class of character highly esteemed among men. I can testify that it is not overdrawn. "Come, come, Murray, don't be a milksop; fill your glass, and be as other young men of your age. Don't make yourself particular. Well, sir, why do you pass the bottle without doing as I tell you? Wilton, fill his glass." Angus looked grave, and coloured slightly. "Wilton," repeated Mr. Arnold, "fill his glass, and fill your own, and show him how to drain it." I obeyed, and filled his glass and mine. "Well, sir, Wilton is only waiting for you, and so am I. I pledge you." Angus took the glass, and raised it to his lips, scarcely touching the wine with them, and then quietly put it down. "Do you call that drinking, man?" "There were two persons to be obeyed, sir," said Angus, modestly, and with his usual sweetness of temper. "I have obeyed them both." "Well, my fine fellow, let me hear who these two persons are?" "One," said Angus, "is yourself. I raised the glass to my lips because you desired me to do so." "But you put it down almost untasted." "Because, sir," said Angus, "I had taken as much or more wine than I like to drink." "And you are afraid of confusing that wise head of yours, I suppose?" "I am indeed, sir," replied Angus, quietly; "I do not know how much my head could bear, and I do not wish to try." "I tell you what, young fellow," cried Mr. Arnold, with a horse-laugh, "I should very much like to make you drunk; and upon my word I've half a mind to do so!"—and then his laugh ceased, and he said, angrily, "I'm sick of your follies; don't make yourself a fool with your absurd singularity! When you come to Rome, do as Rome does. You are always setting yourself up as wiser and better than any one else. You can't go with us to the play or to the opera. You set your face against races. If I ask you to come and pass a quiet Sunday with us—you had rather come on some other day. When is there to be an end of this puritanical folly? When shall we ever make a man of you? But come, sir, do you mean to drink or not; answer one way or the other—yes or no?" A flash of manly fire glanced from the eyes of Angus, and his brow was slightly knit with an expression of determination. This was but for a moment, his look of gentle sweetness was only to be seen as he replied clearly, distinctly, but very mildly, " I say most respectfully, but most decidedly, no!"

Mr. Arnold stared with astonishment, and after pausing a moment, as if he was about to give way to some violent expression of anger, he filled his own glass to the brim, passed the bottles with a frown, and drank off his bumper. Before he could put down his glass Mr. Tresham laid his hand on Murray's arm, and rising up, said, with a look and voice of marked kindness, " We will go to the ladies, Murray."

The next morning, when Angus and I were standing together, Mr. Arnold came up to us, and said, " Murray, I have something to say to you. Don't go, Wilton; I hope I'm not ashamed to own myself wrong before you. I ask you to give me your hand, Murray," he continued, " and to forgive me for speaking to you as I did last night. It was unjust, unkind, and most ungentlemanly. You were right, and I respect you for your firmness. The fact was, though not positively drunk, I had taken too much wine, or I think I should not have forgotten myself as I did." Surely it was an argument against excess in drinking, that it could lead a man like Mr. Arnold to forget himself in the way he did on that occasion.

Angus had proved how truly he could read my character, when he had told me, at the very commencement of my acquaintance with Desmond, that he was a far more dangerous associate for me than any of my other companions; and if this had been true when he was, like myself, a merchant's clerk, how greatly was the danger increased by his altered position. I look back with amazement to the influence he gradually acquired over me. There was indeed scarcely a species of dissipation to which I was not introduced by him. I shall not take my readers into the various disgraceful places and practices with which I became acquainted through his means. I was not at times without a feeling of shame; I suffered from the stings of an accusing conscience; but these inward restraints all gradually gave way, and I was soon initiated in the mysteries of profligacy. I give no details of this portion of my life; but my reader must not suppose that I have none to give. Alas! I could fill not only pages, but chapters with them; but I will not (if I know it) write a word which may offend the delicacy of my youthful reader, or bring before him any lines or tints of pictures which would leave a corrupting stain upon the mind of those who are at present, and, I trust, may ever be, unacquainted with such scenes. I pass over as rapidly as I can, not only the weeks but years which it took to bring me down to the state of a poor wretched profligate, enfeebled both in mind and body. I had fallen into evil courses while associating with Hanson and his set; but then I had secretly felt a kind of natural disgust both at their ways and at themselves, even when most familiar with them : but now all sense of disgust was gone—literally worn away. I loved and revelled in the vices in which I indulged. Is it to be believed, that attached as I was, and bound by an honourable engagement, to a modest and lovely young woman, I could still keep up anything like a feeling of true affection for her—still indeed persuade myself that I really loved her, and yet be at times enjoying the company of abandoned characters? It has been said that an engagement to a virtuous woman is one of the best preservations of a young man from an immoral course. And so it may be, and, doubtless, has been in some instances; but perhaps some of my readers may feel their cheek as deeply flushed with the crimson of shame as mine is at this moment, when I affirm that it is possible—nay, that it is common—for a profligate man to be so self-deceived as to continue in his iniquitous courses, while he professes that his heart and its affections are devoted to the amiable and gentle being who has pledged her pure and maiden troth to him. But I did not become what I was all at once. During the first month, or even the first year after my engagement, I should have turned with indignant anger from the idea of so degraded a state, had it been hinted at. But Desmond, not Angus, was now my chosen companion. I had no standard of high godly principle within me, and gradually but surel I sunk lower and lower, deceiving and being deceived; charmed with the pure-minded and lovely Janet Arnold when with her, but when absent from her, secretly false to her and to myself. Let some of my readers pause on this sad and disgraceful avowal; its truth will be acknowledged in their bosoms.

Alas! at the very time that my letters and my personal attentions to Miss Arnold appeared to her to be animated by the very enthusiasm of tender affection, I was revelling with Desmond, and some of our associates, in the haunts of intemperance and impurity! There are many, I am well aware, who will say with a sneer, that such are the ways of the world, and that young men will be young men, and that many a fine, honourable fellow, has lived the life that I lived; and sobered down into an excellent husband and father, and has become an ornament of society. It is, no doubt, perfectly true that some bad men have repented, and reformed; but it ought not to be tolerated among men of common morality, to say nothing of Christian men, that such practices should be spoken of in any way whatever that may seem to justify or extenuate them. The thing is common enough, we all know, if we know anything of the ways of the world; but the number of the offenders, instead of palliating, adds to the enormity of the offence. There are hundreds of persons, sensible men—men of reputable character, and high respectability in the world, who would loudly express their disapprobation and displeasure against any glaring excess of profligacy, any flagitious breach of morality; but who might be told, with all solemnity, that they are themselves the connivers and abettors of a course of proceeding which, if allowed to grow up to its rank but natural height, would fill them with disgust and abhorence. Are there not many, to use the words of the good Dr. Chalmers, who, while they would mourn over it as a family trial, should any son of theirs fall a victim to excessive dissipation, yet are willing to tolerate the lesser degrees of it—who, instead of deciding the question on the alternative of his heaven or his hell, are satisfied with such a measure of sobriety as will save him from ruin and disgrace in this life—who, if they can only secure this, have no great objection to the moderate share he may take in this world's conformities—who deceive themselves with the fancied impossibility of stopping the evils in question, and say that the young man's hours of companionship must not be too jealously watched or inquired into, nor must we take him too strictly to task about engagements and acquaintances and expenditure. They will tell you that sobriety has its time and its season in one period of life, and that indulgence has its season in another—that they were no better themselves when they were young; and yet point with no little self-approval to themselves as they now are; and, they will add, that in short it is no use arguing about the thing, because that there is in fact "no help for it." We meet these men, the whole body of them—and their name is legion—with the plain precept of that sacred volume, which they now profess to admire, and to obey—with these words of immutable wisdom, and divine and unquestionable authority:— "Rejoice, O young man, in thy youth, and let thy heart cheer thee in the days of thy youth, and walk in the ways of thine heart, and in the sight of thine eyes; but know thou that for all these things God will bring thee into judgment!"

The Head of Tancred's Mere

~~~~~~~~~~~~~

CHAPTER X.

FOR some considerable time I had seen and heard
nothing of Hanson, though I could not help sus-
pecting that the feats which were from time to time
recounted in the public papers of a certain notorious
highwayman, in various parts of the country, might
be attributed to him.

In one of my short, but occasional visits to Tancred's Ford, an event occurred, in which he was again
brought under my notice, when indeed he may be said
to have filled up the cup of his iniquity.

I had written home, to beg that a horse might be
sent to meet me at the Hammer Ponds, a well-known

spot on the Portsmouth Road, by which the coach passed, and had often set me down, within a few miles of Tancred's Ford.   The path which crosses the broad heath, and passes over one or two steep and picturesque hills, is wild and solitary, and would not easily be found after dusk, except by those well acquainted with the country.   I was on the top of the coach, and we had scarcely proceeded a mile beyond Godalming, when my attention was called to a gig and horse, which we were overtaking.   Two men were in the gig, and one of them was lashing the horse (a roan horse) in the most savage way, uttering and using, at the same time, loud and horrible oaths.   Just as we came up with the gig the horse started off again, but not till I had recognised Hanson in the driver, and in his companion the young man whom I had met with him at the house of Wallis.   They had not seen me, and I had no wish to be recognised by them.   In a few minutes they were out of sight, and not long after, the coach had set me down at the little way-side public-house, where I expected to find the horse and servant waiting for me.   I found, however, that no horse had yet been brought, and I sat down in the parlour to wait for its coming.   While there, my curiosity was excited by the conversation that was taking place among some men in the kitchen, and which I could not help hearing, as the door was open.   They were talking about a family who had lately taken the old red house, at the entrance of the heath.   They seemed to think that there was something suspicious about them; and after some discussion they came to the conclusion that the master of the house was a smuggler. At that time smuggling was extensively carried on over the greater part of that wide and unenclosed district. The booty was brought inland by night, and dispersed, it was strongly suspected, among some of the insulated cottages, which were to be found scattered here and there over that broad expanse of wild heath country. I have often heard my mother say, that she and others have seen parties of smugglers pass quietly along through the grounds of Tancred's Ford, within a short distance of the house, soon after daybreak; and that, though thus exposed to apparent danger from the near approach of men of so lawless a character, there seemed to be a kind of methodized understanding among them, so that no act of offence, or annoyance of any kind, had ever been known to occur in the neighbourhood. The little party at the public-house spoke of the irregular hours of these supposed smugglers, and mentioned a circumstance which excited my curiosity not a little, that one, or more, of the household were ladies. I waited till after sunset for my horse, and at last made up my mind to wait no longer, but to set off on foot, without losing any more time, to Tancred's Ford. The night was dark and stormy, but I knew well the various paths that cross the heath; and those points in the way which had served me as land-marks, lead by the head of

Tancred's Mere to my grandfather's house. I was walking briskly on, and had just crossed the broad stone that forms a foot-bridge over the clear brook near that old red house, of which mention had been made that evening, when I saw, with astonishment, the same gig and horse which Hanson had been driving. The gig was standing in the turf-house, behind the building, and the horse was grazing in a little green meadow, which had been enclosed from the heath. The light was still sufficiently clear for me to recognise the animal, whose peculiar colour had attracted my notice on the road. I paused for a few minutes, under the dark shadow of the two old Scotch firs which stand on the smooth turf at a short distance from the house, and looked up at the windows, half expecting to see the painted face and long black ringlets of Mrs. Wallis at one of them; but all appeared to be silence and darkness within. An unnatural stillness seemed to prevail, and feeling, I scarcely knew why, oppressed by it, and anxious to escape the notice of any of the party by whom I now suspected the premises were inhabited, I walked fast from the spot. I had soon ascended the first hill, over which my path lay. As I walked onwards, I could not help asking myself what could have induced Wallis to come to that out-of-the-way spot. But I came to the conclusion that a man of so fraudulent a character was very likely to seek concealment; and that Hanson, his degraded associate, who had had opportunities of observing the peculiarly secluded character of our wild, heathy country, had recommended the place to him, where they were probably residing together, while they wished to remain undiscovered.

Evening was now veiling, with its dark shadows, the features of the surrounding landscape. The clouds were scudding fast over the sky, and here and there a twinkling star shone out, and was quickly hidden. The wind, which had blown strongly, was beginning to subside, and a gentle rain was falling. As I descended into a deep hollow between the hills, I thought I had never seen so dreary a place; or rather, that that desolate spot, where nothing is ever to be seen but the brown and barren slopes of the meeting hills, had never seemed so dreary. Once or twice I stopped, for I thought that I heard voices; but soon after the loud hooting of an owl, which was too plain to be mistaken, made me think that I had heard no other sound. I had scarcely reached the bottom of the hollow when two men suddenly passed me, walking at a rapid pace, and scarcely muttering the usual good-night. I looked round, but in a few moments they were hidden from my sight. I scarcely knew why at the time, but I now began to walk faster up the hill, and by the time I had reached the deep sandy gorge, called the Lion's-mouth, at the summit, I was glad to stop and take breath. The sky was now clearer, the rain had ceased, and the moon began to rise over the hills. I saw before me my well-known land-marks, and found the path which I knew would take me by the best and shortest track across the heath, when just as I was descending the hill a man rose up from the heather, and I heard the well-known voice of Will Chase, the servant who had been sent to meet me from Tancred's Ford. He seemed unusually rejoiced at meeting me, and yet I saw at once by his manner that something had occurred to alarm him exceedingly. My first thoughts were about my family, and I hastily questioned him on the subject, and asked if he had left any one ill at home? He told me that all were well, but that the horse which he was to have brought for me had fallen lame, and that he had been on his way with a message, to tell me of the disappointment, and to carry my valise. He said that he had scarcely reached the summit of the gorge, and turned aside into one of the deep and narrow hollows, where the sheep love to lie in hot weather, and the path is on the fine short turf, when he heard a loud and piercing cry. He started up to see whence the sound proceeded, but saw nothing. After a few minutes, he plainly distinguished, at some distance to the right, on the ridge of the hill, the figure of a man, running as for his life. The man stopped for an instant, and seemed to look round him on every side, and then darted down the slope, and he saw him no more. He stood wondering at what he had seen, when two other men appeared on the very spot where he had seen the first. They were evidently in pursuit of him, for, after halting also there, they rushed forward on the same track. Will Chase told me that he paused some considerable time, irresolute what to do, and had just made up his mind to hasten on to meet me, when on looking once again in the same direction, he observed the two men appear again, and gaze stealthily around. Will now determined to crouch down behind the bank of the narrow pathway, which had hitherto, he supposed, hidden him from their sight, and watch their proceedings. The twilight was beginning to give indistinctness to every object, but he was sure that he could see the men dragging what appeared to him to be a dead body, along the ridge of the hill, till they came to some stacks of turf, which were scattered about over the heath. There they moved about among the stacks for a considerable time, sometimes opposed to the pale crimsoned sky, sometimes almost confounded with the brown and shadowy hill side. He then again lost sight of them; but as he was descending the hill as quietly and as quickly as he could, he was suddenly stopped by seeing them walking forward in the very road which runs parallel to the path in which he was. He again crouched down, trembling and shaking, as he owned, with terror, till, thinking they were out of hearing, he stole back up the hill. There he remained, resolving at first to hasten back to Tancred's Ford, and tell what he had seen; and then again, calling up his courage, he made up his mind still to go forward to the Hammer Ponds, where he supposed I should be waiting for him.   Just as he had come to this conclusion, I appeared; but he lay still among the heather till he could be certain who it was that approached, and soon recognised me by the moonlight. What was now to be done?

We did not long deliberate.   There could be little doubt, that if a murder had been committed, the body was concealed under one of the turf stacks, and that Will Chase would be enabled to point out the spot. We knew also that the murderers were not likely to be found by us that night, or if found, we had no warrant to apprehend them, and that we could neither of us swear to their identity.   We determined, therefore, to hasten, without loss of time, to Tancred's Ford, to give the necessary information to my grandfather, who was a magistrate.   As we walked along I could not help thinking to myself that Hanson, and perhaps Wallis, were the perpetrators of the dreadful crime, and that they had been the men who had passed me in the hollow between the hills!   There was something about the gait of one of the men, especially, which had at the time struck me with the idea that I had seen him before, and then it suddenly occurred to me that Hanson and Elrington had been seen by me that same afternoon in the gig which had so rapidly passed the coach, the same gig and horse which I had seen afterwards near the old red house.   Elrington, therefore, was probably the victim, for Chase had described the man whom he had seen running so swiftly, and endeavouring to escape, as tall and slight; Wallis, on the contrary—a stout and heavy man—corresponded with his description of one of the supposed murderers! All these thoughts, however, I kept to myself, and horror-struck as I felt, I determined, whether right or wrong, to leave to others the detection both of the crime and of the criminals.

Before daybreak the following morning a party of armed constables, guided by Will Chase, were at the place where the latter had seen the two men moving about among the turf stacks. They approached cautiously and silently, and came suddenly upon two men, who were just covering up with their spades what was soon found to be the grave in which they had buried their murdered victim. The turfs of one of the stacks lay scattered about, having evidently been just removed; and the ruffians had chosen a sandy spot, where no heath was growing. They made a desperate resistance with their spades and with pistols, with which both of them were found to be armed. They were dressed like countrymen, with smock-frocks, and old straw hats, and refused to give their names. But after they were taken, they were recognised in the course of the morning, by the ostler belonging to the public-house at the Hammer Ponds, as the mysterious tenants of the old red house. Their examination took place in the justice-room, at Tancred's Ford, where I purposely avoided being present. My good old grandfather was deeply affected in dis-

covering that one of the murderers was, as I had suspected, my former associate, Hanson. Neither my
aunt nor my sister had mentioned to him till after that
morning, that he was also the man who had stopped
their carriage on Bagshot Heath. That very night
Hanson and Wallis were lodged in Horsemonger Lane
prison, and fully committed for trial for the wilful
murder of Elrington.

It is painful to myself, and, in my opinion, unprofitable to others, to dwell more than I am obliged
to do on the details of this horrible story. It is well
known that the circumstances I mention came out on
the trial. The wretched victim, Elrington, had been
a young man of weak mind and profligate habits, and
his acquaintance with Hanson and Wallis had proved
his ruin. He had possessed some property, and was
in expectation of much more at the death of an uncle.
It appeared that his uncle had died but a few months
before the murder of the nephew, and that the sister-
in-law of Wallis (the only person of the party who was
at all respectable), who was attached to Elrington,
deeply shocked at the conduct of her relations, had
been anxious to quit their house, and to induce her
lover to separate himself from his infamous companions. By her advice he had consulted a lawyer of
high respectability, and put his affairs into his hands.
Her plans had been discovered by her unprincipled
sister, who had intercepted and opened a letter from
Elrington to her. The information thus cbtained

had been disclosed by Mrs. Wallis to her husband, and
by him to Hanson. The guilty parties were well aware
that in a very short time disclosures would inevitably
be made which would involve them in open disgrace
and ruin, and that all the particulars of Hanson's and
Wallis's course of iniquity would be laid before the
public.   They determined, therefore, to take immediate
steps to get Elrington out of the way (his property, on
which they had counted, being lost to them); and their
diabolical schemes had but too well succeeded. Hanson had induced him, with many professions of friendship, to accompany him from London, telling him that
Miss Flower was anxiously expecting him at the
house on the heath, though he well knew that the poor
girl had refused, when urged by her sister, to write
a note to invite him, and did not expect him to come.

On the arrival of Hanson and Elrington, they
found Wallis alone in the house, and, in answer to their
inquiries for the ladies, they were told by Wallis that
his wife and her sister were drinking tea at a farm-
house in the neighbourhood, and that he had promised
to bring Elrington and Hanson (such was the plan
they had settled), to join the party and walk back
with the two ladies. They had thus led their unsus-
pecting companion to the spot where they had agreed
to murder him. Elrington was conversing cheerfully
with Wallis when Hanson commenced the attack—
sprung upon him, and stabbed him in the back·
There was a dreadful struggle, for the wretched young

man was stronger than they had supposed; and feeling that the contest was for life or death, he broke from them, and fled with such swiftness across the heath, that had it not been for the loss of blood from his wound, he might have outstripped his pursuers. But he fell fainting to the earth, and was just recovering when the two wretches came up, and Hanson, heedless of all his entreaties and promises, completed his horrid work.

It seems that the whole plan for the murder of poor Elrington had been arranged with great forethought, and had it not been for the providential circumstance which brought the servant over from Tancred's Ford to meet me, the disappearance of Elrington might have been to this day involved in mystery. Anxious to get the women out of the way, and to keep their horrid design a secret from them, Wallis had taken them the day before to the Isle of Wight, saying that he intended to join them there in a day or two with Hanson and Elrington, that they might together make a tour of the island; and they had fully purposed to join them at Cowes, and to account for Elrington's absence, by pretending that they could not prevail on him to leave London with them. These circumstances came out from the confession of Wallis, who had offered to turn king's evidence against his friend, and who positively denied having lifted his hand against Elrington. They were both hung—Hanson in chains—on the spot where the murder was committed.

I found on my return from home to London that Angus Murray had left our counting-house, and accepted an offer from Mr. Foster, the banker, whose wife was sister to Mr. Maxwell, and thus related to Angus. He now held a situation of high confidence and responsibility under Mr. Forster, with the prospect of a partnership in the house at no very distant time. Not long after this change in his prospects, I heard from Angus, with as much pleasure as surprise, that he was about to write to my mother to seek her consent to ask my sister in marriage. He had, he told me, for some little time been much attached to her, but not having anticipated such a change in his circumstances as that which had now taken place, he had therefore said nothing to us of his attachment. I assured him of my hearty concurrence, and a few days afterwards he received a reply from my mother, which he brought to me with a joyful countenance. He went down to Tancred's Ford, and wished me to accompany him; but I was unable to do so. From that time I regarded him as my future brother-in-law. But we were no longer in the same counting-house, and our daily intercourse was now interrupted. This was at first a source of real regret to me, but I own it with sorrow and with shame, that many weeks had not passed away before I began rather to shun than to seek his society.

As I said before, from the time of my more intimate association with the Arnolds, a kind of estrangement from Angus had sprung up on my side. Alas, there was now another cause which separated us still more widely; and that was my increasing intimacy with Desmond. I had found a note from the latter at my lodgings, inviting me to a quiet dinner-party, on the very day that Angus left Town for Tancred's Ford. The invitation was accepted; and I returned home from that party more pleased than I had ever been with Desmond. I had never found him so agreeable; and I said to myself that it would have been almost impossible for the most fastidious judgment to have found fault with anything, either in himself or in his guests. Mr. Tresham was one of the party; and there were one or two other persons whom I had never met before, but whose names were well known at that time in the best society. The conversation had turned on the literature and politics of the day; and the modest ease with which Desmond might have been said to take the lead in it, and to draw out each of his guests, quite surprised me. Mr. Tresham left early; and cards were introduced after his departure, but no one played high. Before I went away Desmond reminded me of the wish that I had expressed to be present at a debate which was to come on in the Commons, and which, he told me, would be introduced the next night; and made me promise to join him at the House, that he might get me in under the gallery.

I met him punctually at the time appointed, and sat listening till a late hour to the debate. Desmond came out arm in arm with an elegant-looking man about his own age; and after introducing me to Lord Alfred T. as his intimate friend, he passed his other arm within mine, saying, " I can give you a lift part of your way home." When we came to the door we found that the rain was pouring, and his carriage was not there. Lord Alfred's servant, however, was waiting; and as his carriage drew up, he insisted on taking us both with him. " I don't know," he said, turning to Desmond, after we had driven off, " whether your friend has any curiosity to see W——'s" (naming a gambling-house then much frequented, but which he termed a club-house); "but if he has, I am going there: and, I think, you, Desmond, are not unlikely to be intending a visit to the same house." I returned some hesitating answer, which Desmond scarcely seemed to hear; for, before I had got the words out, he said, " Oh! Wilton, you should go for once, for really the thing is worth seeing." No further remark was made on the subject; but Lord Alfred soon after said, " I think you reside in Surrey, Mr. Wilton; somewhere near the borders of Hampshire, is it not? Did you see that account of the murder which has been committed near Hindhead? Perhaps you know the spot? I rather think one passes near it in going to Portsmouth." Before I could answer, Desmond interrupted, and began to speak very coolly of Hanson as a low fellow whom he had once met with—a very low fellow! I was silent; but I remembered, with a shudder, that it was in Hanson's company, and as Hanson's friend, I had first met Desmond.

I had not said that I would go with them to W——'s, but it seemed that both Lord Alfred and Desmond took it for granted; for when the carriage stopped at the door of the club-house, Desmond's arm was again passed through mine, and he said, " You 'll let Lord Alfred introduce you; but, take my advice," he added, in a whisper, " and don't play." I had made up my mind to leave them at the door, but we know how soon a man can change his mind who has not the manliness to say, " No"—so I merely replied, also in a low voice, " Nothing would induce me to play, I assure you;" and together we ascended the broad and brilliantly lighted staircase. Ah! how well I now remember the feeling that came over me, as, with my two companions—who were laughing and talking gaily—I entered the splendid saloon! I thought of the grave and beautiful countenance of Angus; and the words, " Lead us not into temptation," in the well-known tones of his voice, seemed to sound in my ears. But I turned from all such warning thoughts as idle fancies, and I said to myself, " I am really glad to be here. I shall doubtless see hideous expressions of eagerness and despair on some faces; and, at least, I shall learn here a lesson, which I shall remember as long as I live: so that it may be a wise thing to do—just to see a party of gamblers for once, as a warning." As it happened, that night I saw nothing of the sort. An elderly man, with sharp features, and small twinkling eyes, but whose figure and bearing were strikingly dignified, was standing near the fire-place, with a cup of coffee in his hand, and a servant in rich livery stood waiting with a salver for his cup.

"Your Grace is early to-night," said Lord Alfred to him. "Or rather you are late, Alfred T.," he replied. "But our house was up early. Who have you with you? Ha, Desmond, how do you?" and he was about to address me, probably mistaking me for some one whom he ought to know, but he stopped and bowed courteously without speaking. "An old friend of Desmond's," said Lord Alfred, "who wished to see one of our dens;" and he presented me to the well-known Duke of ——. "I'm not well to-night; I've a headache," said the Duke to Desmond, "and was thinking of going. I don't like the men who are here to-night. But this cup of coffee has almost set me right, and now you two are come, I shall stay half an hour longer. There is that old dotard, De Mirabel, looking like a venerable monkey in a court dress, with all the airs and graces of a petit maitre, his poor old fingers sparkling with diamond rings, and his whole person stinking with musk. Faugh! the very sight of him makes me sick! Here has he been for the last half hour wearying me with his stories of Madame du Barry's charming petits soupers, and his gallantries towards her, and a hundred other old twaddling French madames, and boasting of his Hotel de Mirabel, and his Chateau de Mirabel, and of his beautiful nephew, the Count de Mirabel, and sighing over his 'grands revers!' Why, the old dog is as rich as Crœsus, and as stingy as a miser, and as sharp as a needle. It's well known that he goes into the City every morning to gamble in the stocks, and comes back to St. James's every evening to gamble with ourselves. Ha, my very dear friend!" he continued, with a sudden change of voice and manner, as the old Marquis de Mirabel (who recognised Desmond, and came forward to speak to him) drew nigh, "we were just talking of you. When did you say that we may expect to welcome your charming nephew? Pray let me see again that beautiful miniature, and let me show it to my friends, Mr. Desmond, and Lord Alfred. Like him! very like him! Who can doubt it?" he said, holding the miniature in his hand, and looking alternately at it and at the old marquis. "It is prodigiously like you! Just what you must have been at his age. What say you to a quiet game at whist," he added, "now our two young friends are come? And here is Leonard; and perhaps, sir," he added, turning to me, "you play whist? Well, my dear Marquis, we wanted hands just now, but here you see we have quite an embarras de richesses." I at once declined playing, and Colonel Leonard said he preferred looking on. The other four sat down to the whist table and played for some hours, and then all the party but myself played at hazard.

The Duke and the Marquis and Colonel Leonard lost large sums. I could not help thinking, after the spiteful tirade of the old Duke against the old French Marquis, as I looked at them both playing together over the card-table, that they were very much alike in appearance and manner, and perhaps it was secretly this consciousness, and the feeling at the same time that the Marquis de Mirabel was a Frenchified caricature of himself, which provoked his antiquated rival to such an effusion of spleen. They were, in fact, so far as such men could be, intimate and familiar friends. Are such cases very rare among the men of the world? Oh, what a sad picture they presented of the frightfulness of evil passions and wretched avarice in old and dying men! Lord Alfred and Desmond won. When parting from Lord Alfred at the door of the house, he smiled, and showing me a bundle of bank-notes, said, "A pleasant way, is it not, of putting a few hundreds into one's pocket?" As Desmond and I walked away together, he said, in a very friendly voice, " I don't know if you want a hundred pounds, my dear fellow; but if you do, don't scruple to say so. That, or a larger sum, is at your service. You know I have been a useful friend in this way formerly, and I know you are a punctual man in paying your debts." I did want money, and I said so; but I declined his offer with warmer expressions of gratitude than were at all necessary.

" Are you for Epsom on the Derby day?" he said,

as we parted; " for if so, I can drive you down. Lord
Alfred goes with me. I introduced you to him, for
I thought you would suit one another. He is as quiet
and gentlemanly a fellow as any I know." I expressed
my admiration for Lord Alfred T. in terms which
were as unnecessarily strong as were my thanks for
the offer of the money. And thus I went on in my
downward course. That was my first entrance at a
regular gaming-house; but I had gone once, and went
again. Desmond lent me money, and I won and lost
in high society of a very low description. I was
pleased and flattered to be on familiar terms with
titled gamblers—some of them little better than titled
knaves—for odd stories were in circulation as to the
ways of that notorious house, and unpleasant ex-
posures have since occurred. Alas! mine is, I fear,
no uncommon case. The love of company above one's
station was, in my case, as it has been in that of many
other wretched worldlings, one of the many causes of my
disgrace and ruin!

I was now involved in difficulties, from which I
could see no possible way of escape. I owed large
sums of money, which I could not pay, and was continually harassed with threatening letters, and with
personal applications from my creditors. I had put
them off with promises, and had given bills, which were
become due. In a word, my creditors had become
clamorous, and I was at my wits'-end. On several
occasions I had been nearly arrested at the counting-

house, and one of my creditors had at last declared that if the whole of his large debt was not paid on a day, and by an hour, which he named, he would wait upon Mr. Arnold, and make him fully acquainted with his claims upon me. On the morning of the day he named I had risen early; I could not rest, and with a sickness and dreariness of heart, a state of feeling which had now become habitual to me every morning on my first awaking, I had thrown on my clothes, and was walking up and down my chamber almost maddened with the oppression and the distraction of my thoughts. Disgrace and ruin from loss of credit and character stared me in the face; and I was too enervated, from my state of bodily health and my agony of mind, to think with calmness on any available means of extricating myself. I was, as it were, brought to a stand. I had returned home the night before, half intoxicated, and had been reading a French novel of the most profane and indecent description, and had gone to bed with my passions inflamed, and yet with an aching head and an aching heart.

The hero of the book which I had been reading on the previous night, had recounted many an act which had shown him to be neither more nor less than the most consummate scoundrel, but all his feats had been made to appear only as proofs of his consummate cleverness; and Desmond, who had lent me that volume, and many like it, had often laughed with me over the adventures of the unprincipled villain. The book was lying open on my dressing-table, where I had left it, and I felt disposed to curse it, and myself along with it, for I was suffering from the reaction of my late excitement. My eyes fell not only on the vile book, but upon a letter which I had put to keep my place in the book. I carelessly took up the letter, having forgotten from whom it came, and unfolded it to look at the signature, and saw the unwelcome name of the creditor whose threat was to be put in execution that very day. While I stood with the letter in my hand, a knock at my bed-room door made me start and tremble with downright nervousness, and the next moment the door opened, and Desmond stood smiling before me. I stared at him, I suppose, with a look of such affright and wretchedness that for an instant he drew back, and a look, which was probably the faint reflection of my own, passed over his countenance. "Come, come, old fellow," he said, quickly recovering himself, "what has happened to you, to make you look as scared as if I were come to murder you?" "Nothing, nothing," I replied, making a wretched attempt at a laugh; "nothing new, only the old story, that I'm done, or rather undone!" "Unwound, you should say," he cried, with a jocular voice; "not undone, but merely unwound—like a clock which has gone down; and now you need, as I do, winding up again. At any rate I can say of myself that the mainspring is sound, and the wheels in order; and I have but to apply the key—wind up the said clock—give the pendulum a swing, and I am going again—and so may you be—in as fine order as ever." "But where is the key to be found?" I said, faintly; "mine is lost." "Leave that to me," he cried. "I think I can produce one that may wind up you as well as me." His eye glanced rapidly over the book—the vile French volume which lay on my table. He took it up with a look which told me that a sudden thought had struck him. While he spoke to me, his eyes were bent upon its pages. "This was a fine fellow," he said, alluding to the hero of the book, "a desperately fine fellow—a fellow of invention—of genius—a glorious fellow!—always successful too, because never daunted!—the architect of his fortune, as Bacon terms it. His was sharp practice, eh, Wilton? They were sharp with him, but he was sharper—a prince of sharpers. How famously he outwitted them all." He turned over leaf after leaf as he spoke. "Ah, here is the passage," and he read aloud. "'Come,' said our hero to the old notary, 'take your pen—take it quickly, or look at this,' and he presented a pistol. 'This little fellow has a voice which may speak more powerfully in your ear, old dotard,' and he presented the pistol to the miser's ear, 'than any voice of mine. Come, come, I do not wish to frighten you, or harm you, but you have more gold than you know what to do with, and can and must allow me to lighten your care by putting a few thousand pistoles into my hand.

Trust me, I shall hold it better than you hold your pen.   There, there, don't let your old hand tremble so, but sit you down, and write an order on the bank of Venice for the sum I claim—two thousand pistoles. Write it clearly, or they may tell me it's not your handwriting, *but a forgery of mine.*'"   As he read these last words, Desmond raised his eyes, and fixed them for a moment intently and steadily on mine. Then he threw down the book, and turning gaily towards my looking-glass, as he surveyed himself in the glass, he said, after a pause, " Our hero was a wonderful fellow, was he not, Wilton?   I have a few slight alterations to make," he added, " and I might as well make them here, for I am off this morning. Do you remember the evening when I dressed for the masquerade, at which I favoured Lady Sussex with my company?   I had Achille then to dress my hair, and I would I had him now, for I must accomplish a metamorphosis of the same description."   Taking a box from the loose great-coat which he wore, he drew out a powder puff, and in a few minutes his dark and curling hair was powdered.   " Almost as good a hand as Achille," he said; " am I not?   The pomatum was rubbed in before I left my house, to which I never return.   I only hope I may make as good a hand of it among the Revolutionists of Paris as my friend Achille. He is now a member of the government, and invites me to come over; and in fact I'm tired of England, and your English parliament.   I would rather take my place among the liberators of that beau pays de France." While he was thus speaking, still standing before the glass, he darkened his eyebrows, rubbed a faint tint of rouge over his pale cheeks, and then turning to me, he said, " My whiskers, you see, are gone;" and unrolling a large handkerchief from his neck, and throwing off his loose great-coat, he stood before me so perfectly disguised in face and dress, that I should scarcely have recognised in him the same man.

" Ah, monsieur," he said, " je vous comprend parfaitement bien, mais je ne puis pas—I am not able—parler—to speak—one word—un seul mot—de votre langue. I came to breakfast with you," he added, resuming his own manner, " and to say farewell. Last night, after we parted, I went to our den, and played high. I can't enter now into particulars—I was there till daybreak, and things went wrong with me. It's all up, and I leave this country to-night. You 'll not betray me, I know. I have been home for a few hours, but not to bed. This disguise is necessary, and if you will, you may give your aid, for the last time. Let me but succeed in what I purpose and I am safe, besides leaving with you enough cash to pay your creditors. Everything is arranged in my plan, which I can explain to you as we go; for go I must into the City by ten o'clock. Rush will be here in five minutes. I hear his step on the stairs, with a cold chicken and a bottle of sherry—the best breakfast for both of us; and when we have breakfasted—for we must force our appetites, and eat and drink—he will bring a coach, and then begins our passage through the straits. There, boy, leave the things," he said, as Rush entered. " There, there, that will do. Now be off—get yourself some breakfast—and be here with a coach at half-past nine, to the minute. But, stop—take that," and he threw the boy a guinea. " Now vanish! That boy," he said, as the door closed on him, " is worth his weight in gold to me. If any one cares for me in this wide, wretched world, he is the one; but no, not the only one. I think you love me, dear Mark, and I am sure my sister does. Poor Jenny! if ever sister loved a brother, she loves me." I looked surprised, for till that moment he had never named her, and I knew not that he had a sister. " Mark," he said, after sitting in deep and silent thought for some minutes. " Mark, answer me: do you go with me? Will you serve—nay, save me? But no," and he seemed as if musing to himself, " no, why should I expose him to such a risk? No, Mark, do not go; I have nerve and skill to play my part alone." Again he seemed lost in thought—then started up, and tossed down bumper after bumper of sherry. " This will not do," he added; " I shall have to colour these sunk cheeks again," and I thought he wiped away a tear, which ran rolling down his face. He rose, and stood before the glass; and after he had just touched his cheeks with the rouge, he laughed aloud, " Capital—capital!" he cried; " I should not know myself! Yes, it will be famous! And so, old notary, this is your handwriting; and this, young gentleman, is your gold? But stop, I had forgotten your difficulties, my dear fellow," and he laid his hand on my shoulder. "I cannot help you but by the same way in which I help myself. You shall have half, and all the blame will rest with me. Come then, say at once—do you go with me, and run the gauntlet with me side by side; or will you stay, and instead of a friend's hand upon your shoulder, look round—as you do now on me—and see a bailiff in my place? You know, old fellow, you are come to your last legs—nay, you have not a leg to stand on. But had I won at the den, as I should have done but for that cursed Leonard, I should have brought you gold enough to set you quite at ease. It was, indeed, partly for your sake that I went, and took so high a stake."

"Whatever it may be," I answered firmly, "I go with you, Desmond, and I stand by you. It is not—no, I'm sure it is not—" and I stopped. "What?" he asked, quickly. "Anything in Hanson's way?" "What could put such an absurdity into your head? No, no, I'm not come to that. There never was, or will be, blood upon these hands! They are clean from that, however," and as he spoke he looked complacently upon his white and taper fingers, and drew down over his hands the ruffles of rich point which he wore as part of his disguise. "Why, Mark, you are density itself! Your brain has lost its powers of comprehension!

Our hero, and the Jewish notary, and the order written with no trembling hand; what is the moral to that fable, as they have it in old Esop? Ha! ha! the moral—an expressive word." "But there was something of a pistol in the story," I said, feeling half ashamed at the moment that he should think my wits at a loss. I had now begun to comprehend something of what we were to do, but not all. "That was in the story—the fable, I mean, but not in the moral to the fable," he replied. "Pistol! no there's no pistol in the case, except indeed for this poor skull of mine, if I fail. You go, then?" "I do," I replied, "Certainly I go with you." "Ha! what is this?" he cried, as the door opened. The servant of the house brought in a letter. "This came by the post yesterday, sir," she said, turning to me; "but you were in so late that I forgot to give it you." I took the letter. "From home," I said; "the Farnham post-mark," and was about to open it, but here Rush entered. "Put it in your pocket, my dear fellow, if you love me," said Desmond; "don't stay to read a long history from home at such a moment, when we have no moments to spare. There, finish the bottle with me." He filled our glasses, and we drank. "Now," he cried, "we are primed." When in the coach, he said, "The old Marquis de Mirabel has money at two houses. I know it from himself. He is immensely rich, and needed not the sums he has managed to win from me to add to his banker's account. Not exactly by his consent, I mean to reimburse myself. I know that he can bear a little fleecing. In me you see his nephew, whom he has been daily expecting from France. He has had much difficulty in effecting his escape, but, as you see, and as they will see in the City, he has reached England, and he brings his uncle's draft to be cashed. Here is his signature"—and Desmond, taking from the breast-pocket of his coat a small note, highly scented with musk, put it into my hands; "and now compare it with his draft—the signature, you see, is remarkable —a fine Italian hand." I now knew well what was to come—I knew it was an act of forgery; but though I had given my promise to stand by him, my heart sunk within me, and a chill struck through me. Desmond saw that I faltered, and looking me in the face, he said, " I warned you, my dear fellow, and I warn you again. It is not too late for you to go back and leave me to my fate. Say but the word, and I will stop the coach and let you out," and he leaned forward and took the check-string in his hand. " *My* mind is made up; but if yours is not—go back, while I go on." "I am not going back," I said, with a low voice, between my close shut teeth; " but it is the first time! I have been bad enough, but it has never come to this." "I tell you what, Mark," he cried, " if you begin in this way, you'll drive me wild, and I will and must stop and *turn* you out. I am wound up to the pitch, and I can't and won't be unmanned at this stage. The die is cast, and—" " I am as resolute as yourself,"

I said. "But how is this? What, are we here already?" cried he. The coach had stopped, and he put the draft into my hand. "I am to present this," I said. "Yes, if you like to do so, and to receive half the money." I looked at the draft—I looked at the door of the banking-house. I had looked at the signature before, but if I had seen the name of the firm, I had not heeded it. It had not for an instant occurred to me that it was in that house that Angus was now placed. "Look there," I whispered to Desmond, and I put the draft back into his hand; "anywhere but here. I cannot do it here: I should betray all were I to attempt it!" Angus was coming out. He stood in the open door-way, holding the door, and waiting for some one, and just then his eyes met mine. Mr. Foster, the head of the firm, and the brother of Mrs. Maxwell, appeared, and taking the arm of Angus, they were descending the steps together. "I was not prepared for this," Desmond whispered; "but let them pass, and we may yet succeed." "It is too late," I replied. "Angus saw me before the other came out, and they are now at the carriage-door." "Who is it, my dear Murray?" we heard Mr. Foster ask, as they approached the coach. "Oh, your friend Wilton! I wanted to see him. You will just have time to introduce me to him, and to ask him to dine with us to-day." Angus opened the carriage-door, and held out his hand with his usual hearty, cheerful manner. "Dear Mark, I am delighted to see you,

and to introduce you to my kindest friend, Mr.
Foster." He saw my companion, but did not recognise him; and Desmond, with a presence of mind that
astonished me, just as Mr. Foster was turning away,
and before Angus, who was now standing behind,
could come forward again, said, " Je crois que j'ai
l'honneur de parler à Monsieur Foster." A pair of
golden barnacles were in his hand, and after glancing
at Mr. Foster for a moment, he held the glasses before
his eyes, and peering intently on the cheque which was
in his hand, he appeared to be reading it attentively.
" Messieurs Fostere, Morton, and Co." "Tenez, monsieur," said Mr. Foster, with a well-bred air of ill-
concealed impatience, replying in French, " you must
kindly excuse me, but I have an engagement of some
importance at the Bank of England, and must refer
you to my young friend, Mr. Murray. He will have
much pleasure in attending to your commands," and
taking off his hat to the pretended foreigner, whose
name he had not even had time to ask, he bowed low
to him. As he walked away, he said to Angus,
" I am already past my time—you will speak to
this gentleman, Murray, and follow me afterwards
to the Bank. I shall be there for the next hour."
Angus now came forward, and again Desmond fixed
the barnacles, and as he seemed to be intently con-
ning over the draft, complained that his eyes had
suffered much during his voyage from France. He
announced himself as Count Armand de Mirabel, and

begged to present the draft of his uncle, Monsieur le Marquis de Mirabel. Angus took the draft, looked at it, and seemed, as he did so, to be deep in thought for a moment; then he said, in French, " It rather strikes me, Monsieur de Mirabel, that the marquis, your uncle, has transferred his money from our house to another banker's within the last few days." " It may be so, Monsieur; and if so, I will trouble you to return me the draft." " By no means," replied Angus, gravely. " I may be mistaken, and if my friend, Mr. Wilton, will kindly come with me into the bank I can inquire, and he shall immediately inform you. I have been out of town for a day or two, and only returned last night; at Tancred's Ford, dear Mark," he added, " where we rather expected you last Saturday. You had a letter from them, I think, yesterday. Come, Mark," he added, pressing my hand, " come, if only for a few minutes." " Mais, Monsieur——" "I will send or bring you word immediately," said Angus. He seized my hand, grasping it tightly, and drew me almost by force from the coach. " Go forward, Mark, into that room, if you please: it is Mr. Foster's, and vacant. I must ask a question, and will follow you in two minutes." I entered the room, but glanced round ere I did so, and as I turned my head I saw Rush standing in the doorway, and intently watching Angus. In another moment Angus had followed me into the room. He closed the door, but did not speak. He went at once to the fire-place—the draft was in his hand, but he quickly thrust it into the fire, and taking up the poker, held the paper in the hottest part of the fire, till every vestige of it was consumed. " Angus, Angus, what are you about?" I exclaimed, hardly knowing what I was saying, or why I said it. " What is right," said Angus, with a solemnity of look and manner as profound as it was touching, while the low, deep tones of his voice were so full of sadness that they affected me almost to tears; "and now what I ought to do, and must do, is to kneel down, and pour out my whole soul in thankfulness and praise. I may have saved his life! I trust I have—and yours—yours also, my friend—my brother—my dear, dear Mark! my first friend and companion on my coming to this country." He clasped his hand over his forehead and his eyes—his chest heaved convulsively — his whole frame shook, and the tears fell fast from beneath the hand that shaded his eyes. This agitation was as short as it was violent; it was suppressed as suddenly as it had burst forth. " Hear me, Mark," he said, calmly, and his countenance seemed to me like that of a reproving angel. " I know all—I know what he—what you were both, perhaps, about to do, for I fear you are in league together. I was at first de- ceived—then perplexed; a second look convinced me of the truth. I had seen him, as you must remember, in that disguise before, and I had seen that innocent- looking servant boy. How to save you both was my first thought; how to get you away from him my next! I told no lie when I said that I was uncertain whether the money of the marquis had been transferred to the other bankers. I could not tell till I had asked our cashier, and I have done so. There were words about some slight mistake, only yesterday — not on Mr. Foster's part, but on that of the old marquis, who is proud and petulant, and he withdrew his money. But here, before another word is spoken, or we enter further"—and he sighed deeply—"into this sad business—promise me, that with the help of God—whatever the consequences may be—whatever the exposure, the disgrace which you may dread—promise me that you will have done with that young man, and with all his ways, and, alas, with all your own past ways of iniquity, for ever! I love you, Mark, but, oh! how with all my heart do I abhor your sin! You are stopped, perhaps on the very brink of ruin! But I say no more; do you promise?"

"I do promise," I replied; "and if the lips of such a wretch as I am do not profane His name in using it, I say most solemnly, as in the sight of God, that with His help, whatever the consequences may be, I have from this moment done with all such ways for ever! But why should I hide anything from you, my own true friend? I shall shock you when I say it; but though my heart is crushed—my spirit overwhelmed within me—though I am suffering more at this moment than I ever suffered in my whole past life, there is no change within! I see not one gleam of hope! I am lost for ever! and were it not for the grief which it would cause to you—were I to follow up the thoughts —the impulse which urges me from within, I should act as he did, who went out and hanged himself! It is no use attempting to conceal the fact, Angus! snatched as I am—I know it—and I own it—even from the gallows, *the burning of that note has driven me mad!* O, that I were dead—that I could kill myself, and then I should be out of this world!" " Out of this world!" said Angus, gravely; "this world where there is yet place for repentance, for pardon—and passed into a state where there would be indeed no hope—where suffering which may be turned into peace, would be exchanged for the woe and the despair which knows no termination. Shame, shame upon you, Mark! your sins have made a coward of you, in the most awful sense! Come, come, be a man, and brace yourself to meet the worst which your infatuated course has brought upon you; aye, submit to anything—to everything—but to the bondage of the Evil One! Say with Luther, ' Burn, Lord, cut—do anything, only save—whatever be the means; only, *if by any means*, let me be saved!' " " But you know not what this day will do for me. In a few hours from this time Mr. Arnold must know all, and his esteem, and his daughter's affection, will be lost for ever!" " No, no," said Angus, clasping my hand affectionately, " as your friend, and as your brother — as the one who will never forsake you, I intreat, implore, nay, I command you to face every difficulty of your present position with a manly spirit. I will stand by you, and sacrifice everything but principle to extricate you." But here he suddenly started, " All this time," he said, " all this time, *he*—Desmond—has been forgotten. He is waiting without—I told him I would return to him at once. I will go, but you must remain where you are." He left the room, and came back immediately. " He is gone," he cried. " He has suspected that the forgery is discovered. He thinks the draft is in my hands, and he has fled—and let him go." With an exclamation of horror, I cried out, " Now, now I remember what had quite escaped me. He told me that the Marquis de Mirabel had money at two houses; and he had cheques prepared—he showed them to me—for both." " Then," said Angus, "it is, I fear, too late to save him. His disguise is perfect, the signature no less so. He has had time to present the other draft—the forgery is fully committed, and he is lost!"

Angus paced the room in silence, every now and then clasping his brow, and muttering to himself: " The first thing I must do," he said, at length, " is to follow Mr. Foster to the Bank." Then he stopped, and placing his hand on my arm, he looked me steadily in the face, and said, "My own brother, I depend fully upon you; you will—I am sure you will, do what I ask. You will go to my lodgings, and remain there; nothing will induce you to stir till I join you. In half an hour at the latest, I will be there. Did you not receive that letter from home?" " I have it with

me," I replied; " but it is as yet unopened." " Go and
read it," he said; " go and think of those you love at
Tancred's Ford. Go," he added, in a lower voice,
" go and pray—for grace, for strength, for pardon. Go
and seek the God whose goodness and whose love to
you you have forgotten."

In less than half an hour he joined me. " All is
discovered," he said. " Poor Desmond is indeed lost!
Mr. Foster told me, the moment I met him, that a
message had come to the Bank, while he was there, to
stop the notes which had been taken for the cheque. It
seems that in less than a quarter of an hour after Desmond
had presented his forged cheque, the old marquis had
come down to Newton's bank, and discovered the forgery,
and the Bow-street officers are already in pursuit of the
offender. Mr. Foster's suspicions," he continued, " fell
also upon you. He could not otherwise account for your
coming with the false count to our banking-house; but
I told him on my word, which he believes, that you
neither signed nor presented the other cheque—that I
received it from Desmond, not from you. He asked
what had become of it, and I told him the truth—I
told him I had destroyed it, and why. With his strict
sense of justice he was exceedingly displeased, and
spoke sharply and angrily to me. He even accused
me of conniving at the fraud. I bore his anger; and I
then appealed to him—not as a banker, but as a
Christian. I asked him to put himself in my place;
I entreated him to tell me how he would have acted

had you been his son—or his brother, as you *are* mine; had he seen you almost involved in the guilt and in the danger of the wretched Desmond. I told him, what I am convinced is the fact, that that designing young man had taken advantage of your miserable weakness of character, and of the ease with which he has before led you astray. The good man was moved —was melted. He now judges you as I do; he blames you, but he pities even more than he blames you. Before we parted, he said to me, 'Tell your friend how deeply I grieve for him; tell him also that neither you nor I will ever mention that we saw him in company with his more guilty companion—that no one but you and myself saw them together, and that we shall not disclose a circumstance which might injure him so greatly.' I have promised to bring you to him when he goes down to his country house, at the end of the week. And now, Mark, let me hear of all your difficulties. I have to-day and to-morrow at my own disposal. Let me hear all, and I shall see what can be done, and do everything in my power." I told him all. He heard me silently and sadly. When all was told, he said, " Bad, very bad! but we must speak of the sin of your conduct at another time. Now, I will set off without delay, and, if possible, see and satisfy the creditor who has threatened to expose you to Mr. Arnold." He left me. When he returned he brought me a receipt for my debt—he had himself discharged it; but he had given all his savings, he told me, and could pay no more. "I was too late," he added, "to prevent the man from seeing Mr. Arnold. He had just returned from a long interview with him. He spoke very kindly and feelingly about you, and told me that he was induced to take the step which he has taken by a hope of saving you from ruin, and especially of detaching you from your unprincipled companions."

Poor Desmond was taken, tried, found guilty, and sentenced to be hanged. It was on the evening of the day that the sentence was passed upon him. I had just heard of the result of the trial, and was sitting half lost in thought in my room, thinking of my own guilt, and feeling how utterly unworthy I was of the goodness and mercy which my Heavenly Father had shown to me. I could not help recalling, in that now silent chamber, the scene which had occurred there on that morning when Desmond had come in his disguise, and had proposed to me that I should accompany him, and present the cheques, on which he had forged the signature of the old French marquis. I looked up towards the glass, almost expecting to see the reflection of his face in it. The servant entered, and told me that a lady, named Smith, particularly wished to see me, adding that she had just stopped in a hackney-coach at the door. My visitor soon after entered the room; an old woman servant was with her. I saw that she was a stranger. She told me that she was the sister of

Desmond, or Mr. Smith, as she called him. She need
scarcely have told me, for her likeness to him had
spoken as plainly as her words. She was a woman
of eight-and-twenty or thirty, and there was a natural
elegance about her which was very striking. Her face
wore an expression of fixed sadness, but she was calm
and self-possessed. She said that her occupation was
that of a milliner, and I afterwards learnt that she was
the celebrated Court-milliner, Miss Smith, and that she
was as distinguished for her excellent character as for the
remarkable talent and taste which she displayed in her
occupation. " She had just left her brother," she said,
" in a state of depression which it was deeply distressing
to witness, but which had not astonished her. He had
spoken to her at other times, as well as on that evening, of myself, as the only friend to whom he was ever
deeply attached, and had bitterly accused himself of having drawn me into many evil ways, which, but for him,
I might never have followed. There was," she continued,
" but one alleviation to his extreme wretchedness, and
that was my having escaped the doom which had over-
taken him, though he had used all his influence to
lead me to become the partner of his crime. He
had expressed so great a desire to see me, if only
once more, that she had resolved to call on me that
same night, and to prevail on me to go to him on the
following day." Her voice was peculiarly sweet and
gentle, and as she continued speaking of him, I could
not help wondering at the composure with which she

was enabled to speak of his state of mind, and of the near approach of his execution. She used the very word execution, with such extraordinary calmness! but suddenly, in the midst of a sentence, she gasped for utterance, and sunk down in her chair. Her old servant, who had stood by her, watching her with looks of affectionate anxiety, hastened to her, but all appearance of consciousness and life was gone. "She will come to presently, sir," she said; "only leave her to me;" and she tenderly raised the pallid face, and laid it on her bosom, and parted and put back the long black silken hair which had fallen over it, and chafed first one and then the other of the white listless hands, and applied her own little blue glass bottle of salts to her mistress's nostrils. "She is coming to herself now, poor, poor dear love," she said, fondly wiping her mistress's face with her own fine cambric handkerchief, as the large tears stole through the long dark lashes, and trickled over her cheeks. I promised to go, without fail, to poor Desmond early the next day, and she only waited for this promise, and departed.

I went to Newgate on the following morning. Desmond was sitting, the very image of overwhelming wretchedness, in the condemned cell; his head was bowed down—his face buried in his hands. He noticed not my entrance. But when I sat down beside him, and looked into his face, and spoke to him, as well as I could speak—for my power of utterance was stopped, even to choking — he raised his eyes, and met the mournful but earnest gaze of mine; and as he did so, his mind seemed to awake up to the consciousness that I was present. With a long and deep-drawn sigh he roused himself, and seizing my offered hand, held it in his forcibly, and with an unrelaxing grasp. " Dear, dear Wilton," he said, " the dream is at last ended;" and he threw himself upon my breast, his head sunk on my shoulder, and he wept like a child. " These are the first tears I have shed," he said, when the violence of his grief had a little subsided; "but thank God for them! My brain has been as if it would burst my very skull asunder! Do not chide me for my weakness, but let me weep."

Never can I forget that morning in Newgate; and though I then learnt for the first time the real history of my wretched companion's life, and was made fully acquainted with the various events of his unprincipled and iniquitous course, it was impossible not to feel an interest, and—as I know I then experienced—an affection for him, which, much as I had liked him before, I had never felt till then. His peculiar charm of manner still remained, but all attempt at disguise or deceit was quite gone. I sat and looked at his fine expressive countenance and graceful person, and listened to the expressive tones of his rich deep voice, and I thought with anguish of heart, that in another week he would be hung up like a dog by the hands of the common hangman, a spectacle of scorn, and perhaps mockery, to a mob of the lowest rabble in London.

Deeply affecting and painfully instructive was the account which he gave me of his past life. It had been spent entirely in the pursuit of one object—pleasure! and the gratification of one idol — self! " I have sought in everything," he said, " to please myself—to enrich and to advance myself. I have scrupled at nothing—stopped at nothing but murder. I have made truth, principle, peace of mind, all yield to this one object —self-gratification! I have taken pleasure in surmounting difficulties—running the most fearful risks, incurring the most tremendous consequences, with this one aim—self-advancement. I set out on my careeer, determined to let no sentiment which men esteem, no usage which society is bound by, no chimera of honour, or principle, or anything of the kind, prove a barrier to me. I determined that each and all, if they came in my way, should be thrown down and trampled upon, and that I would stand and triumph, with that success to which I felt sure of attaining, above them all. I knew that such a career needed the exercise of consummate skill, and of artifice and tact the most exquisite. You, Mark, have seen how far I did succeed, up to a period which is not far distant. But you see the climax now; you find me a felon, under sentence of execution, in the condemned cell of this horrid Newgate. And when another week has passed away, this throat," he said, clasping his hands round his neck, " will be clutched by the hangman's grasp, and throttled by the hangman's rope; and I shall hang dangling, a swollen and

bloated carcase, till I am *dead, dead, dead!* Take,
O take the warning, dear, dear, Mark," he added; and
as he spoke he took both my hands in his, and looked
up into my face with such an expression in his large
dark eyes, which it is impossible to describe, but which
I can never forget. " Take the warning while there
is time; you see what want of principle, and the love
of self, and the license of the pleasures of the world,
have brought me to. It is not too late with you,
though all is over with me. But a few words more.
I wish just to tell you who and what I am. You shall
know all. I was born of poor and honest parents: my
father was a warehouseman at a wholesale slopsellers
in Wapping; my mother a semptress. Their characters stood high, and they were loved and respected;
and owing to the esteem of his employers my father
obtained for me the place of a clerk in the office of the
great establishment to which he belonged. I had been
an errand-boy, and I was elated by my rise. I was
much noticed by my employers for my intelligence
and personal appearance. I soon met with some companions older than myself, who were idle and profligate, but whose ways were pleasing and seductive to
me. An old drawing of a coat-of-arms, with many
quarterings, hung over our chimney-piece. It had
been once richly emblazoned, and some of the azure
and gold and crimson still remained. It was the only
relic remaining of my father's family, which had once
been of some rank in the world; and my mother, who

was a distant cousin of my father, had belonged to the elder branch of the same family. They were connected with the great Desmond family, and one of the quarterings in the old escutcheon was that of Desmond. I had begun to read novels — nay, I devoured them in secret, for my worthy parents would not tolerate such trash under their roof. My reading was of as unprincipled a character as my associates. I began at this time to imagine myself a hero, like some of the absurd personages I read of. My father died when I was about fifteen; and my outward deportment and character (for I was already practised in deceit) were so fair, and apparently so estimable, that out of regard to him I was again advanced; and from that time I managed to recommend myself so skilfully and so speciously, that on the application of my master's brother to a correspondent at Liverpool, I obtained the situation of a clerk in one of the first counting-houses there. But I did not like the place. I set my wits to work to return to London, expressing an anxious desire to my new employers to be near my widowed mother and unprotected sister. They procured me a situation in a well-known London house, and from thence, after a few years, I became a clerk at the house of Simon and Co. My poor mother died the year after I returned to London; and my sister, who had commenced her life in the world on principles the very opposite to mine — in strength of mind, high principle, energy, modesty, and sweetness she has not perhaps her equal!—has attained almost the first place in that occupation which she adopted, and for which she had ever shown a peculiar talent."

Here we were interrupted by the entrance of the turnkey. I had already outstaid the time allotted to my interview. Again Desmond took my hands in his, and said, as we parted, "You will see me again; if not before—on the last night. Promise me this."

It was the night before his execution, and I went, according to my promise, to take my last leave of Desmond. I turned out of the Strand into the Old Bailey, and saw, with horror, that a large wooden bar had been thrown across the street, to prevent the passing of carriages on the following morning, and that a crowd of the very refuse of the people was already gathering in the street, to wait during the whole night—with a frightful eagerness for such sights—in order to secure the best places at the execution. I cannot describe the sickness which overpowered me, and I felt once or twice as if it was almost impossible for me to proceed. The low wretches who surrounded me were laughing and talking with utter recklessness of the sufferings and death of my poor unhappy friend. I can't repeat the speeches which reached my ears on every side: they were too loathsome and too dreadful to write down. Suddenly I heard a stir in the crowd, and many voices exclaiming, "She is coming now!"—"She went in just half an hour ago," said a decent-looking woman to a man next me. "She is his only sister, they say, and a rare pretty one she is. I hear she is the famous Court-milliner, Miss Smith, and her old nurse is with her. A cousin of mine knows Mrs. Benson, the nurse, well. Poor thing, there she comes," and the two pressed forward, and I followed them. "What a tall, lovely lady," said the man. "What a noble figure." "But what a poor, pale face," observed the woman; "and yet how handsome! And see, the black lace veil tied under her chin, and the beautiful dark curls falling over her cheeks, and the elegant white handkerchief that she holds in her hand! and see how daintily she lifts-up her black silk gown, as she comes down the steps! Yes, let me see—and a crimson silk quilted petticoat, and a short satin cloak, and large silver buckles to her shoes. Yes, now I have it, to tell my master all about her. God bless that dear old nurse, say I! How she seems to guard her from the crowd, whispering comfort in her ear, as she comes out into this noisy mob!"

I had stood waiting to see them come down the steps; and now I hurried forward to offer my services if necessary through the jostling crowd, as they went forward to a coach which was drawn up beyond the bar. I spoke to them, and they turned, but quickly passed on. In another moment, however, the old nurse turned back, while her mistress went on alone, and seizing my arm, she said, hurriedly, "He begs you not to go to him to-night. No," she added, in answer to my question, "I can tell you nothing now—only don't stop me—but promise me, on your sacred word—only promise, that you will not go. He cannot, must not see you. To-morrow morning, at seven, if all is well, I will see you at your lodgings, and explain all." I gave the promise. The boy Rush stood at the coach-door, the nurse entered, her mistress was already in the coach; the boy mounted the box, and the coach drove slowly off. I followed down Ludgate Hill, and I saw that when they came to the corner of Bridge Street the coachman urged on his horses, and they went off at a rapid pace towards Blackfriar's Bridge.

At seven the next morning I was up and dressed, waiting for the old nurse, and wondering what she had to tell me, and what she could possibly mean by say-ing, "If all is well, I will come." She came, however, as the clock struck the appointed hour. "They are gone," she whispered, as I closed the door, and made her sit down beside me. "Gone! who?—what do you mean?" "My poor boy—my young master— Mr. Desmond is off," she said. "It was he, not my dear, sweet mistress that you saw come out from that horrid prison last night. My mistress has the courage of a man, though she is as gentle as an angel. She thought it so hard that he should die, and be cut off in his sin, that she was determined, if it could be done, to save him, even if she suffered in his stead. They are as like as two twins," she added; "only his hair is a dark auburn, and hers is as black as the raven's

wing. Almost as quick as I can speak it, she dressed
him in her gown and petticoat, and darkened his eyebrows, and put back his hair, and put the black hair,
with its long ringlets, which we brought with us, upon
his head, and tied her black veil, just as she wears it,
under his chin, and threw her short satin cloak on his
shoulders; and I managed to shift his shoes for ladies'
shoes and silver buckles, for we attended to everything,
even to the black velvet round the throat. And when my
poor dear mistress had hurried away into the sleeping cell,
and hidden herself under the bed-clothes, and Mr. Desmond stood before me, dressed like a lady, even I could
hardly have told them apart. And so I begged him not
even to raise the handkerchief to his eyes, and to take
short steps, and to speak to no one; and we passed by
them all; and bolts were undrawn, and heavy doors
unlocked, and turnkeys stared at us, and at last we
were out in the free air of heaven; and we got out
of the coach in the Westminster Road, and walked a
little way, and took another coach, and then we drove
into the Borough, and there got out again in a dark
street near the Old Kent Road, not far from a lane
where a daughter of mine is living—one who would
give all she has in the world to serve my mistress—for
she is her foster-sister; and there a sailor's dress was all
ready, and he and Rush put on the dress of sailors,
and set off together in the dark. And now, sir, be
silent—only be silent as the grave. All this is safe
with you; and my poor young gentleman wished you

to know that he was gone, and said that you should hear from him when he was safe out of the country. But good-bye, good-bye," she added, without giving me the opportunity of saying a word; "I must be down ·to Newgate, to do and dare anything, so that I can see and help my poor mistress. I shall go to a lawyer's in the way—a great, good gentlemen, whose lady knows my mistress well, for she works for her; and I am to tell him—so my mistress ordered if Mr. Desmond got off—all that she has done, and to beg him, for pity's sake, to put forth all his skill, and help her if he can. I trust that I shall get him to go down with me to Newgate, and he will see what can be done."

Hanson hanging in chains.

CHAPTER XI.

THE full exposure came at length; it was perhaps the inevitable consequence of the course I had run. Mr. Forster and Angus had supposed that Desmond and I had not been seen together in the coach on the morning of the forgery—they had wished to conceal the disgraceful fact; but whether one of their clerks had passed and seen us, or in whatever manner the thing had been known, it matters not—it *was known*, and it got wind, and was talked of throughout the City. As it usually happens, a story loses nothing in the telling, and untrue and exaggerated accounts of my share in the sad transaction were circulated. They went even so far as to say that I had been taken up, and carried to Bow Street, and that undue influence had been used, and that even a large sum of money had been paid that I might be screened and liberated. The story was improbable and absurd enough, but that was no hindrance to its being told— and it *was told*. I saw, or fancied I saw, that some looked at me, and whispered as I passed by; that some stared at me, as if curious to see me; that others, who had known me, looked another way, and would not notice me as formerly. Alas! how little was I then able to discriminate between the sin and the shame! Had I continued in the former—undiscovered, I should, doubtless, have gone on in the same utter recklessness as to the iniquity and guilt which gathered thick upon me; but I quailed, and almost sunk under the shame of exposure. I felt myself a degraded creature. I had drained the cup, and all its fatal sweetness and spirit was gone, and nothing was left me but the vapid dregs. I believed, in fact, that every one looked down upon me with the contempt which I deserved; and I wished that I could shrink away from the notice of every one. I became suspicious and distrustful; and even Angus, my noble, delicate-minded friend, who sought in every way to sustain and comfort me, was at times suspected by me. If a remark was made by him which could in any way be distorted by my morbid, over-strained imagination to apply to a course of action at all similar to my own, I at once secretly accused him of an intention of reflecting upon myself. I had been permitted still to remain at Mr. Arnold's office, but it seemed to me that I was merely tolerated there. I do *now* believe that more of sorrow than of contempt was felt for me; but my heart was full of bitterness towardse very one. Stanley, for instance, pitied me sincerely, and was greatly softened towards me; and good Mr. Dawson, the head clerk—that one among the clerks whom I had always looked down upon as having neither sense nor feeling, except for the dry details of his department in the office—he, above all others, went out of his way to show kindness to me. But all was in vain. I was in fact not only grieved and wounded in spirit, but my nerves were shaken past recovery, and my bodily health was fast breaking. They all saw how wretchedly ill I was, and how unfit for business I had become. I endeavoured to rally, and, by attention and diligence, to prove how anxious I was to regain the confidence and esteem of Mr. Arnold and his partner, Mr. Tresham, who both treated me with extraordinary kindness. But the exertion was too much for me. I began to feel conscious that the time was for ever gone by for me to prove the sincerity of my repentance, and the reality of my amendment. Alas, it was now indeed too late! The excesses to which I had yielded during my late career of profligacy, and the anguish of mind I had suffered, had quite undermined a constitution which was naturally good. Still for some time I endeavoured to hide from myself the conviction which was daily

gaining ground upon me, from symptoms too evident
to be mistaken, that my strength was fast failing me.
But this soon became apparent to every one. My
once vigorous frame was gradually wasting, and my
face had lost every appearance of health and freshness:
a dull but constantly returning pain attacked me whenever I bent over my desk in writing for any length of
time; and a short dry cough seldom left me. Mrs.
Arnold, with a mother's anxiety, was the first to notice
the change that was taking place in me; and she begged
her husband to call in Dr. B., and to take his opinion
about me. That celebrated physician said at once that
my recovery was almost hopeless, and that the only
chance of saving my life was my entirely relinquishing
business, and going without delay into my native air.
He insisted on my setting out the following day for
Tancred's Ford. It is not my intention to dwell here
on the distress that I suffered on parting with Miss
Arnold, and on finding that, notwithstanding her unaltered and tender affection for me, my state of health
was such, that it was almost certain my funeral might
take place at the time when, under other circumstances,
our marriage might have been celebrated.

My never-failing friend Mrs. Arnold, however,
comforted and delighted me on the morning of my
departure, by telling me that she and her daughter
proposed following me in a short time to Tancred's
Ford, that they might help to nurse me there.

Accompanied by Angus, I returned to that dear

home. I saw the shock which my altered appearance produced, though they all endeavoured to conceal it from me, and received me with affectionate tenderness. Ah, I could only feel that they who welcomed me had indeed caught something of the spirit of that Father's love whom our blessed Saviour has described as running to meet his returning but prodigal child, and almost overpowering him with the tokens of his unchanging love. It was with me as with that prodigal—I heard not a single reproach. The only feeling that seemed to predominate was this: "The wanderer is returned—the lost is found!"

It was now absolutely necessary to make some arrangement for the settling of my debts, for my creditors were applying to me almost daily. Angus knew this, and it was partly on this account that he remained for several days at Tancred's Ford after he had brought me home. I cannot bear to dwell upon the details of the consultations which were held among us, at which Mr. Morland, my grandfather's solicitor, and the old and tried friend of our family, was kindly present. My debts were examined into, and paid. But never can I forget the sorrow and the shame which I felt when I found into what perplexities I had brought all who were dear to me; and how large the sums were they were compelled to pay to save my name from dishonour, and my person from prison. My kind good aunt made great sacrifices, and my dear sister (as I afterwards found, with the full approval of Angus) gave up the whole of her portion, only too delighted, by doing so, to be enabled to extricate me. Angus left us then for a short time, but a few weeks afterwards he returned; for, at my dear grandfather's particular desire, his marriage with my sister had been fixed for that time. Mrs. Arnold and her daughter accompanied him, and their wedding took place. Miss Arnold and Miss Trafford were the bride's-maids, but besides them and Mrs. Arnold, no one but my own family, and Mr. Morland, were present. The marriage ceremony was very trying to me. It was impossible for me not to think that I had once hoped to stand with that sweet and gentle girl who was then present, but who was, I feared, never to become my wife, as Angus and my dear sister then stood before me, and to be united in the same holy bands of matrimony with her. I saw, from the delicate and tender attentions which they all paid me, how sincerely they felt for me; and, oh! how grateful did I feel to them—how much I loved them! I endeavoured to be cheerful, and I hope that I was so. No one rejoiced in that marriage more than myself; and the union of Angus and Alice threw indeed a transitory gleam of happiness across my gloomy path, and led me to forget my sorrow and my shame for a little season. But a few weeks afterwards, the sudden death of my grandfather plunged us all in the deepest grief; and when I accused myself—and, alas! with justice—for having brought down his grey hairs with sorrow to the grave, the whole of the mournful group were silent: they could not gainsay my words; they could not reassure my troubled spirit, or banish, by a word which was not true, the agony of my remorse. My aunt at last spoke. " This is no time," she said, ' for recrimination: we know how you suffer; we feel for you, my poor Mark, more than for ourselves. But this stroke is immediately from God; and you must learn to say with us, ' His blessed will be done !' "

Another trying scene still awaited me. The will of my grandfather was to be read. We were all, of course, required to be present. Every one but our family lawyer was in entire ignorance of its contents. My grandfather had consulted no one but that old and confidential friend. In a low and gentle voice he read the whole. It was short, but explicit. I was as one disinherited ! The whole of the paternal property, with a life interest to my mother, and a legacy to my aunt, to whom my grandmother's fortune had before devolved, was settled upon my sister and her heirs, with a request to Angus and herself that they would allow me a small annuity during my life, which I was positively forbidden to anticipate, on pain of forfeiting the whole. Oh, how can I find words to express the tenderness, the affection, with which they all gathered round me, or to do justice to the noble spirit with which my sweet sister and her husband, as if actuated at once by the same impulse, declared that they could not, and would not, abide by the will, but that Tancred's Ford should be mine, and mine alone, whom they regarded as its rightful owner. But on this point I was inflexible. It was now my turn to be calm and even cheerful. I could tell them, as I did from my heart, that my dear grandfather's just will met with my full concurrence, my entire approval; that I loved, honoured, thanked him for it; that nothing could make me so happy as to receive what I might need from their dear hands; and that if they would grant me but one request, the only one I had to make, they would make me as happy as it was now possible for me to be in this present world, and that was, to reside with them at Tancred's Ford till the short time of my sojourn on earth should be ended.

They reasoned with me, and entreated, but I only replied, " You wish to make me happy, and in this way alone can I be happy." They saw that it was in vain to attempt to change me; and at last they ceased to urge me. I felt that, although they would not say it, I had prevailed.

For some time after this period I revived in so wonderful a way, that my beloved relations began to hope that my complete recovery was more than probable. Whether such would have been the case, it is impossible for us to know; but an incident occurred which entirely threw me back; and as my illness proceeded from sorrow of heart even more than bodily disease, it was out of the power of medicine to administer relief to such an ailment. I was sitting one delightful morning on the lawn near the house, under the shade of one of the spreading cedars. I was quite alone, and was reading a volume of Cowper's poems, which, strange to tell, I had never opened till then, when I heard a voice addressing me by name; and on looking up, I saw standing before me a slight and delicate-looking boy in tattered clothing. So changed was his appearance, so piteous the expression of his countenance and the tones of his voice, that I did not at first recognise the lightsome and intelligent lad whom I have frequently spoken of as the servant of poor Desmond. He came to tell a melancholy story; for he came to tell me that after having wandered about for some months, hiding themselves with difficulty as they proceeded from place to place, they had at length reached the sea-coast in the neighbourhood of Folkestone. They were well provided with money, which Desmond's sister had sewed in their clothes; and finding a fisherman quite alone on the shore, Desmond had prevailed on him to set off without a minute's delay in his open boat, for the coast of France. A sudden squall came on—the boat was upset. The honest fisherman had, by extraordinary exertions, saved the life of the poor child. They were both, in fact, taken up by another fishing boat, when their strength was almost exhausted. Desmond had sunk, to rise no more. At the commencement of their danger, it seemed that he had spoken to his youthful servant in a most impressive way, though the boy could never be prevailed upon to disclose what his master had said to him; the effect, however, appeared to be truly marvellous. He seemed from that moment a changed character. He had come to me in obedience to Desmond's last words; and the first request that he made was, that I would give him, what his master had desired him to ask for—a bible. He added, at his own request, another petition, that he might be permitted to remain with me as my servant, and never to quit me while he lived. My sister and Angus came while the poor youth was speaking, and found me in such an agony of grief that they feared for some time I should not have strength again to rally.

I have been very ill—too ill indeed to continue this narrative, for many months. I wish to leave some account of my past life as a warning to others—to the young and heedless—now, perhaps, as self-willed, as self-confident, and as devoid of godly principle as I once was. To-day, for the first time, I have left my chamber, and I sit down to continue my narrative. Since I have been lying on my sick bed, attended almost daily by good Mr. Trafford, my mind has been, by the goodness and grace of God, gradually brought to a right understanding of myself and of my sins. God is indeed merciful to me. But though I feel deeply grieved for the past—though I may repent, and, oh! how heartily do I repent, and thank God that He has turned me, and given me grace to repent — though I trust God has graciously forgiven what I have

humbly confessed, and do confess, my deep and
aggravated offences against Him—though I know that
my gracious God has declared to us, that if we
confess our sins, He is faithful and just to forgive us
our sins, and to cleanse us from all unrighteousness in
that blood which cleanseth us from all sin;—still the
effect of sin, my own sin, on my own body and my
own mental faculties, cannot now be undone; the
work, both bodily and mental, has been done. I can
never be again *on earth* what I was, and might have
been. This wasted and enfeebled frame, with its fever-
ish languor—these impaired and blunted faculties, are
injured past recovery; and my own experience
fully confirms the opinion of the eminent medical
men whom I have consulted. Nor can I ever lose—
nay, I may say from my very heart, I do not wish
to lose—the deep-rooted recollection of the past. I
am at times tolerably cheerful; I am always grateful
for the blessings which I still enjoy in this world—
they are more, many more than I deserve. But,
no; the vigour of limb, the glow of health, the
elasticity of spirit which I once possessed beyond most
other men, are irrevocably gone. I look forward to a
brighter world, where, after this poor tenement has
been laid low in the dissolution of death and the decay
of the grave, I hope, through the mercy of God in
Christ, to expatiate in eternal strength and gladness!
But till then, and not till then, the blight must be
upon the branch, the canker in the very core of the

fruit: and I write to warn and to entreat those who are still in the possession of health and strength, in the freshness of youth, or early manhood, to reflect upon my sad story, and be wise before it is too late.

If you, my reader, be a youth, or a man of unbridled temper or passions—intractable, and intolerant of contradiction and opposition, oh, think of Hanson! He determined to take his own way. He yielded to the Evil Spirit, whose slave he was; for, "he that committeth sin is the servant of sin." He served a hard master, and one who effectually succeeded in deceiving him; for, while he whispered, "Take your own way—give as wild a licence as you will to your violent temper, your stormy passion, your lusts, and your intemperance; be as wilful and as stubborn as you please; dare everything, and boast of your daring —you are your own master!"—that father of lies— that murderer of the souls and bodies of his deluded and miserable bond-slaves—was all the while entangling him in his fatal snares, and winding round him, more and more closely, his hellish chains, till at last he sunk a fettered and a helpless victim beneath his power. The gaol, and the felon's dock—the awful sentence of the earthly judge—the hangman, the rope, and the gallows, were the only recompense which he received for the brutal licence which for a time he gained and gloried in. Or it may be that you are naturally the very opposite of what Hanson was; you may be gentle, refined, and eminently pleasing—but secretly intent on

one subject, self-gratification—devoted to one pursuit,
that of ungodly pleasure! Are you aware of your
danger? Think upon Desmond! You can scarcely
be more fitted than he was to ingratiate yourself with
those around you, and to win your way with graceful
ease to the eminence which he reached; but your fall
may be as sudden—your death as desolate as his!

Or, perchance, you may be really well-disposed—
amiable—full of all generous impulses, but the mere
creature of feeling and imagination—with no settled
principles, no resolute purpose to do what is simply
right in the sight of God and man, let the consequences
be what they will—unstable, and yielding like a fool to
the influence of the present associate, whether for good
or evil—blown hither and thither like a weathercock
by every breath of the inconstant wind that trifles with
it. Then reflect on my story. Sometimes the prodigal, who claims the portion of his father's goods that
falleth to him, and departs to the far country, and
wastes his substance in riotous living, till he has spent
all, and there ariseth a mighty famine in that land—
sometimes the prodigal comes back, but not often.
The common case is that he dies famishing in the
barren fields, the swine his only companions—their
food his only fare. He may *come to himself*, but all
hope has died within him; the will and the strength
to arise and go to his Father are gone; enfeebled and
exhausted, he has fallen to rise no more. He would
fain fill his belly with the husks by which swine are

satisfied; but such food cannot nourish him, or give him strength to rise. And there—where there is not an eye to pity him, nor a heart to feel for him, nor a hand to raise or to relieve him—there, amid the dreariness and desolation of that mighty famine, prostrate and helpless, he perishes.

The following letter was written about four years after the conclusion of the narrative of Mark Wilton. It is dated Tancred's Ford :—

FROM ANGUS MURRAY TO MR. MAXWELL.

Your letter, my dear and valued friend, to our beloved invalid, came, alas! too late for him to write in reply. He read it, or rather it was read to him; but he was too ill and feeble to do more than beg that I would assure you how deeply he valued your friendship, and how much consolation he derived from your letter. He desired me to give his most affectionate remembrances to yourself, and to the Forters, and every member of your family, and to say that he looked forward to a world where all who are now one *in* Christ, will be with Him and with one another for ever.

He had been unusually well, *for him*, during the last few months, and less subject to those seasons of deep mental depression which at times brought on such great prostration of bodily strength. You were witness to one of them when you were last with us.

He had been lately more calm, more cheerful, and seemed to take more interest in the little events of our quiet domestic circle. Nothing, however, seemed to please him so much as to have one of our children with him; and Mark, who is named after his dear uncle, was, if possible, even more a favourite than his sister. At times he was sad and thoughtful with the elder members of his family; but he was never so if the children were with him: yet even with them, I, who could at all times read his character better than others, always observed that touching humility of spirit which so peculiarly characterized him, and which imparted to his words, and even to his looks, a gentleness and even tenderness, inexpressibly interesting. He realised, more than any one I ever met with, during the latter years of that earthly course, which is now, as you have already heard, come to its peaceful close, the disposition of one who goes and sits down in the lowest place; in lowliness of mind literally esteeming all others better than himself. My hasty letter, announcing his unexpected death, crossed yours on the road, and I now sit down to give you, as I promised in that letter, some account of the distressing occurrence which appeared so entirely to overcome him, that his enfeebled frame was unable to resist the shock. Since my last return from town he had taken to gentle horse exercise, which appeared to be accompanied by less fatigue than any other, so that he usually came home, even after our longest rides, refreshed and invigorated.

About a week ago he proposed that we should order the horses after our early dinner, and take a favourite round of his—setting out in the direction of Headley, and returning by the paper mills and the beautiful Chert lanes; and so back, across the heath skirting Tancred's Mere, home. We were tempted by the loveliness of the day to turn into a lane over which the hedge-row trees formed a continued arch by their interlacing branches, and we rode slowly on—farther than we intended—deep in conversation about many circumstances connected with our youthful days, every now and then interrupting our discourse with expressions of our admiration of the wild and lovely scenery that burst upon us. Suddenly a thunderstorm came on, and the rain began to fall in such torrents that we took refuge in an old farm-house by the road-side. The storm continued to increase, and was succeeded by a pouring rain, during which I positively refused to leave the house, feeling that it would be highly imprudent for Mark in his state of health to be exposed to such inclemency of weather. At length the rain ceased, but not until the shades of twilight were spreading around us. When we set out on our return home, we took, as we thought, the most direct way, till, on coming to a place where two roads met, we became much perplexed. There was no house near, and we could only guess which was the right turning; we took it, as we supposed. But after wandering on for some distance, Mark, who knew the

country better than myself, said that he was sure we
had lost our way. Once or twice I insisted on his
riding more slowly; but he was in higher spirits than
usual, and though, with his accustomed gentleness, he
promised to obey, and did obey me, he laughed and
said that he felt no fatigue, and that, as a clear moonlight was beginning to light us on our way, he
rather enjoyed the adventure. "I have often told
you, dear Angus," he said, "that here there are
always new haunts to explore, and new beauties to
admire. And look," he added, riding foremost, "we
are evidently coming to a charming spot, of a more
wild and picturesque character than any we have yet
passed." But just as we turned the corner of a hazel
copse, where a large oak cast a deep shade over the
road by its spreading branches, and came out upon a
glade where the intermingled heath and green sward
was reposing in the calm moonlight, he abruptly ceased
speaking, and his horse stopped short. Wondering what
could have happened, or what he could have seen, I
was instantly at his side. Ah, I soon ceased to wonder
at the effect which the sight now before us had oc-
casioned! My eye turned first on the appalling object,
and then instantly to my beloved Mark. He had
clasped his brow with his hand, and was evidently
hiding his eyes, as if to shut out the spectacle which
had struck him with horror. For some minutes he
continued speechless—motionless;—for there—in the
full light of the moon-beams—and close to the spot

where we had stopped—stood a lofty gibbet, on which, slowly moving and rattling in the gentle breeze, hung the body of a man in chains. I knew at once that it could be no other than the body of the wretched Hanson, and that we stood on the very spot where the murder had been committed. "Mark, dear Mark," I said, as I leaned forward, and clasped the hand which held his bridle, speaking soothingly to him, "let me take you instantly from this frightful spot." But for some time he appeared too overpowered to speak. "Angus," he at length replied, in a hollow voice, "this is worse than death. I know the spot too well, though I had never come to it by this side before." Horror-struck as I was, I thought more of my poor Mark than of my own feelings. I spoke to him at once on the highest and holiest subject, and said, "Let us endeavour, with this frightful spectacle before us, to fix our whole souls on Him who died a viler and a far more dreadful death than this, that he might bring the vilest and the worst to God. Let us think what sin has done, in looking here—what God has done, in looking past this murderer's body—to Christ crucified. We cannot tell whether this wretched man did or did not cry to Him for pardon before he was brought here to suffer; but this we know, that if he did so—yes, even he! the Lord has put away his sin, and washed him in His own blood. This is a subject for our consideration here— one that will raise our minds above the frightful associations of such a spot—one before which the dismal shadows of the valley of death must pass away." While I was thus speaking, I had taken his bridle in my hand, and gently guiding the horse, and passing my arm through his, side by side we turned away from the place, and were soon riding quietly over the broad heath, with the full beautiful moon shining in the blue and cloudless heavens above us. He appeared tolerably composed when we arrived at home, but he said little. He drank tea with us as usual, and was present at our family worship. I went up with him to his chamber, and we conversed together for some little time. I returned to him when I thought he would be in bed, and in bed I found him. I thought it would be a comfort to him if I knelt down beside him and prayed with him, and I did so. When I left him, I thought I had never seen so calm and beautiful an expression of peace upon his fine countenance. In the dim light of the chamber-lamp he looked almost as he did when we first met at your house many years ago, and when I thought I had seldom seen so handsome or so ingenuous a youth. His eyes beamed with affection as he looked at me; and the words "God, even our own God, for ever bless you, my own friend," rose in a soft whisper from his lips. It might be half an hour after that I was passing his door in my way from my dressing-room to my bed-room, and I thought I would pause and listen at the door to hear if he were sleeping undisturbed; all was stillness, and I was just turning away, when I fancied a low moan rose upon my ear.

I listened with breathless anxiety—it was no fancy—the moan was again heard. I opened the door as softly as I could, and entered the room. The first thing which met my sight was blood; the sheet and counterpane were soaked with blood, and my dear brother lay pale and almost lifeless, the dark blood oozing from his mouth. He could not speak, but his languid eyes fixed their gaze on me, and a faint smile played for a moment over his features; but as it died away, the low and piteous moan succeeded. He had broken a blood-vessel, and if I had not—by God's gracious providence—gone to him when I did, he must have died before morning. Medical aid was instantly sent for, and in the meanwhile our dear aunt, who is an excellent doctor, with her usual strength of mind and calm self-possession, used the best possible means to stop the bleeding. Thank God, he revived, and was so much better for the next few days, that our medical friend gave us some hope, humanly speaking, that he might have strength to overcome the attack. Alas, he was mistaken! the frightful bleeding did not return, but three days after he gently fell asleep in Jesus. Alice and I and his poor mother were sitting by his bedside; we had sat there all the night, and he had slept calmly, with some intervals of restlessness all the time. Soon after six he woke, and turning to his dear sister, he said, " Are the children dressed—may I see them?" Mark and Agnes were instantly brought to him. They came in hand in hand, on tiptoe, holding in their breath; and Mark's finger was lifted up as a sign to Agnes not to make the slightest noise. Their fresh rosy cheeks and glowing lips were pressed for a moment to their beloved uncle's sunk and pallid face; and they stole out of the room as softly as they entered. "Where is my aunt; my dear aunt?" he said, faintly; she was already in the room. "You will all kiss me, for the last time," he said, as a few large glittering tears stole trickling from his eyes, and he looked at us with the same soft, yearning gaze, which he had fixed on me on the evening of this last attack. We all did so; but when my lips touched his calm, clear forehead, its damp and icy coldness told me that the chill of death was there. Afterwards he slept quietly for at least an hour; and if he dreamed, his dreams were sweet and peaceful, for smiles played gently over his face, and from time to time his lips moved, and the names of those who had been dearest to him rose like a soft murmur from his lips: Halsted, the friend of his childhood; my own name; his sweet Janet; his mother; his aunt; his sister,—all, were, it seemed, present with him—he was conversing with us all; but at last his features assumed a more solemn and yet a still sweeter expression—and another name hovered upon his lips—it was the name dearest to all our hearts, and, oh, how I bless the God of all grace, dearest to his own! that name which is above every name!—the name of Jesus! A smile, bright as a beam of sunshine, passed over his face, and opening his eyes and looking upward, he said, "I come!"—"Come, Lord Jesus—come—come!" The Rev. Mr. Trafford entered the room as he expired, and heard his last words. At my brother's earnest desire he had been frequently with him.

———

Several years have passed away since the pages which are now presented to the reader were put into my hands, by Mr. Wilton, of Tancred's Ford. He was then lying on his deathbed. He had been seized with a sudden attack of bleeding, from the breaking of a blood-vessel. I was sent for on the following morning, and was constantly with him during the few days he survived. On one occasion when we were alone together, he begged me to unlock the drawer of his writing-table, and to take from it the manuscript of this narrative, which he told me he had written of his past life. He put it into my hands, and requested me to publish it, unaltered, at some future time—leaving that time to my own discretion. I have now fulfilled my promise, adding to the manuscript a letter which I obtained from my valued friend Mr. Maxwell, without which the narrative of the life of Mark Wilton would be incomplete. A loose page was lying with the manuscript in the same packet, headed "The Balance Sheet;" and as it was in his handwriting, I have attached it to the other pages.

THE BALANCE SHEET.

The Single Crime.

Character.

Credit.

Health.

Fortune.

Respect.

Confidence.

Friends.

Peace of Mind.

Hope.

Mortal Life.

Heaven.

"God be merciful to me a sinner."

"Having forgiven you all trespasses, blotting out the hand-writing that was against us, which was contrary to us, and took it out of the way, nailing it to his cross.,"—Colossians ii, 13, 14.

I trust the volume may possess more than a common interest with the class of readers to whom it was offered as a warning, and perhaps something better than a warning, by the writer. I hope and think that others may also find much to interest them in it. To myself it has been deeply interesting, from my long and personal acquaintance with Mark Wilton. I have seen several of the individuals mentioned in the narrative, and I well remember, soon after my return to this parish, the two young men named Hanson and Desmond, whom I found, on the occasion mentioned in the narrative, in the drawing-room at Tancred's Ford. Their appearance and their manners in that short interview left a lasting impression on my mind. I think I could almost have foretold the character of their future career. Both of them came to an untimely end. As for my dear son in the faith, Mark Wilton —for though I fully believe that he was a true penitent, and, through the mercy and grace of God and the finished work of that great Redeemer who died for our sins, and rose again for our justification, a pardoned and accepted believer—still, with regard to this our mortal state, what was his death but an untimely end? His friend Angus has, on the contrary, realised in his whole life the truth of that grand and inspired assurance that "godliness is profitable for all things; having the promise of the life which now is, and of that which is to come." He is at this time one of the highest in station and in character of the mercantile

world; and those who would wish to describe real domestic love, and peace, and happiness, might find them in the happy circle at Tancred's Ford.

Mark Wilton is not forgotten, the remembrance of him is cherished in all our hearts; though all that remains of him on earth is in its quiet resting-place, beneath the tablet of white marble, placed by Sir Angus and Lady Murray on the southern wall of my church. The inscription is short and simple, but it appears to my mind just what it ought to be.

WALTER TRAFFORD.

Sacred to the Memory of

Mark Wilton,

AGED TWENTY-SEVEN YEARS,

Unforgotten, and regarded with undying affection.

A broken and a contrite heart, O God, thou wilt not despise."

The Parish Church

VIZETELLY BROTHERS AND CO. PRINTERS AND ENGRAVERS, FLEET STREET.